After the Storm

After the Storm

Dan Marshall

Onion River Press
89 Church Street
Burlington, VT 05401

info@onionriverpress.com
www.onionriverpress.com

ISBN: 978-1-966607-13-7 Paperback // 978-1-966607-14-4 eBook
Library of Congress Control Number: 2025920094

To Jude

1

Chief Bridger sat in his cruiser at the top of the hill for a few minutes and just watched. A short football field away, where Tower Road and Cramer Hill Road met in an awkward intersection, a woman was trying to back her Volvo, with horse trailer attached, from one road into the other. She was apparently trying to turn around and making a bad job of it. As the car and trailer came to almost a right angle, he spotted the Connecticut plate on the back of the car and chuckled.

Well, he thought, *some things never change. Guess it's time to offer some help.*

Kate Stone saw the police car rolling slowly down the hill towards her and sighed. *I guess I need some help*, she thought, *and maybe this is it.*

She was out of her car, standing with hands on hips, before the chief emerged from his parked car. He took a minute to size her up before opening his door. About five-eight, he thought, and nicely shaped. Late twenties or early thirties, casual slacks and blouse, pretty face, with blue eyes and dark hair. She looked like she was fit and could afford to dress fashionably, but she didn't look too glamorous or flashy. All in all, just who you would expect to step out of an out-of-state Volvo in the middle of a small town in Vermont.

"Good morning, officer," she said with a smile. "I guess I've got myself in a jam here."

"Chief Les Bridger, ma'am," he said, extending his right hand, "I'm the Chief of Police here in Merryfield."

"Oh, well I'm pleased to meet you, Chief. My name's Kate Stone, and I'm new in town and a little bit lost."

"Pleasure to meet you, Miss Stone. New in town, you say? Visiting, or..."

"No, actually, I'm going to be living here. Just arrived."

"Say, are you the one bought the old Andrews place?"

"Yes, yes, I am. I've been there, of course, and I know how to get there from the highway, but I thought I would deliver Dolly—that's my mare—to the farm where I'm boarding her..."

"Sunrise Farm?"

"Yes, that's it. Am I anywhere close to it?"

"You sure are, and I've got good news for you. You don't need to turn around at all; you were headed in the right direction, and it's little more than a mile."

"Oh. My GPS told me to..."

"To go up over this hill?"

"That's right."

"Well, I guess it's shorter, as the crow flies, but it's damned twisty and steep in some places. No need to try that road pulling a trailer; just stay right on Tower Road and you'll be there in a few minutes."

"Oh, thank you, Chief; I'm so relieved!"

"Les, Miss Stone; just call me Les."

Sunrise Farm was a real farm, but no longer the dairy farm it had been for several generations. The dairy herd had been sold off in the late nineties, and the owners—the Norman family—now made their living with a mix of sheep, pigs, and organic crops. They also had a big horse barn, which accommodated their own horses and several others. They offered riding lessons and had several miles of trails for pleasure riding.

Kate Stone arrived at the farm at about one-thirty and was greeted by Linda Norman, who helped her park the trailer and lead Dolly, her grey mare, into the barn and to the stall that would be her new home.

"She's a beauty, Miss Stone," said the short, red-haired woman in dirty overalls and barn boots.

"Yes, she is, and call me Kate, please."

Linda, who had lived with horses all of her thirty years, patted the mare affectionately as she walked around the mare from front to back.

"Gentle, too."

She looked appraisingly at Dolly and said to Kate, "I think she's pregnant."

"Yes, I think so, too," Kate said with a laugh. "A little bonus for me."

"A bonus?"

"Well, you see, Linda, in my 'less-than-friendly' divorce settlement, Jim ended up with 'General Patton,' the stallion, and I ended up with Dolly and that old trailer. If Jim had known she was in foal…"

"Ha, ha, ha!!" Linda laughed, slapping a knee in delight. "I love it!"

Linda Norman had given Kate directions back to the village center and recommended that, if she was hungry, she should stop at the Maple Leaf Café, right on Main Street. It was easy to find; in truth, everything in Merryfield was easy to find, as long as you didn't venture too far out of the village and end up on the dirt roads—such as Kate had found earlier.

It was a nice little café, with tables for about forty and a long counter with eight seats. The lunch rush was over, and there were only a few people sitting at the tables and no one at the counter. Before Kate could even decide where to sit, a cheery waitress with a big, friendly smile said, "Hi! Have a seat!"

"Thank you, I will."

Kate took a seat at the counter, where a cup and saucer sat waiting for her, alongside a knife, fork, and spoon sitting on a little white napkin.

"Coffee?"

The cheery waitress was right in front of her, with coffee pot in hand and poised to pour.

"Sure, thank you."

The waitress poured the coffee with her right hand while sliding a menu across the counter with her left.

"This is the regular lunch menu, and there's specials on the board."

Kate looked up at the chalkboard on the wall behind the counter and saw two handwritten specials—one sandwich and one salad.

""You're Miss Stone, aren't you?" said the waitress confidently.

"Umm, well, yes and no. I guess I haven't decided yet."

"Well, the chief was in for lunch and he said he saw you out on Tower Road. You're the one who bought the Andrews place, right?"

"Yes, I am. What I meant was, I've just gotten my divorce and I haven't decided yet what to call myself. All of my documents and credit cards and stuff say 'Stone,' and it's easier to keep that name rather than my maiden name, even though it's a constant reminder of a life I want to forget. And I'm not sure if I'm a Miss or a Mrs."

"Oh. Yeah, I guess I never thought about that. I mean, I've never been divorced before, so I don't know."

"Are you married?"

"No. I've never been married, either. I'm Bitsy, by the way."

"Bitsy?"

"Yes, that's my name. Bitsy."

"Okay. Well, it's nice to meet you, Bitsy. I'm Kate. Tell me about that salad special."

Kate was still finishing her steak salad when the blonde came in and swept imperiously to the end of the counter where the cash register sat. The newcomer was tall and slender and beautifully dressed. In her tight skirt and heels, she didn't exactly look "small-town-Vermont," at least not to Kate's eyes. Bitsy was momentarily back in the kitchen, and the newcomer began impatiently tapping a knuckle on the counter while her right foot bounced up and down in rhythm.

Bitsy quickly appeared from the back.

"Hi, Miss Thompson. What can I do for you?"

"You know what you can do for me; it's the same every time. I want to make sure Paul has my order for the meeting tonight."

"Of course. Two pots of coffee and a tray of two dozen cookies."

"That's right. I'll pay for it now."

She handed Bitsy a credit card and glanced casually around while she waited, her foot still bouncing up and down. Her glance did not rest on Kate, at least not apparently, but Kate felt sure that she had been observed and appraised, nonetheless.

When Miss Thompson had signed the receipt and handed it back to Bitsy, she said, rather sharply, "The meeting starts at seven and I want the order delivered at six-forty-five."

"Of course."

The blonde swept out without another word.

Kate looked questioningly at Bitsy, who quickly supplied all the answers.

"Her name's Tiffany Thompson. She owns the antique store, 'The Tiff-Toff Shoppe,' and she's the chairman of the school board. Chairperson, I mean." Bitsy looked around; there was no one else in the cafe. "She's supposedly the most beautiful woman in Merryfield. At least, that's what all the men say, and she never contradicts them. She claims to be twenty-eight, but my mom says she's thirty-two, and my mom's the Town Clerk, so she should know."

"I see. She's single, I take it."

"Yes. She's had her claws in Ben Fremantle for a couple years now, but she can't seem to pin him down to an actual engagement."

"Ben Fremantle?"

"He's a lawyer; really handsome and a super nice guy. He comes in almost every day for lunch. The Fremantles have lived in Merryfield for, like, two hundred years, and Tiffany wants that, you know, old-family class and the money, of course."

"I see. Well, I guess there's a lot to learn about Merryfield. Bitsy, this place does dinner, as well, I take it."

"Oh, of course. You gonna come back tonight?"

"Well, I was thinking, if you guys do delivery..."

"We don't normally, but since we have to deliver the order for the School Board meeting, maybe the kid could drive up to the Andrews place, too."

"It's just that my moving van arrives tomorrow morning, and I don't have much with me..."

"Sure. Let me check with Paul."

"So, Boss, how was your first day in Minnyfield?"

"It's Merryfield, Millie, and stop calling me 'boss.' We don't have to be formal anymore. My first day has been interesting. I learned a few things, met a few people, had a couple of really nice meals..."

Millie Halpern was the office manager at Kate's literary agency and a good friend.

"What about men? What are the men like up there in the wilds?"

"It's not the 'wilds,' Millie. It's Vermont, and it's just as civilized as Connecticut. I haven't met any men yet; that's not what I'm here for."

"Of course it is! You're single, you're hot, and you need to meet someone! You haven't met even one?"

"Actually, I met the Merryfield Chief of Police, but he's in his fifties, has a big beer belly, and he's married."

"Well, then, you'd better start getting around tomorrow!"

"Millie, how can I convince you that's not what I'm here for?"

"You can't, so get your booty out there!"

2 |

The moving van was scheduled to arrive at nine-thirty, so Kate, having brought her basic survival kit, got up from her inflatable mattress and sleeping bag, spent half an hour in the bathroom, dressed, and was at the café for breakfast at eight o'clock.

The Maple Leaf was one of two places to have breakfast in Merryfield, so it was busy, but there were a couple of spots open at the counter. She sat down next to a couple to her right, engrossed in each other, and a bearded young man in jeans and a Carhartt shirt to her left. Bitsy was pouring her coffee before Kate was even seated.

"Morning, Kate! How was your dinner last night?"

"Oh, it was wonderful, thanks! Richie brought it to the house right at seven; he's a good kid, isn't he?"

"Yeah, he is. He's Paul's nephew. Take a look at the menu, and I'll be back in a minute."

At a corner table, Tiffany Thompson watched Kate walk from the door to the counter and take a seat. Her companion across the table noticed her gaze and asked, without turning around, "Who's just come in, Tiff?"

"It's the one I told you about, of course. Kate Stone, the rich divorcee from Fairfield County."

His interest peaked, Ben turned around and watched her sit down.

"She looks nice," he said and took another bite of his omelette.

"*Nice*? She looks *nice*? Ben, that naive shtick of yours is getting a little old. 'Nice' people do not leave their husbands behind and buy a mansion in Vermont."

"You know, these homefries are fantastic; and I'd hardly call it a mansion. More like an old wreck."

"Well, it was a mansion once, and it will be again when she's poured half a million into it."

Bitsy was carrying a full bus-tub through the swinging doors into the kitchen and almost bowled over Richie Pratt, who was staring at someone at the counter.

"Jesus, Richie! You can't stand there when it's this busy; don't you know that?"

It was obvious that the boy's stare was fixed on someone at the counter, and a quick glance back and forth confirmed who it was. Bitsy set the bus-tub down then grabbed Richie by the arm and pulled him back away from the door.

"Richie Pratt, you little fool! You are 'head-over-heels,' aren't you?"

"She's the most beautiful woman I've ever seen."

"Well, maybe she is, but she's at least ten years older than you and she's just been divorced! She's way out of your league, kid! And why are you still here? You're late for school!"

"I'm going, I'm going!"

Kate ordered her breakfast and was sipping her coffee when the man sitting to her left scraped his stool back and stood up. He hadn't said a word or appeared to notice her at all, but now that he was finished eating, he pulled out his wallet, flopped some bills on the counter, and slid a business card over in front of Kate.

"You're the lady that bought the Andrews house, right?"

"Yes, yes I am. I'm Kate Stone."

"My name's Chris Doran. I know that house inside and out. You're going to need a handyman, and I'm the one. Ask anyone. Ask Bitsy."

He pointed to the card, which advertised "carpentry and other services."

"Nice to meet you, ma'am."

"Thank you."

Among the thirty-five to forty people sitting in the Maple Leaf Café that morning, almost everyone knew who Kate Stone was. It being late May, there were not a lot of tourists in town yet, so everybody knew everybody. Kate had spoken to only a few people the day before, but others had seen her, and word had gotten around quickly.

Those who had spoken to Chief Bridger heard some variation of: "Seems like a nice lady, and she's a looker, for sure. Rich? Well, she might be, but that Volvo she drives is at least fifteen years old."

Those in Linda Norman's circle heard, "Good-looking lady with a four-year-old grey mare—beautiful horse. From what she told me, sounds like her husband was a real prick and maybe she didn't do so well out of the divorce."

Seventeen-year-old Richie Pratt, a month away from graduating high school, told his friends, "I almost dropped her dinner when she opened the door and smiled at me. She's gorgeous! Gave me a nice tip, too!"

Bitsy told her customers, "She's really nice. My mom said she got a good deal on the Andrews house; didn't pay as much as most people think. Hot? I'll say. I think the men are going to change their minds about who's the hottest chick in town, as soon as they've got a look."

But most people believed what they heard from Tiffany Thompson: "You know the story; it's the same old script. Her ex-husband is a financial advisor in one of the richest counties in America. She took him to the cleaners in a divorce, bought a two-hundred-year-old house in Vermont, and waltzed into town in a Volvo, pulling a horse trailer! Well, if she thinks she's going to be the biggest thing in this town, she's got another think coming!"

The movers showed up right on time. They were a professional outfit, and well-paid, so with Kate there to direct them they had all the furniture unloaded and in the right rooms in two and a half hours. When they had gone, she heated up a can of soup and brought it out to the porch, along with some crackers and a can of ginger ale.

The old Andrews house, now the Stone house, overlooked about half of the town of Merryfield from a plateau north of the town center. Wooded hills hid the rest of the town. Her winding driveway was about sixty yards long, so she could see any vehicle that turned off Locust Road to approach the house long before it arrived. Having visited twice while she considered the buy, she was familiar with the view, but this was her first opportunity to actually sit and enjoy it; her own view, from her own house.

Kate had visited Merryfield for the first time just about a month before, having seen the property listed on a real estate website. Before that, the only times she had been in Vermont were for a week at a summer camp when she was eight and a weekend at a ski resort shortly after she had married Jim Stone. Neither of those visits had been very memorable, but then, she hadn't really left the interstate other than at her destination.

But that first trip to Merryfield, to view the old Andrews house, had opened her eyes. She had driven through plenty of "picture postcard" villages in Massachusetts and a few in southern Vermont, but when she'd reached the valley where Merryfield, Wayford, and Petersford nestled in the shadow of surrounding mountains, she'd found a different kind of charm. There were neat little houses and antique stores, to be sure, but there were also sprawling farms with barns that hadn't been painted in years and old abandoned tractors left to rust in a corner of a pasture.

She'd even had to stop and wait for a herd of dairy cows to cross the road. It was that first drive up from Darien to Merryfield that had convinced her that Vermont could be a place to live, not just a place to visit. It was the kind of place that Arnold James Stone, Jr. would scorn to visit, much less live.

What to do first, she mused as she ate. A lot of unpacking to do, a lot of arranging, and a lot of assessing. That business card from Chris Doran was sitting on the kitchen counter; she had already decided to give him a call. Bitsy, the café waitress who was already her primary contact in town, had recommended him highly. There were a lot of jobs to do, some big and some small.

Thinking of jobs, she really wanted to do some "work work," even though she was supposed to be off for the week. A big file of queries was sitting in a folder on her PC, just waiting for her attention. She would have to call Millie tonight and see how the office was functioning without her. The plan was for Kate to do most of her work remotely but to spend one week a month back in Darien managing the office.

Kate chuckled as she thought about all of those locals watching her in the café this morning. What did they think about her? It had been pretty obvious that everyone, or nearly so, knew who she was. At least, they knew that she was "the divorcee from Connecticut who bought the old Andrews house." But what did they think about her? *They probably think I'm a rich bitch with a heart of stone, ready to rule this little town from the "house on the hill," she thought. Well, let them think what they will; I'll just live my life and let them discover who I really am.*

The real story of Kate Stone was more complicated. Some of what the townsfolk believed was true—her ex-husband was a very wealthy financial adviser in Darien, Connecticut, and she had certainly divorced him to buy an old house in a country town in Vermont. But she had certainly not "taken him to the cleaners." In her determination to escape an intolerable marriage, she would have settled for far less.

The good advice of friends, and a certain amount of righteous pride, had given her enough resolve to fight for a decent settlement. She had gotten enough money to buy this house, enough of her own furniture to be able to settle in, and a chunk of extra cash for renovations. At the last minute, however, an opportunity had arisen to buy out the literary agency where she worked. It was what she had always wanted, and she had no doubts about doing it. But it took most of her money, so now she was going to have to live on her earnings from the agency and try to fix up this old house bit by bit.

"So, how was your first full day in Vermont, boss? What did you do today?"

"Well, I watched the movers bring all my stuff in and made sure everything made it to the right room. They were good; nothing broken or lost. Still a lot of work to do unpacking and organizing."

"You can leave some of that, you know. I'll be up to help this weekend."

"I know; I appreciate it, Millie."

"So, who did you meet today?"

"Well, a lot of people saw me at the café this morning and I got the impression that they all knew who I was already."

"Small town gossip—word gets around fast."

"It sure does. I met a handyman; he was sitting next to me at the café. He gave me his business card, and Bitsy said he was really good, so I called him this afternoon and he's coming over tomorrow."

"Progress! What's he look like?"

"Don't get all excited, Millie. He's about thirty, kind of rough looking, and Bitsy says he's married, with one kid and another on the way."

"Too bad. Who's Bitsy?"

"The waitress at the café. It seems to be 'gossip central' in Merryfield, and she seems to know everybody."

"Is that café the only place to eat there?"

"No. There's a diner—the Miss Merryfield Diner—that serves breakfast and lunch, and there's a restaurant called the Tranmere. They serve dinner only and it's supposed to be really nice—that's what Bitsy told me, and Linda Norman at the farm said the same thing. Not a place I would go by myself, though. The Maple Leaf Café is open from six-thirty in the morning until ten at night. They're a little more 'upscale' than a diner, and the meals I've had have been really good."

"Did you go there for dinner tonight?"

"No. I felt like having something from my own new kitchen. The moving van had a refrigerated section, so they brought all the stuff from my fridge and I had some chicken and rice."

"Okay. Anything else happen today?"

"Well, I had some interesting visitors. This afternoon, at about three-thirty, I was out in the yard, looking over the shed, when a car drove up the drive. It was the same Subaru that delivered my dinner yesterday, and the same driver, but this time there were three other boys in the car with him."

"Boys?"

"Yeah, this kid, Richie, works at the café. When he stopped, he leaned out the window and asked if I needed any help moving things. I'm pretty sure he's got a crush on me."

"Ha! And he was showing you off to his friends!"

"Yeah. I said, 'No, but thanks for the offer,' and he drove away. Took a little more time turning around than he really needed to; it was kind of weird. Sort of halfway between flattering and creepy."

3 |

Kate was in the cafe for breakfast again the next morning, but a little later this time.

"Not as busy today?" she asked.

"It was earlier," Bitsy replied. "It's always busy between six-thirty and nine, then it slows down until lunch time. You should try the turkey hash today; it's really good."

"Turkey hash? I've never heard of such a thing. Sure, I'll try it."

"With a couple eggs?"

"Just one egg, please—over easy."

Kate's plan for today was to go out to the farm after breakfast and bring Dolly out for some exercise. Chris Doran was coming out to the house at one, so she had plenty of time for a ride and a stop for groceries after.

"Bitsy, is the IGA the only place in town to get groceries?"

"Yeah. There's a bigger store in the next town, Wayford, and most people go there if they need to load up, but the IGA's not bad. So, what's your horse like?"

"She's a beautiful grey mare, four years old."

"I love horses. Never really had many chances to ride, though. Be right back!"

This Thursday morning, a couple actually stopped to introduce themselves as they were leaving the café.

"Miss Stone?" the elderly woman said, her voice as crackly as her skin.

"Yes, I'm Kate Stone."

"I'm Lila Bennett, and this is my husband, Tom."

"Pleased to meet you, Miss Stone," the man said, extending his right hand.

"Thank you, I'm pleased to meet you, too."

"You know," Lila said, "we used to go up there pretty regular, when Margaret and Stanley still lived there. Margaret and Stanley Andrews, that is. They were the last of the family to live there."

"Course, that was quite a few years back," Tom added.

"They used to have dinner parties, you see," Lila said.

"Really nice parties," her husband said. "And Christmas, too."

"A big Christmas party every year."

"Just about everyone in town would be there."

"Just about everyone."

It seemed that Kate would never get a chance to say anything, but Bitsy arrived with her breakfast and, knowing full well who she was dealing with, the waitress immediately jumped in to break up the conversation.

"Here's your breakfast, Kate. Hope you had a nice breakfast to-day, Mr. and Mrs. Bennett; so nice to see you again."

"Yes, it was lovely, Betsy. Well, I guess we'd better get going."

"Better get going."

"Lovely to meet you both. Bye!"

When the elderly couple had left, Bitsy simply said "They like to chat."

"I gathered."

"And they always call me 'Betsy,'" she said, with a roll of her eyes and a helpless shrug.

Ben Fremantle had a secret. It wasn't intended to be a secret; his brother, Rory, hadn't asked him not to tell anyone else. It was only a secret to Ben, and there was a good chance it would remain a secret for a week, because Ben knew that Rory would almost certainly not contact anyone else. Rory was notoriously uncommunicative, and the only other person he might have told—his former girlfriend, Christine Plouffe—had vowed never to speak to him or hear his voice again.

Ben didn't want to tell his girlfriend—Tiffany Thompson—that Rory was coming back to town, and if he told anyone else, she would surely hear of it quickly. She would find out in a week's time, obviously, and there was a chance she would find out sooner, but Ben was the kind who needed time to mull things over. He very much wanted as much time as he could get to determine in his own mind what the impact would be on his relationship with Tiffany and what he should do about it.

He was leaning on a fence outside the stable on his family estate, waiting for Tiffany to arrive for their regular Thursday morning ride. He and Billy Tourville had already saddled both his mount and Tiffany's, knowing how she hated to be delayed. The Fremantles maintained six horses of their own as well as boarding Tiffany's, and Billy was their almost-full-time groom/stable hand.

Right on cue, Tiffany's Saab pulled into the barnyard just as Billy was leading both horses out to them.

As always, the tall, slender blonde looked perfect in her chic riding habit, and she flashed that trademark smile at Billy as she took the reins from his hand.

"Thanks, Billy; you're efficient, as always."

Billy grunted and sort of grinned.

"How's my man this morning?" she said, turning her attention and her smile to Ben.

She came right up to him and, not the least bit shy about public displays of affection, threw her arms around his neck and planted a full kiss on his lips. As he responded fully, he asked himself—for the thousandth time, it seemed—why he couldn't just go ahead and ask her to marry him? This was the woman for him, no doubt. Why couldn't he get over that hurdle?

Again, as always, there was no logical answer, but the hurdle remained. It wasn't Rory; he had put that behind him, behind them. That's what he kept telling himself.

Kate was enjoying her morning ride, as was Dolly, although the trail was, of course, new to both of them. It was a five-mile loop that wound through woods and meadows and crossed several small streams. There were other trails with more elevation, but Kate had decided to start with this fairly easy ride their first time out in their new home.

Linda Norman had explained that part of this trail and some of the others crossed through the Fremantle estate. The two families for several generations had happily shared trails, to their mutual benefit.

Kate and Dolly came up a slight rise out of a wooded section and came to a "tee" where they could go left or right. A log fence outlined a semi-circular flat; a perfect spot to stop for a rest and enjoy a spectacular view.

That was where Ben Fremantle first saw Kate Stone to full effect, leaning up against the fence, with Dolly's reins casually looped over the top rail. She was about Tiffany's height—perhaps an inch shorter—and, in her riding habit—not as fashionable as Tiff's—she looked fantastic. In spite of the studied calm that was Ben's seemingly permanent attitude, there was a decided change in his body language, and he knew it.

Tiffany knew it, too.

They exchanged greetings—friendly, of course. They all knew who was who, but formal introductions were begun and completed. The tension was palpable, however, and none of them really wanted to linger. So Ben and Tiffany continued on their way, and Kate remounted and rode off to the left.

Back at Sunrise Farm, Linda Norman had a good laugh about it while they gave Dolly a good rubdown in her stall.

"I suppose it's not really funny," she said, "but it's funny as hell!"

"Okay. Well, let me in on the joke, please, so I can know what I'm laughing about."

"See, Ben and Tiffany have been going together for three, maybe four years. He is the town's 'biggest catch,' the eldest son of Mrs. Fremantle. The family is rich, owns the biggest piece of land in Merryfield, and even if Ben inherits only half of the estate, he'll be the richest man in town, by far.

"Not that Tiff is poor, herself. She owns that antique store and everything in it, plus the house right behind it that she lives in. But she wants more; she wants Ben, and she's made it clear that she deserves him and nobody else. Well, who wouldn't?"

"He's very good looking."

"He sure is. Tall, slender, face like an angel, and he's more than that. He's an attorney; graduated Vermont Law School, specializing in Environmental Law, and he's already taken on some major litigation against developers and polluters."

"Sounds like a dream come true. Are they engaged?"

"No, they're not and that's the funny thing. See, last spring, Tiff got tired of waiting, apparently, and she had a fling with Rory—that's Ben's brother. She only did it to make Ben jealous. She even told him so, and it worked. Ben was furious and he told her he wanted her and swore if she ever did anything like that again, he'd drop her like a hot potato."

Linda stopped talking for a bit.

"So? What happened?"

"She went back to Ben, of course. But he still hasn't proposed."

"Maybe they have a secret engagement."

Linda snorted.

"Not likely. When Ben finally gives her a ring, she'll shout it from the highest hill in town."

"What happened to the brother? Is he still around?"

"Nah. That's the sad thing. See, Ben and Tiff and everybody in Merryfield knew she did it just to make him jealous. Everybody except Rory. It broke his heart and broke up a long relationship he had with Christy Plouffe. He's gone off to work on an oil rig down in the Gulf of Mexico. Been gone a year."

"That's sad. What a bitch!"

"You can say that again!"

Chris Doran arrived right on time, rolling up the driveway in his pickup truck at one o'clock. Kate was sitting on the porch, enjoying a cup of coffee and a cookie. She got up and walked down the steps to meet Chris, holding a small plate of cookies in front of her.

"Don't mind if I do, Miss Stone."

"I can't claim to have made them myself, I'm afraid; they're from the café."

"Mmm... I know these cookies—good."

"Would you like to sit on the porch and talk?"

"Sure."

He cast an appraising eye over the steps and the deck of the porch as he followed Kate and sat down on one of the wicker chairs.

"You said you know this house inside and out, right, Chris?" Kate asked.

"Yeah. Haven't been here since last fall—October, I think. I did a temporary repair on the roof in the back: the northeast corner. Just to get through the winter. That's one of the things you'll have to have done."

"Yes, I know. I had an inspection done before the closing. Would you like to see it?"

"Sure."

"It's on the kitchen counter; I'll get it. Say, I should have offered you something to drink. There's more fresh coffee in the pot. Or…"

"Oh, coffee would be great. Just black, thanks."

She came back in a minute with a cup of coffee and the inspection report.

He looked at the information on the front page and made a bit of a sour face, just sour enough to be noticeable.

"You know the inspector?"

"Bill Donohue. Yeah, I know him. A lot of people around here use him. He's perfectly capable, don't get me wrong, it's just that…"

"Yes…"

"Well, it's always the same, isn't it? *You* pay the inspector, but he's working for the realtor or for the bank." He immediately raised his hands with a gesture that seemed to disavow what he had just said. "Now, that sounds like an accusation, so let me rephrase that. It *seems* like they're working for the realtor or the bank. The realtor in your case, since you don't have a mortgage."

"How did you know that?"

He just shrugged.

"Well, you're right, Chris. Anyway, would you like to read it through? I need to make a phone call that will take ten to fifteen minutes sometime this afternoon. I can do that right now while you read the report."

"That works. Okay if I walk around and check out a few things at the same time? I know my way around."

"Sure."

Chris was coming up the stairs from the basement when she finished her phone call, and they walked back out to the porch together.

"Listen, Chris," she said, "I have to tell you before we get into details that I have a budget. I'm sure most people in town think I'm filthy rich, but..."

"I'm not most people, Miss Stone. Just tell me what you can spend, and we'll figure out where you should spend it."

"Just what I had in mind, and I think you should call me Kate."

"Thank you, Kate; I will."

"So, I have six thousand dollars to spend this year on repairs. I hope to be able to spend more than that next year, but that's my limit for this year."

"Okay. Well, here's what I think are the most important things to get done. That corner of the roof, for sure. The patch I did was never meant to be permanent, and Bill's report says the same thing. I can't get up there today; the ladders on my truck aren't long enough, but I can take a look tomorrow. But I know what needs to be done anyway. It's about a two thousand-dollar job, and if you put it off you could have a lot of damage."

"Okay."

"This porch—the deck, the railing and the steps. It's a safety issue, so you shouldn't put it off. That's another two thousand, and I can make it look a lot nicer, too."

"Okay."

"I'm concerned about the furnace. I think Bill's estimate that you can get five years out of that furnace is optimistic, to say the least."

"Oh. That's disappointing. That's going to cost a lot, isn't it?"

"Yes. A lot to replace the furnace. But there is an alternative. You've got a wood stove in there, sitting in a corner of the cellar."

"But it's really old, isn't it? The inspector thought it wasn't usable."

"He don't know wood stoves. It's old, alright—practically an antique. But it's a really good stove, and all it needs is a good cleanout and some grates replaced. Your chimney is fully lined already; that lining was put in six years ago, before the old Andrews couple left.

"What I'm saying is, you can be pretty sure your furnace will make it through next winter, but if you start using wood, it will take some stress off the furnace..."

"You mean use the furnace as a backup?"

"Exactly. It will save you a lot of money on oil. If you don't mind carrying wood, it's a good option for you. And that furnace will last a lot longer the less you use it."

"How much does firewood cost?"

"Well, I've got pretty good connections. I can get you wood for two hundred a cord, split and dried. You've got almost a cord there in the shed already. It's been in the shed and covered, and it's perfectly fine. Another cord should get you through the winter. If you can swing it, get two cords and you'll be ahead for next year."

Kate smiled. "I always wanted to be able to heat with wood, but I didn't think I'd be able to. Can you do that? Clean up the stove and put it in place and working?"

"Sure I can. Here's what I figure; I can do the roof, do the porch, get that stove sorted and a couple cords of wood, and..." He gazed over at the shed. "And I can get that shed painted; it needs it. If I do all that, you should have maybe five hundred left in your budget, more or less."

"I think we've got a deal, Chris. Thank you!"

"Carry wood? You're not exactly a country girl, boss. What are you thinking?"

"Maybe I'll get that high school boy to haul wood for me; I bet he'd do it for nothing."

"Kate Stone, are you kidding me?"

"Yes, I'm kidding you, Millie. It's a joke."

"Well, that's a relief. I think your sense of humor is changing from that country living. So, this Ben Flanigan sounds like a dream."

"Fremantle."

"Whatever. But his girlfriend sounds like a nightmare."

"She sure is. I got a vibe of pure hatred from her."

"Well, her beau got a look at you in that riding habit and it probably knocked him for a loop. You should have arranged a private meeting."

"I didn't arrange anything, and I'm not going to. Believe me, Millie, I'm not setting my sights on Ben Fremantle."

"More's the pity. I sure would."

4 |

On Wednesday, Chris Doran asked her to meet him at the hardware store to look at some materials with him, and afterward, they went to the Miss Merryfield Diner for lunch.

"I like to spread my custom around," he said. "Nothing against Bitsy or Paul."

"Oh, I understand. I haven't been to the diner yet."

"It's...well, it's a diner."

It was, in fact, a classic old diner of the type that resembled an old railroad dining car—in its shape, anyway. There were about sixty seats inside, and there was an attached deck with outdoor seating for twenty-five, but the entrance was blocked off, and the sign read: *Opening for the season soon.*

As they took their seats at a two-top, Kate remarked, "I'm still trying to get used to the seasons here. I've been here eight days and it's only really been warm once. And it's almost Memorial Day!"

"Well," he said with a laugh, "I could try to entertain you with all the clichés about Vermont climate and weather, but it really just comes down to a shorter season than you're used to. We have some beautiful weather here, for sure; you just have to wait a little longer for it."

A waitress came over to pour coffee and take their orders. There was nothing "upscale" about the menu here at the Miss Merryfield: burgers, sandwiches and salads made with shredded iceberg lettuce. The Wednesday special was Maple Baked Beans with Macaroni and

Cheese and Ham. That's what Chris ordered, and he said it was the best thing on the menu.

"I don't often miss Wednesday lunch here, and that's the reason."

"I'll have the same, please," Kate said as she handed the menu back to the waitress with a smile.

"Speaking of seasons," Chris said. "You've still got time to plant a garden if you want."

"I've been thinking about that. As I told you when you first mentioned it, I know absolutely nothing about gardening, but I look out at that plot every day and wish I were doing something with it. I hate waste, you know."

"So do I. I'll tell you what. We could clear off as much of that garden plot as you want to use. The fenced plot is about a hundred feet square, but if you wanted to start small, we could till just a small part of it—say, ten feet by twenty—and you could give it a try. If it doesn't suit you, you won't have wasted much time or money to find out."

"'Till' meaning plow? I'm afraid I don't know much…"

"Yes. We have a big rototiller at home and I, or my wife, could turn over a ten by twenty plot for you in twenty minutes or less."

"Really? That's all it would take?"

"Well, we'd have to clear the brush off first, but that's only two years' growth. The last tenant used it three summers ago. My mower would clear that whole plot in half an hour. The soil underneath is fine; it's been planted off and on for years and it's pretty much rock-free. As much as any field in Vermont can be rock-free."

"You mentioned your wife…"

"Patty. She could come over with the tiller and show you how to do it, or just do it herself."

"Isn't she…"

"She's six months pregnant, but that don't stop her. Nothing stops her."

"Could I grow tomatoes? Lettuce? Basil?"

"All those things. Tomatoes and basil you wouldn't have wanted to plant before now, anyway. Lettuce and other greens can go in when it's still cold, but it don't matter; plant them now and they'll catch up."

"What about corn?"

"Well, you could, if we cleared more space, but why bother? Come August, there will be four farm stands selling fresh corn within three miles of here. You can buy all the fresh corn you want for pocket change, without any work."

The waitress arrived with their lunch, and Kate gasped in astonishment.

"Oh, my God! All this?"

The waitress chuckled, as did several people at neighboring tables.

"A little more than you expected, honey?" the waitress asked.

"Just a little."

Kate was back at the cafe for breakfast Thursday morning.

"Hey, Kate. How are you?" Bitsy asked with a big grin.

"I'm fine this morning, Bitsy. How about you?"

"Great. I heard you had lunch with Chris at the Miss M. How was that?"

"Bitsy, do you hear everything that happens in this town as soon as it happens?"

"Pretty much. Was it your first time there?"

"Yes. But didn't you know that already?"

"Yeah, but sometimes it's better to pretend I don't know things."

"Alright, I get that. Yes, we were looking at some stuff at the hardware store together and then we went for lunch. I suppose everyone in town knows?"

"Pretty much. It's not much of a scandal, though. The 'upper crust,' Tiffany's friends, don't go to the diner. A few people seem to think that you and Chris are an item, but everyone who knows Chris knows he's true blue."

"Good. He's helping me out a lot."

"Yeah, he was a good find for you. There's a lot of so-called handymen out there and you met the best one right off the bat."

"So, what's good today, Bitsy?"

"How about a brie souffle with asparagus?"

Tiffany kept trotting out ahead of Ben on the trail and then slowing down until he caught up. It seemed deliberate to Ben and it seemed to match her mood. Outwardly, she was all smiles, but the pre-ride embrace and kiss had been rather unenthusiastic, he thought.

She's been cool all week, and I know it's about that woman. Of course I reacted when I saw her; what healthy male wouldn't? Kate Stone, the new woman in town. She's not more beautiful than Tiffany. Nobody's more beautiful than Tiffany. She's just different, and why can't a man look at something different?

Jesus. Why can't things be simple?

Tiffany had disappeared around a corner; they were in pretty thick woods and he couldn't see her. He turned the corner and stopped. There they were; his Tiffany and Kate Stone, standing still where the trail forked, forty yards ahead. Tiff's black stallion and the new woman's grey mare, standing nose to tail and pointed in opposite directions. They seemed to be chatting.

Ben started slowly forward. Before he had gone far, Kate turned her horse's head and trotted off, down the left-hand fork. Tiffany waited for Ben, and when he reached her, she gave him a big smile and said, "Come on, hon."

As they rode silently along the right-hand trail, side by side now, he wondered. That smile seemed almost triumphant, as if to say: *I've settled her hash.*

At one o'clock, Chris Doran pulled into Kate's yard in his pickup, followed closely by a small car driven by a woman. Kate walked down from the porch to meet them, nearly tripping as a rotting step crumbled under her foot.

When the Subaru came to a stop, Chris went right to the back as his wife got out of the driver's seat, and the reason became apparent when he emerged holding a small, laughing child.

"Hi, Miss Stone," said the clearly pregnant but not-too-huge woman, "I'm Patty. Nice to meet you."

"Nice to meet you, Patty, and please call me Kate."

Patty was short and pretty in her jeans and sweatshirt and her long hair restrained by what looked like a tie-dyed kerchief. The first thing that came to mind for Kate was: *Phish came to town for a concert and left one of their followers behind.*

"You gotta meet our little girl, Kate," Patty said as Chris approached carrying the giggling child. "This is Beth."

"Well, hi, Beth."

"Hi!" the girl shouted, followed by a big laugh.

"She likes people," Chris explained.

"Apparently."

"Until she doesn't like them anymore," Patty added.

"Okay; I'm forewarned. Can I get you anything? A lemonade? Iced tea?"

"Well, I've got juice for Beth. Lemonade would be nice, especially after we've worked for a while. I think Chris wants to get started."

"Right," Chris said. "Why don't you three get settled at the picnic table while I get the tiller out of the truck. But here's the thing, Kate, I really don't think you should use the front steps anymore or that end of the porch."

"Yeah, the steps..."

"I saw. I really want to get the roof done first; you never know when we might get a storm that could do some real damage. So how about if I rope off the porch and you use the back door for now. You can still use the other end of the porch and come around from the back."

"That sounds like a good idea; I don't want to have anyone get hurt."

Kate went around to the back door, which led right into the kitchen, and when she came out with a big pitcher full of lemonade and ice cubes, she found Patty seated at the picnic table, which Chris and Kate had retrieved the day before from behind the shed and set up right next to the garden fence. Beth's stroller was set up right next to the table, but the girl was, for the moment, up on the table, dancing and singing.

They talked for a few minutes, but Chris wanted to get going unloading the materials he had brought, so as soon as he had wheeled the tiller over to the garden plot, the ladies got up for Kate's first lesson in using the rototiller. Kate expressed her concern for Beth, who was walking along beside them, but Patty reassured her.

"She helps me in the garden all the time, and she knows enough to stay out of the way."

Patty fired up the tiller, which looked way too big for the small area Kate intended to use. Speaking up to be heard over the noise of the gas-powered machine, Patty asked if she was starting in the right place and, when Kate nodded an affirmative, she glanced quickly at her daughter to make sure she was safe then flicked the lever to lower the blades and started off.

Kate was astonished at how easy it looked and how well it worked. The sod was disappearing into furrows of turned-up soil that looked dark and rich. In little more than a minute, Patty had reached the end of the ten-by-twenty-foot area and turned to come back.

"Wow!" she exclaimed when Patty had come back to the starting point and stopped.

"Ready to give it a try?"

She wasn't really, but she gave it a try anyway. It turned out to be more difficult than she thought, but it was doable. The arm strength required was a bit surprising, but Kate was not a weakling; she had often mucked out the stalls in their stable back in Darien and that was no easy task. When she had finished a double row, Patty looked at her with raised eyebrows, but she shook her head, turned the big machine around and headed off to do another double row. After that she did stop for a break, and Patty took over to finish it.

That was all it took. Twenty minutes of work, and she had a garden plot ready to be planted.

"Yay!" Beth shouted as her mother shut off the machine and wheeled it back out of the garden plot.

"Well said!" Kate answered with a laugh.

They returned to the picnic table, which was only a few feet away, and sat down for more lemonade and juice and chatter. This time they had a much longer talk about the garden and about Merryfield and about each other.

It turned out that Patty was the daughter of a woman who had followed the Grateful Dead to Vermont back in the nineties, which explained why Beth had been singing "Sugaree" while dancing on the table earlier. Patty was twenty-six and Beth was three and a half.

Kate explained about her divorce, without going into detail, and about her horse and her clothing.

"This is what I used to wear in the stables back in Darien."

"I thought those boots looked like shit-kickers. You should get some other boots for gardening, though. Those must be a little awkward."

"Yeah, I need a few things. This is the only shirt I have that I don't mind getting dirty. These jeans will do, I guess, but maybe I should have another pair."

Chris interrupted with a shout then climbed into his truck and drove away.

"He's got to meet someone at two-thirty and he's coming back with roofing tiles. They've got a pretty good selection of gardening gear at the hardware store. Why don't you follow me there when we leave and I can show you what you need. So what do you want to plant?"

They talked about what to plant and where to put it. Beth had been dozing in her stroller, but she woke up briefly to yell, "No carrots!" before falling asleep again.

They talked about the town and the townspeople.

"You've made quite the impression in just a week," Patty said.

"Oh? Well, that wasn't my intention."

"I'm sure it wasn't, but people don't care about intentions; they only care about what they see and hear. It seems, so far, that all the people you've actually met seem to like you—except for Her Highness, of course—and everyone else seems to think you're an evil schemer out to steal every man in town away from their women."

"Well, I'm not really surprised. I'm not, though. I mean I'm not out to steal..."

"Oh, I know. But—to most people—you are automatically suspect. You're from out-of-state, you're divorced, you divorced a rich man, so everyone assumes you have a shitload of money, and you're beautiful. It all adds up to a big threat."

"What do you mean, you've met another friendly *woman*? Boss, you're supposed to be meeting *men*."

"Oh, stop it, Millie. I'm not trying to meet men, and the ones I've met don't appeal to me anyway."

"Oh, come on. That dreamboat lawyer doesn't appeal to you?"

"Well, at another time and in another place, sure he would. But I'm not out to steal anyone's man, no matter what they think."

"Is that what they think?"

"Some of them. I had another encounter with the blonde bitch today."

"Hey, careful what you say about blondes!"

"Sorry. I was out riding, and I ran into her on the trail. He was quite a ways behind her. I was stopped at a fork in the trail and she stopped beside me, looked me right in the eye and said, 'Mrs. Stone, I've got some friendly advice for you. That carpenter you're hanging out with is married, and people in this town don't like that sort of thing. You'd better watch your step.' That's all she said. I turned Dolly's head and rode away."

"As if it was the carpenter she was worried about."

"Exactly. Hey, you're still coming up for the weekend, right?"

"Absolutely. I should be there between twelve and one."

"Great. I've made reservations for us. Hey, call me once you get off the highway. The GPS won't like these country roads."

5

Millie Halpern arrived in Merryfield without incident just after noon on Friday and even found her way to Kate's house without having to ask for directions. She found Kate leaning against the garden fence, a steel rake in her hands.

"Look at you, boss! You're like a real farmer!"

"Hardly. I've learned more about gardening in the last twenty-four hours than I ever knew, but I'm still a rank amateur."

The women shared a quick embrace, and Kate helped Millie get a couple of bags out of her car. They walked around to the back door, Kate explaining as they went about the front steps and why they were roped off.

"Is that something you knew about before you bought the place?"

"Yes. It's one of the reasons the price was so good."

The back door led into the kitchen, and Millie immediately proclaimed it an awesome kitchen.

"It's so big and airy! And sunny!"

"Yeah, it's great, isn't it? It gets the morning sun through that window and the midday sun through this one."

"Hey, I gotta look around; give me a tour!"

So Kate led her around the five spacious rooms on the ground floor then up the wide staircase to the four rooms upstairs.

"Jesus, Kate! This is like that B&B I stayed at with that guy—what was his name?—anyway, it's fabulous! It just needs fixing up. But what the hell are you gonna do here by yourself?"

"I'm just going to live here, Millie, all by myself."

"Yeah, right. Listen, when you hook that good-looking lawyer, you and he can sink some of his money into this place and it'll be spectacular!"

"You're dreaming, Millie. Hey, this is your room. I made the bed, and the closet and the bureau are clean, though I don't suppose you need much space for a weekend."

"Not much. Hey, we're going out tonight, right?"

"Yes, but… listen, Millie, the place we're going is supposed to be really great. I mean, a destination restaurant with a French chef, but going out in Merryfield, Vermont is not the same as going into Manhattan for dinner."

"Sure, I know, but we've got to look good, boss."

Tiffany was a little peeved. "Six o'clock, honey? Why so early?"

"I know it's a bit of a pain, but I have to take a phone call in the office at eight-thirty. It's that client in California, and he swears he can't be ready before then. I don't know how long it will take, so there's no way we could eat after."

"Okay, I guess it's alright. What about after?"

"Why don't I drop you at your place after dinner, then I can go back after my call for a nightcap and whatever?"

"A nightcap and whatever sounds nice."

Ben hung up the phone and leaned back in his chair. The phone call from California *was* important; he hadn't made that up. But it was an earlier call that was weighing on his mind. Rory had called again. Ben's younger brother was flying into Burlington on Saturday, and he wanted Ben to drive his car—Rory's restored '65 Mustang—up to the Burlington airport to pick him up.

No problem with that; there was no rancor between the two—not now—and Ben could easily arrange his schedule to take most of the day off. But Ben still hadn't told Tiffany that Rory was coming back to town.

He got up and walked over to the window. His office was located on the second floor, over the bank, and overlooked Main Street. The town of Merryfield had a population of just over three thousand, about half of them scattered over a grid of residential streets on either side of Main and the rest on farms and isolated homesteads farther out. Most of the businesses in Merryfield were concentrated right here, either within his field of vision or nearby. The drug store was directly across from him, and he could see the hardware store to his left and the Maple Leaf Café to his right. Two church steeples were in clear view on this bright, sunny day, as well as an old rusting water tower by the railroad crossing.

Fremantle and Burns was the only law office in town, and he and Clem Burns the only attorneys. Of course, the town of Wayford was only six miles away, and Wayford had twice as many people and twice as many businesses of every kind. Folks around here liked to "keep it local," but the definition of local could be easily expanded to suit the needs of the moment.

Ben liked his life here very much. It was quiet, it was comfortable, it was secure. People liked him and trusted him and he liked the people of Merryfield. He was going to marry Tiffany Thompson, eventually, and raise a family right here in the place he loved. He was going to age gracefully, have lots of grandchildren, and die in his bed a respected patriarch of the town of Merryfield.

He guessed he'd better tell her about Rory. Tonight, over dinner. Or maybe later.

* * *

After a sandwich on the porch, Kate and Millie spent the afternoon moving things around and arranging. With few exceptions, every piece of furniture was in the right room, but not necessarily in the right place. Kate had situated the kitchen: her kitchen table, with chairs for four, was in the southwest corner, the sunniest spot in the house.

But there were boxes and boxes of china, glasswear, cutlery, and pots and pans, only a few of which Kate had pulled out and used thus far. It took almost all of Friday afternoon to get everything in its place. Finally, all that remained was Kate's nicest, and most expensive, dinner service and the set of wine glasses that went with it.

"It's got to go in your awesome china cabinet, right?"

"Right. It's in the living room."

Kate's awesome china cabinet was a seven-foot-tall oak antique with glass doors.

"Boss, I'm so glad you ended up with this. It's insured for like…"

"Four thousand. Well, it was mine before we married; it was my mom's. I let Jim have so many other things, and he decided not to fight for this."

They carried the boxes of Kate's best china carefully into the dining room and placed them in the cabinet. When the wine glasses had gone in as well, there was still a lot of empty space to fill. A few boxes on the dining room table held some ornamental pieces and those were put in the cabinet. It still looked half empty.

"Jim took all those nice silver pieces?"

"Yeah, they were his. It's going to take me a while to fill this thing."

"There's an antique store in town; I drove by it. You can maybe pick up some things there."

Kate laughed out loud.

"What's funny?"

"'Her Highness' owns that antique store—the blonde who belongs to the hunk lawyer. Or he belongs to her. Anyway, I can't be buying much of anything right now."

They heard the toot of a car horn outside, followed by a door opening and closing.

"Kate, it's Patty! I've got some starts for you!"

Patty Doran came around to the back door and into the kitchen, carrying a cardboard box.

"Oh, Patty, that's so good of you! Come on in!"

The kitchen door flew open, and a wild-looking child ran in, arms outstretched, and headed right for Kate.

"Hi, Kate!" she shouted, a big smile on her face.

"Hi, Beth!" Kate responded, lifting the little girl up and into her arms. "I'm so happy to see you again!"

"Me, too!"

Patty had followed her daughter through the door, and she introduced herself to Millie while setting a tomato box filled with small plants on the table.

"Nice to meet you, Patty. And this is your daughter, I take it."

"Yes, that is Beth, the wild one. She likes Kate. And I suppose Kate told you about the hippie farmer she met. That's me."

"Yes, she did. What did you bring?"

They stood around the kitchen table while Patty pointed out the little seedlings she had brought.

"Well, like I told you, Kate, I always start more than I'll need, because you never know how many will survive. These are what's leftover: four tomato plants, two cucumbers, three lettuces, and a bunch of herbs."

"No carrots," Beth said emphatically.

"No, no carrots," Patty said. "But, honey, if Kate wants to plant carrots, that's up to her. This garden is for her, not for you."

"I don't like carrots."

"Understood, Beth," Kate said, still holding the child. "No carrots. Patty, this is great. Are you sure you don't need any of these?"

"I'm sure. I've got everything I need. I'll be planting my tomatoes and the rest of my herbs over the weekend, and these are extra."

Millie looked skeptically at the limp little seedlings. "They look, umm..."

Patty laughed. "They don't look as nice as the plants you buy at a garden center, but they'll grow just as well. See the ones that are still kind of limp; I have them tied loosely to popsicle sticks with twist ties. You can leave them like that until they're strong enough to stand on their own."

"That's great, Patty," Kate said. "Millie and I can plant them tomorrow. Right, Millie?"

"Umm, well, I brought some casual clothes, but not that casual. And if you think the dress I brought for going out tonight is too 'over the top' for this restaurant we're going to, then I'll have to wear my 'casual' stuff tonight."

"Well, we'll figure it out, Millie."

"You're going to the Tranmere tonight?" Patty asked.

"Yes, we are," Kate said. "What can you tell us about it?"

"Oh, well, Chris and I haven't been there for a couple years. We went for our anniversary once, but it's a little out of our price range. I sold them some spring lambs, though; you'll probably see a lamb special on the menu."

Ben and Tiffany had a splendid time at the Tranmere. The place was nearly full, it being the Friday night of a holiday weekend, but Ben had had no difficulty getting a reservation. Later in the season, when all the B&Bs in the county were full and the tourists were every-where, even a Fremantle would have to book a table at least a week ahead.

Tiff was in a good mood, which made everything more pleasant. The scallop ceviche appetizer was one of Ben's favorites, and the rack of spring lamb with rosemary was superb. They talked about horses quite a bit; Ben had plans for renovating the stables and Tiffany was always talking about buying another horse, or two. She loved her black stallion, Jet, but she always wanted more of everything.

They talked about the Memorial Day festivities, which interested Ben more than Tiff. He was on the committee that organized the whole thing. She was proud of him, of course; it was part of being one of the town's leading citizens. But she thought the parade on Monday was sort of "provincial." Most of the businesses and orga-nizations in Merryfield had some kind of float entered in the parade, but it wasn't the kind of thing that a first-rate antique store did.

She did her share of people-watching and dishing. She talked about who was overdressed and who was underdressed; who had clearly had a few drinks before they got there; and who should have gone to the diner for the meatloaf special instead of taking up space at the Tranmere. Ben wasn't really interested and she knew it, but as long as he smiled politely and didn't interrupt, she didn't mind.

Ben had thought, before they got there, that if Tiffany was in a good mood, he would tell her about Rory coming back over dinner. He certainly didn't want to tell her when she was in a bad mood. But then he thought— *We're having such a good time, why ruin it? I'll tell her later.*

Another glass of wine, a splendid dessert, and all of a sudden it was quarter to eight. Ben paid the check and Tiffany headed to the ladies room. When she emerged, she was putting her compact back in her bag and didn't look up until she reached the foyer. Right in front of her was a curvy blonde in a low-cut, very tight dress. She was flirting shamelessly with the maitre d' and when they stepped aside to let Tiffany pass, there, right in front of her, were Ben and Kate Stone; smiles on both their faces and appearing to have a friendly chat.

6

"Oh, my God, Kate! Here's your coffee, and I'll be right back. It's busy, but boy do we have things to talk about!"

Bitsy had managed to get Kate and Millie two seats at the counter. The café was packed, but the Saturday morning rush was just dying down and everyone waiting at the door had finally been seated. Almost every eye in the place had followed the two women from the moment they walked in. Now that they were seated, almost every tongue in the place was talking about them.

It was nine o'clock Saturday morning and the café had opened at six-thirty, so, by now, everyone had heard some version of what had happened at the Tranmere the night before. Some of the café patrons had actually been there, but most of the information came by way of the staff. One of the café's servers bussed tables at the Tranmere on weekend nights and one of the dishwashers did double duty, as well. So the rumors were flying, even if only a small part of what was being said was true.

"She was flirting with Ben Fremantle and Tiffany caught them at it!"

"That other one—the blonde—she was practically spilling out of her blouse and she was all over anyone in pants! Waiters, busboys, anyone!"

"I heard Tiffany stormed out and wouldn't even let Ben drive her home. She got a ride with someone else."

"Well, who could blame her?"

Kate could certainly feel the vibe, but it was clear, especially at the counter, that not everyone had the same attitude. Bitsy had a gleam in her eyes and couldn't wait to talk about it, and two of the men sitting at the counter smiled and said good morning.

"This looks awesome, Kate," said Millie, who seemed oblivious to the vibes—good and bad—swirling around them.

"Everything I've had here has been really good. Look, they've got a smoked salmon and chevre omelette."

"Ooh; that's for me."

Bitsy set down plates for a couple to their left and stood in front of them, grinning.

"Bitsy," Kate said, "this is my assistant and friend, Millie. She's up from Darien for the weekend."

"I know; you told me. Great to meet you, Millie!"

"Great to meet you, too, Bitsy. Kate's told me you know everything that happens in this town almost before it happens."

"Almost." She looked left and right, the expression on her face clearly saying that she couldn't talk about things with this many people within hearing distance, but she was practically bursting.

"I think we're both going to have the special omelette, right, Mill? Mine with fruit, please."

"Yeah, I want the same thing but with home fries."

"Okay, you got it. Back in a jiff."

As the two women sipped their coffee and waited for their meals, the crowd in the café gradually started to thin out. Only a couple of people had come in after them. By the time their omelettes arrived, only two other customers were still at the counter, although there were plenty still at the tables. When the manager of the hardware store paid his check and got up from the other end of the counter, he smiled widely at the two of them and gave them a "thumbs-up" as he left.

"He can't stand Tiffany," Bitsy said when he had gone.

The omelettes were wonderful, of course, and Millie could scarcely believe there could be food this good in a backwater place like Vermont, but she didn't say it out loud. Soon, they were alone at the counter and, when Bitsy was caught up with everything, she leaned over, hands on the counter, and said to Kate, "So, what really happened?"

Kate had finished eating, so she was free to talk.

"Almost nothing happened, Bitsy. Really."

"Almost nothing," Millie agreed, but she was chuckling.

"We got to the restaurant a few minutes before eight. The maitre d' greeted us, checked our reservation, then told us our table was just being cleared and it would be five minutes, at the most. We were standing in the foyer when Ben Fremantle came out of the dining room. He smiled and said, 'Hello.' I smiled and said, 'Hello.' I said, 'This is my friend, Millie,' and they said 'Hello.' Then he asked if it was my first time at the Tranmere. I said it was. Then Tiffany Thompson walked out of the dining room. She stopped, looked at me, looked at Ben, and walked out without a word. Ben followed her out.

"I don't know what anyone else has told you about it, but that was the sum total of any interaction between the three of us. Then Millie and I went in, sat down, had a beautiful dinner, a bottle of wine, and a great time."

"That's right," Millie said. "Of course, Kate didn't mention that the temperature in the foyer dropped about thirty degrees as soon as Tiffany saw those two talking. The chill she threw was incredible!"

"Ha ha! It's so funny you put it that way," Bitsy said, "because the maître d'—Albert—told Mary Ann it was like someone had just opened the door to the walk-in freezer! And one of the dishwashers was outside the back door having a smoke, and he said when Ben caught up to Tiffany she turned around and told him off! Then she waved to somebody she knew who was just leaving and asked for a ride home. And Ben left by himself."

"Well, that's all very interesting," Kate said, "but I didn't do anything. Neither did Ben."

"Hey, Bitsy?" Millie said. "There's somebody peeking at us through the kitchen door."

Bitsy strode quickly to the swinging doors and just growled. The face disappeared, and she came back.

"Richie?" Kate asked.

Bitsy just nodded.

"Oh, is that the high school boy who's got the hots for you?"

"Yeah. Jesus, I seem to be disrupting lives left and right, and I haven't done anything!"

Ben Fremantle was sitting by himself on the back veranda, admiring the view and considering his fate, when he heard the sliding glass door behind him open. The distinctive rhythm of his mother's walker made it obvious who was coming out.

Robert arrived at the little table first with the coffee and pastries and then assisted Mrs. Fremantle to sit.

"Thank you, Robert; you may pour and then that will be all."

Ben wasn't really in the mood for coffee and buns with his mother, and he had to leave soon to drive up to Burlington, but there was no arguing with the head of the family. When Robert had disappeared back into the house, Doris Fremantle sipped her tea and spoke.

"What time are you leaving to pick up Rory?"

"In about forty-five minutes."

"I think you had better tell me what's going on, Ben."

"Mother, I don't know what..."

"Benjamin, I spoke with Tiffany this morning, so don't pretend you don't know what I'm talking about. She was quite distraught."

"But there's no reason…"

"Let me finish. Rightly or wrongly, she is convinced that this Stone woman has set her cap for you and that you—at the very least—have failed to put her off."

"'At the very least?' What is that supposed to mean?"

"Are you attracted to this woman?"

"Mother, Kate Stone is a very attractive woman, and I am a normal, healthy male. As a casual observer, of course I am attracted to her."

"'A casual observer?' When it comes to male hormones, there is no such thing as a 'casual observer.'"

You can say that again, he said to himself. *How do I get out of this?*

"Mother, Tiffany is the only woman for me; she has been, is, and always will be. Just because a good-looking woman smiles and says 'hello' to me…"

"You said 'hello' first."

"Maybe I did. Should I have been rude and ignored her? You're the one who taught me manners, Mother."

"This is about you, Benjamin; don't try to shift the focus." She paused for a nibble and a sip. "I told Tiffany about Rory coming back."

"Shit!"

"Benjamin! Do not use such language when you're speaking to me. Why didn't you tell her?"

"I was going to, last night, but…"

"Yes, that didn't work out, did it? Listen, Ben. I've done my best to mollify Tiffany, and she will be sitting beside us in church tomorrow, as usual. I've told her what she already wanted to hear; that this woman is trying to maneuver you and make it look like you're interested in her."

"But she hasn't..."

"Whether she has or hasn't is immaterial. The only way to minimize your guilt is to maximize hers. You're an attorney; you ought to understand the tactic. We also need to set up another target for her."

"Really? Do you have someone in mind?"

"Rory."

"Rory? Mother, is that really fair to anyone?"

"I'm not concerned about fairness. I'm concerned about your future. And I wouldn't worry too much about Rory. I think he'll rather enjoy it."

It was hard for Kate not to laugh at the spectacle Millie presented when trying to help her in the garden. While Kate was on her knees in her new gardening duds and boots, Millie was standing up, holding a rake, her Ann Taylor slacks ludicrously tucked into Kate's barn boots. She had actually pulled the rake over some of the garden plot, following her boss's instructions, but now, while Kate was putting seedlings into the soil and mounding the dirt around them, there wasn't much for her to do except try to keep herself clean.

"Boss, can we go to the restaurant again tonight?"

"No. You know I've got a couple of steaks for us. Besides, just because I've got a company credit card doesn't mean I've got unlimited funds."

"That maître d' is single, you know."

"Yes, I know. You've pointed that out several times. But you're driving back to Connecticut Monday morning."

"Right. So there's no time to lose."

"Anyway, you can't show up in the same dress two nights in a row."

"That's true, and I certainly can't fit into any of yours."

"That's the last one; my garden is planted!"

"Great! Can I get out of the dirt now?"

"Yes, you can. I'd like to get a few boxes of books unpacked, and by then it will be time to start dinner."

"Okay. Hey, we're going riding tomorrow, right?"

"Yes, in the morning. You did bring your riding clothes, didn't you?"

"Sure did. Do I get to pick out a horse?"

"Linda has one picked out for you, but I'm sure she'll let you look over the others."

"Do you think those two will be riding tomorrow?"

"Linda said if they ride on Sunday, it's always after church, so I want to be off the trails by one o'clock. I really don't want to meet up with them again."

7

en Fremantle had no difficulty spotting his brother walking out of the loading ramp and into the arrival lobby at Burlington International Airport. He would have known that figure anywhere. The confident stride, the head held high, as if daring anyone to challenge him. That smile, as Rory recognized him and walked briskly toward him.

"Ben! It's good to see you, man! Thanks for driving up."

A handshake, a man-hug, and it was like it had always been. It was a huge relief to Ben that there was no apparent rancor or ill-feeling about what had happened. He so badly wanted to have the old brother/brother relationship back again. It was like nothing else, and he had missed it terribly.

It wasn't like either of them had done something terrible. Couples had fights all the time, and it just happened that he and Tiff had had a fight just when Rory and Christy had one. Tiffany had stormed out, declaring that it was over, and Rory had left his girlfriend at the same time.

Rory and Tiff were together for only a week before all three of them had realized that wasn't going to work. Ben and Tiffany were right for each other, plain and simple. So she came back to Ben and Rory decided to go away for a while.

Ben had heard that the Plouffe girl was devastated, but what could she have expected, after all?

"Welcome home, Rory. Let's go get your bags and you can tell me all about working in the Gulf. You look great, man!"

He did. Rory was an inch shorter than his older brother but broader in the shoulders and chest, and his arms, never less than impressive, looked more powerful than ever. As they walked side by side down the stairway to the luggage carousels, anyone seeing them approach would probably conclude that they were brothers. Their faces looked very much alike, their voices were similar, the way they laughed was almost identical, and the difference in physique was no more than might be expected.

Rory only had one bag—a big duffel bag, fully stuffed, plus the carry-on that hung by a strap from his left shoulder. Ben grabbed the duffel bag from the carousel, and they walked out to the parking lot.

It was a drive of more than two hours from Burlington to Merryfield, but neither of the brothers considered it a burden or a chore. Ben was happy to have his brother back home, and Rory was delighted to be driving his vintage Mustang again.

"I have missed you, Beauty!" he had exclaimed as soon as he saw her. Ben's passion for cars was not as extreme as Rory's, but he had been happy to spend a couple hours the day before getting the Mustang out of winter storage, replenishing all the fluids, and getting her ready for the road.

Rory talked a lot as they headed down the Interstate: about hard work alternating with boring drudgery on the oil platform, and about the weekends in New Orleans.

"Too few, for sure. Four weekends out of a whole year. I made the most of them, though!"

"I'm sure you did, brother."

"It's a good life, brother. Working the rigs, I mean. Not for a long time, but a year was good. You work hard, stay in shape, make a lot of money, and then you go back home."

"Sounds great. Not for me, though."

"No, not for you. You've got the life you want and it's all in front of you: a straight road."

Rory and Ben drove right down Main Street before turning off toward the Fremantle house, and a lot of heads turned and hands waved. Both of the boys had always been town favorites their whole lives and still were. Everyone in town knew about the scandal and why Rory had left town, but it hadn't changed most people's opinions about him. Those who knew Christine Plouffe well might still harbor some ill feeling, but those were few in number. As for Ben and Tiffany, well they didn't seem to act like their hearts were broken. Besides, some people said, nothing mends a broken heart quicker than a lot of money!

Ray Everett watched from the front steps of the hardware store he had managed for seventeen years and waved heartily as "the boys" drove by. Ray had known them their whole lives and had coached both of them in youth soccer and was immensely proud of them. Merryfield's best, in his opinion. They both deserved better than that bitch, Tiffany Thompson.

Tiffany watched from the Tiff-Toff Shoppe. *Well*, she thought, *it's no big deal. So I slept with Rory a few times. It's all forgotten now and all of us are in agreement as to the best way forward.* Doris had told her that they were all having dinner at the Tranmere tonight. There would be tongues wagging, especially among the restaurant staff who had been there on Friday night, but who cared what those people thought?

The best table at the Tranmere was reserved for seven o'clock. Reserved for four people; the most important people in Merryfield, at least in their own estimation, and to those whose business depended on the wealthy and important. In another month, and for several months afterward, more than half of the restaurant's business would be big-spending tourists from out of state. But, until then, the Fremantles were *it*.

The three Fremantles and Tiffany Thompson would be seated personally by Albert, the maître d'; would be visited by the Tranmere's General Manager; would be served by the most experienced professional waiter; and would also be visited by the chef, who would personally discuss the menu with them.

They arrived precisely on time, and two of the staff rushed out to assist Mrs. Fremantle in navigating the ramp with her walker. Rory, however, waved them away and insisted on doing it himself. Albert was delighted to welcome them as they entered the foyer, and Doris greeted him almost as an old friend, with just the right note of condescension in her voice. Tiffany was treated almost as royally, but she must, of course, accept second billing whenever Doris was present.

It was a gay evening, with very little of any importance discussed. Rory entertained them with stories of working on the oil rig, describing the colorful characters he worked with and the hilarious things they did. He made it sound as if he were a "gentleman ranker" out of a Kipling poem, working alongside men of a distinctly lower class, and that was exactly the way Mrs. Fremantle wanted to think of him. He talked about the wild weekends enjoying the nightlife in New Orleans. In his practiced way, he managed to convey that he had enjoyed the more sinful activities of that city without actually saying it, sparing his mother the sordid details.

He did not mention how much money he had made, since his mother would have thought that rather vulgar. They all knew he didn't need the money anyway.

Tiffany laughed along with the others; there was not a hint of any feeling other than the happiness of being in a loving family. But she never made eye contact with Rory, not for a second.

8

The three women rode briskly across a broad meadow and into the woods: Linda Norman on Roadrunner, Millie on Prince, and Kate on Dolly. It was a beautiful day; the warmest day of the year so far. That made everyone in town happy; great weather on Memorial Day weekend made it feel like the summer season was finally here.

Millie was not what you would call an experienced rider, but she had ridden with Kate several times back home in Connecticut and was perfectly safe on a gentle horse like Prince. Linda had decided to join them and show them some of the trails Kate hadn't seen yet.

Linda was attempting to explain some of the geography of Merryfield; at least, this part of the town. The trails wound in and out of woods and across meadows and over small brooks. At several places, there were open areas with excellent views, and they had stopped at each one so she could tell them where they were.

"From here," she said, from a knoll where they had stopped for a drink of water, "you can see, across these two hay fields, the Fremantle house. We're still on their property here, and their land goes on about half a mile behind us."

"It looks twice as big as your house, boss," Millie said.

"It is, at least." said Linda. "Although the Andrews house—your house, Kate—was one of the nicest in town, and could be again. But the Fremantle house is a real mansion with twenty-two rooms."

"Like some of the ones in Darien," Millie said. "There's lots of old money in Darien," she explained.

"Lots of new money, too," Kate added.

As they rode, they crossed the same brook over and over again, first one way and then the other.

"It's called Wandering Brook," Linda explained.

"Good name," Kate said. "It keeps turning back and forth."

"It used to be called Wander Brook, and supposedly it was a phonetic spelling of an old French name, but people started saying 'wandering,' for obvious reasons, and it stuck."

After a mile or so through the woods, they came out into another clearing and stopped at a place where a rise overlooked the brook. There was a wooden railing along the top of the bank and two picnic tables had been set up here, where people could sit and enjoy a splendid view in all directions.

"Sometimes riders like to bring a lunch with them, and we put these tables here for them. Want to sit for a few minutes?"

They dismounted and Kate walked over to the railing and looked down on the brook. At this point, the brook turned at almost a right angle and below the railing where she was standing a concrete wall reinforced the bank.

"Linda," Kate asked, "why the wall? The brook looks pretty tame here."

"It is now," Linda replied, "and it stays that way most of the time. But every now and then we have a flood and the erosion kept eating away at the bank. We put that wall in so we wouldn't have to keep repairing the trail along here."

"So, where are we now?" Millie asked.

"Well, we're back on Norman family land now." Linda pointed back over her shoulder to the east. "Back there where we came from is the Fremantle estate. Now, over there, straight ahead where the brook is coming from, is the Plouffe farm."

"Plouffe?" Kate asked. "Haven't I heard that name?"

"Yes, you have. Remember I told you about Rory Fremantle? Well, Christine Plouffe was his girlfriend. She's a single mom, about twenty-six, and she was going with Rory for a long time before he had the affair with Tiffany. Christy is a great gal—friendly as hell—but nobody ever sees her anymore. She stays at home on the farm."

As the congregation left St. Thomas Episcopal Church, there were a few quiet whispers about Ben and Tiffany. Everything seemed to be fine on the surface; lots of smiles from the three of them and the same friendly greetings to old friends and fellow parishioners. But everyone knew what had transpired Friday night—or thought they knew—so of course they all wondered. People also knew that Rory was back and that naturally added fuel to the fire of speculation about the goings-on of Merryfield's First Family.

Robert was waiting, as always, to help Mrs. Fremantle into the Lincoln Continental that idled gently in its preferred spot. Ben and Tiff waited politely beside the car until the door was closed behind her, then they walked casually to Ben's car for the ride home.

Tiffany was in a surprisingly good mood. Perhaps "placid" would be a better description. She was outwardly calm and wasn't displaying any of the usual clues of a hidden fury that might erupt at any moment. Ben was feeling pretty much the same way. They had had a quiet talk over breakfast at the Fremantles. Doris had wisely decided to let the two of them talk this out alone; she had made her opinions perfectly clear and would not hesitate to do so again, if necessary.

In a surprisingly pragmatic and emotion-free discussion, they had made it plain to each other that they were in complete agreement on the one thing that mattered most—their future. Ben was the only man Tiffany wanted, and she was the only woman for him. It was precisely the kind of agreement that the best old families always came to. They would unite to defeat any challenge to their path to happiness.

Tiffany had very much hoped that this discussion and agreement would conclude with a marriage proposal. Ben had almost decided the same thing. But, somehow, he couldn't quite say it.

Chief Bridger noticed the Subaru parked in a turnout off Livingston Road that Sunday afternoon but didn't think too much about it. He knew it was Mary Pratt's car, and he knew she was a "birder." She must be up in those woods with her camera. There were a lot easier places to look for birds, but then, birders weren't known for doing things the easy way.

After a couple of hours of unpacking boxes and moving things about, Kate and Millie decided that a glass of chilled wine with cheese and crackers would be a fine thing, so they spent the last part of the afternoon on the east end of the porch, sitting in the warm sun.

"I wish I'd brought some shorts," Millie said. "I thought it was going to be cold up here."

The two were lounging on partially reclined deck chairs, with a little table between them.

"It's the first time I've worn shorts since I got here," Kate said. "It has been too cold until this weekend."

"Well, you've certainly got the legs for it, boss, but you need to work on your tan, ASAP. I don't suppose there's a tanning salon in Merryfield."

Kate laughed. "I highly doubt it. I'll just have to do it the natural way."

"Well, it works, but it takes too long. This is a really beautiful spot here, Kate; I think I appreciate it more today, with the clear sky and the warm sun shining down on us. Tell me again how far your property goes."

"Okay. Straight ahead, you can see Locust Road, or a short stretch of it, about sixty yards from the house. That's the boundary of my property, and where the road turns into that patch of woods, the line goes along the edge of those woods towards the east, our left. This ridge, on our left, hides the rest of it, but you can see, just beyond the garden plot, where a path leads around the point of the ridge. There's a hay field over there; that's mine, too."

They sat and talked until the sun was low and the glasses were empty, then they got up to go in and change. The plan was to go to the café for dinner for Millie's last night in town. As they gathered up their stuff to go in, Kate paused to point up towards the ridge.

"They say this ridge looks spectacular in foliage season, especially this time of day, with the sun shining on it." As they looked, a little flash flickered across their eyes, reflecting off something up in the trees. "Must be something shiny hanging in a tree up there."

They sat at a little corner table in the café, rather than at the counter. Bitsy was off on Sunday night, and their waitress was Mary Ann, the same one who had been bussing at the Tranmere on Friday night. They both ordered Chicken Dijonnaise with rice and a salad with locally grown mesclun.

Mary Ann was pretty busy, but when she came back with their drinks and fresh bread, she paused to ask if Millie was going back to Connecticut the next day or if she was staying for the parade.

"I'm going back tomorrow morning. You're the one who was at the restaurant Friday night, aren't you?"

"Yes, I bus tables there some nights. Good money on a Friday night."

"I'm sure. I'm looking forward to going there again next time I visit. That maître d' is quite attractive."

"Albert? Yes, he is."

"He's not married, is he?"

"Oh, no. Albert's not exactly the marrying kind."

"Good. Neither am I."

The food was excellent, as always. After a dessert of profiteroles and ice cream, they left with Mary Ann's friendly advice: "Get to the Interstate as soon as you can, because every little town will have their own parade and roads could be blocked for hours." Then she added to Kate, "I don't know if it means anything to you, but Ben Fremantle's brother, Rory, is back in town. He just got back yesterday."

9

Kate was reading a submission Tuesday morning while sitting on her front porch with a cup of coffee. It was another mediocre mystery, with trite situations and overused tropes, but the murder itself had an interesting twist.

The wife waited for her husband to climb up the ladder to the pier then struck him a heavy blow to the head with a rock. He fell back into the swiftly moving river and floated downstream. The wife put the rock into a plastic bag then got in her car and drove downstream about half a mile to where the rapids were. She saw her husband's body hit the rocks several times and then float free into an eddy downstream. She walked to a spot as close as she could get to the rapids then took the rock she had struck him with out of the bag and threw it as far as she could into the river. She had previously taken the rock from the river at this same spot, and she knew it was of exactly the same material as the rocks in the rapids. She knew her murder weapon would be washed completely clean by the river and that there was no way it could be determined that her husband had not simply been carried along by the current and struck his head on the rocks in the river.

Unfortunately for the woman in the story, she had failed to make sure there were no blood stains on the ladder at the pier, but still, it was an interesting device. She marked the passage with a red pen, wrote "interesting" in the margin and continued to read.

Chris Doran was up on the roof with his brother, nailing down the roofing tiles. He expected to be finished by noon and would shortly start working on the porch.

She looked up as she heard a car turning onto her gravel driveway. It was a police car. Chief Bridger pulled up between Chris's truck and Kate's Volvo and slowly got out of the car.

Kate got up, walked over to the railing, and said, "Good morning, Chief."

"Good morning, Ms. Stone. You've got to start calling me Les."

"Okay, Les, I will. What brings you here?"

"Oh, not anything important; not police business at all, really. I just need to talk to Chris for a couple minutes. He's doing a job for me, too."

"Well, he's up on the roof. Why don't you come around to the kitchen door. Can I get you a cup of coffee?"

"Don't mind if I do, ma'am."

"Kate."

The chief knew the house from many visits over the years, and he came right around and into the kitchen.

"The coffee's pretty fresh, Les," she said as she poured him a cup. "Why don't you take this out to the porch and sit down, and I'll go stick my head out of a window upstairs and tell Chris you're here."

"Thank you, Kate."

The chief sat down at the little table on the east end of the porch. It was nice and cool here in the morning. In a little while the sun would be high enough to warm the whole porch. Kate had left the manuscript she was reading on the table, folded and open to the passage she had just read and marked.

Curious, he picked it up and read it. Well, he thought, that was one way to get away with murder; interesting, indeed.

He had finished it and put it back when Kate reappeared.

"Chris says he'll be down in five minutes."

"Thank you, Kate."

Kate was standing at the counter in the hardware store, discussing lighting fixtures and bulbs and such with Ray Everett when the Mustang drove by. She wasn't what you would call a car enthusiast, but a 1965 Mustang, restored to near-mint condition, would turn anyone's eye, and Ray's reaction interrupted their conversation anyway.

"There's Rory! Good to have him back in town, and what a car!"

"So, that's the prodigal son I've heard about?" Kate asked with a smile.

"Oh, yes, that's Rory Fremantle. Those boys, I tell you... I coached them both in youth leagues, you know."

"Football?"

"No, soccer. We're too small to have a football team. But we've had some good soccer teams over the years, and when those two were in high school... Well, Ms. Stone, we were Division Three State Champions the year Ben was a senior and Rory a junior. Best team we ever had; put Merryfield on the map!"

"They were that good, huh?"

"Oh, they were the best. Ben and Rory played side by side—central defenders—and we only gave up two goals the whole season! They were a perfect pair, you see, Ms. Stone." Ray's eyes were gleaming, and it was obvious that this meant the world to him. "Ben was so smart, so cool, so solid; never out of position and never panicked. But Rory was the fiery one—very aggressive. He would charge into a tackle, and sometimes he would over-commit and miss his mark, but Ben was always there to cover.

"It will be a while before we see a pair like that again. Course, it was sad; the championship game, I mean. Rory got a red card in the semi-final and was suspended for the final. The coach had to put Billy Tourville in to take his place. He held up fine, and we won, two to nothing, but it was sad. Rory shrugged it off—said it didn't matter—but it broke my heart, for sure."

Kate was not much of a sports fan and knew nothing at all about soccer, but she smiled and nodded in sympathy.

"Well, Mr. Everett, I think I'm going to take these bulbs for now because I know they're what I need for the bedroom, then I'll go online and check out those bathroom fixtures you told me about. If I see something I like, I'll come back in and you can order it for me."

When Kate walked into the café a few minutes later, Bitsy was having an animated conversation with a brown-haired, broad-shouldered man who was sitting at the counter, and she knew before he turned around that this must be the man Ray Everett had been talking about. Bitsy had a big smile on her face and gave Kate a quick wave while she listened.

Rory Fremantle turned half around to see who had walked in, continuing to tell his story, but he stopped speaking when he saw Kate. There was a moment of silence as they looked at each other, then Bitsy broke in to introduce them.

"Rory, this is Kate Stone. She's new in town; she's the one that bought the old Andrews house. Kate, this is Rory Fremantle, just come back from New Orleans, or somewhere down there."

The younger Fremantle lad was no stranger to beautiful women, nor was he often lost for words, but this dark-haired, blue-eyed beauty was like no other woman he had ever seen. Kate was as taken aback as he was; she hadn't had any specific expectations, but she was surprised nonetheless. While he looked very like his brother Ben, his grey eyes had a different aspect and the aura he projected, while decidedly virile, was warm and more comforting than threatening.

It was obvious to Bitsy that this was a "moment," and she let it last just long enough before speaking.

"Why don't you have a seat, Kate?" she said as Kate was already sliding into the seat next to Rory.

The two recovered their composure quickly; they were not moonstruck teenagers, after all.

"You're Ben's brother, aren't you?" Kate said.

"I sure am. So you've met Ben."

"Yes, I've met Ben, and Tiffany."

Something in her expression spoke volumes, and Rory broke into a big laugh.

"Don't tell me; let me guess. Tiffany already hates you."

"Apparently. She seems to think that I'm after her man."

"Of course she does! Why else would a beautiful woman appear suddenly in Merryfield? It couldn't be a coincidence; you must be here to break up her relationship and ruin her life!"

Now Kate burst out laughing and Bitsy was chuckling, too.

"Hey, guys," Bitsy said, "I've got an order up, but I'll be right back. Check out the specials!"

Kate and Rory quickly filled each other in on their recent pasts—how and why they came to be where they were right now—discussed the menu and ordered lunch then launched into a friendly discussion as if they had been friends for years.

"Tell me about your horse, Kate."

"Oh, Dolly's a four-year-old grey mare. She's beautiful and very sweet."

"Have you been riding long?"

"Oh, yes, since I was a girl. I competed in shows until after high school, but I haven't done any competitive riding since then. After I graduated from Penn, I married Jim Stone and life got more complicated."

"Marriage does that, I've heard."

"It sure does. Anyway, Jim—my ex—got it into his head that he wanted to own a thoroughbred and eventually become a breeder, so he bought a grey stallion at a claiming race and he let me buy a matching grey mare. But Dolly's not a thoroughbred. She's pregnant, though, which Jim didn't know."

"Ooh, so not a planned pregnancy."

"No, but Jim would still want the foal if he knew. I'm not going to tell him."

Lunch, another cup of coffee, a piece of raspberry pie, and an hour later, they went their separate ways, having agreed to meet for a ride the next morning.

One could not spend an hour in the Maple Leaf Café without being seen by a considerable number of people, and the staff at the café were not exactly prone to secrecy, so, within a very short time, everyone in town knew that Rory had met Kate and they were instantly "an item."

Tiffany heard about it very quickly at the Tiff-Toff Shoppe, and was suitably outraged—on the surface.

"My God, the woman is an absolute harpy! Rory's only been back two days and she's got her claws into him already! I said it from the start; she's on the loose and she's got her eyes on the prize!"

Inside, she was delighted. If that bitch was after Rory, then she was safe with Ben. But how did Doris arrange this so quickly?

Ben heard it from his law partner, Clem Burns, who came back from lunch at the café and said it looked like that Stone woman had fallen for Rory hook, line, and sinker.

Ben's reaction was the same as Tiffany's. Not her outward reaction; he would never say things like that. But he, too, was wondering if his mother had somehow arranged for them to meet, and how could she have done it that fast?

Unlike Tiffany, Ben did consider the possibility that it was just coincidence, but he wouldn't bet on it.

At the Fremantle mansion, the lady of the house knew about it even before Rory came home. The man who delivered their weekly supply of milk, eggs and cream had just come from the café. He told the cook, the cook told Robert, and Robert informed his mistress when he brought her tea and cakes out on the veranda.

Doris laughed out loud.

"I didn't even have to do anything! Robert, this is perfect."

"Yes, ma'am."

"When Rory comes in, tell him to come see me, and... no, wait. On second thought, don't say anything. We'll just let this play out. That will do, Robert."

"Yes, ma'am."

When Rory returned home, he drove straight to the stable and parked his car there.

"Billy! Where are you?" he shouted.

"I'm coming."

Billy Tourville ambled slowly out from behind the stable, a pitchfork in his hand.

"Billy, I'm going to take Jagger out tomorrow, around ten o'clock."

"Okay, sir, I'll have..."

"For Christ's sake, Billy, don't call me 'sir.' You can play the servant with Ben and Tiff, but cut that crap out with me."

"Okay, Rory; I guess I've kind of got used to it."

"Well, I'm back, so get unused to it. I just met this fantastic woman, Billy, and she rides. I'm going to meet her on the trails tomorrow."

"That sounds good. Where'd you meet her?"

"At the café. Her name's Kate Stone, and she bought the old Andrews place."

"Oh."

"Do you know her? Have you met her?"

"Uhh, no, I haven't, but Ben and Miss Thompson met her out riding one day last week. Twice, I think."

"And?"

"Well, the first time, Miss Thompson came back looking furious, and your brother was looking like—well, the way he looks when she's furious and he doesn't know what to do about it. The second time was on my day off, so I don't know what happened."

"That's funny, Billy. I can just see Tiffany's reaction meeting a woman more beautiful than she is, especially if Ben was with her. Tiffany doesn't like competition!"

"No, she don't, for sure."

"Do you know anything about her? Miss Stone, I mean?"

"Well, I haven't seen her, but I've heard she's drop-dead gorgeous."

"She is, for sure."

"She's divorced, from Connecticut, and most people think she's rich, and, well, you know what people think about divorcees."

"Oh, that's just old soap opera stuff, Billy, you ought to know that."

"Yeah, sure. I mean, most of the people who've met her say she's really nice, and I talked to Chris Doran; he's doing some work for her and he says she's not rich at all."

"Well, Chris has a good head on his shoulders; I expect he's right."

"Oh, my God, boss! This is it! He's the one!"

"Calm down, Millie; I just met the man this afternoon."

"Listen, boss, I know you, and I can hear it in your voice. You can't fool me, Kate Stone; you've already decided this is the man for you!"

"That's silly, Millie; I haven't decided anything yet."

"When are you seeing him again? Tonight?"

"No, not tonight, of course not. We're riding together tomorrow."

"Oooh...romance on the trail! Sounds perfect!"

"C'mon, Millie, it's not like we're going to jump out of the saddle and... Oh, God, I can't believe I almost said that."

"Ha! Well, why not? Tell me more about him. He's really buff, right?"

"Yeah. He's just been working on an oil rig for a year, so he's really fit. He looks a lot like his brother, but Ben's a little taller, more slender. Rory's stockier, looks a little rougher around the edges."

"*Rougher*. Oooh, I like that."

"I'm talking about the way he looks, Millie. He just looks like more of a free spirit than Ben."

"Okay, okay. So, you go riding tomorrow, which is Wednesday. Dinner tomorrow night?"

"Mmm... not sure yet. We'll see how it goes. Maybe Saturday. You know I'm driving down Sunday."

"Well, then, don't waste the weekend!"

10 |

Kate decided to have breakfast at home on Wednesday morning. She knew she would be feeding a great deal into the gossip machine later in the day and thought she'd better just stay out of it until then. Her pantry was not fully stocked yet, but she had bread and eggs and granola and some good coffee.

She ate her breakfast out on the porch as she had been doing while this good weather lasted, and she was sitting there when Chris Doran drove up the driveway in his truck.

"Good morning, Chris! Coffee's on!" she called out.

"Thank you, Kate! I'll be there in a minute."

Chris was starting on the porch today and all of the lumber he needed was already stacked on the ground next to the porch, covered with a tarpaulin. He lowered the back gate of his pickup and grabbed a toolbox, set it down next to the lumber pile, and then headed around to the kitchen door.

It was another beautiful late-May day in Vermont, and Chris was in a mood to get things going.

"A fine day to get some work done," he said.

"Yes, the weather's been beautiful. I'm so glad you got the roof done."

"Yeah, well, as I told you, that was the most important job, and we were lucky with the weather."

"Is your brother helping you today?"

"Yes. He should be here in a while. We've got to tear out these rotten deck boards and the steps first thing. It'll be a lot faster with two. Most of it I can do by myself. What time are you headed to Sunrise farm?"

"Well, I plan to get there at ten-thirty. How did you know I was going to the farm?"

He shrugged, mildly abashed but not very. "You hear things in town."

"Of course. So, the whole town must know I'm going riding with Rory Fremantle this morning."

"Of course they do."

"Do you know Rory well, Chris?"

"Pretty well. He's always been a lot friendlier with folks than the rest of the family, you know."

"I don't really know at all. I met Ben twice, but we didn't exchange more than a dozen words, total. And I just met Rory yesterday."

"Rory's okay. Both the boys are okay, really. Neither of them are as 'self-important' you might say as their mother is and the old man was. Like I said, they're both nice enough, but Ben's more reserved and he doesn't mingle much with folks like Rory does."

Chris didn't say any more; he just looked kind of sad and sipped his coffee.

Kate wanted to know more, but she didn't feel that Chris was the one to press for more information.

The trusty old Volvo brought her to Sunrise Farm at ten-twenty, and Kate was pleased to see Linda Norman walking Dolly out of the barn, already saddled.

"Good morning, Linda! You didn't have to do that."

"Oh, that's no problem, Kate. I like being with Dolly; she's a nice lady, and it's all a pleasure for me anyway."

Kate spent a few minutes stroking Dolly and whispering to her while Linda disappeared into the farmhouse, which was only a few steps away. She returned quickly with a mug in each hand.

"I figured you could use a hot drink before you start. This is hot chocolate with a little maple syrup in it."

"Ooh, thanks, Linda!" She took a sip. "Gosh, that's good! I'm going to have to stock up on maple syrup; we have it in Connecticut, of course, but..."

"But it's too expensive and it's probably too bland. Don't you worry, Kate, I'll give you a jug to take with you when you leave. So, tell me, where will you be riding today?"

"I'm not sure; I'm supposed to meet Rory Fremantle at that spot where the brook takes that big bend."

"Right. Well, I wondered if he might be taking you on one of the longer trails. You've seen a couple of places where there's a trail that's blocked off? Those go up through the woods and over towards Wayford. They're all on Fremantle land, and they keep those private."

"Oh. He did say something about showing me a new trail. That's probably what he meant."

"Why don't you sit down and finish your cocoa."

They sat down at a picnic table and drank their sweet, hot, mapley cocoa together.

"Linda," Kate said, "you know I just met Rory yesterday."

"I know."

"You told me something about him before, and other people have told me things, too."

"About him and Tiffany."

"Yes. And about the girl Rory left."

"Christy. Christine Plouffe. Nicest woman I know. She's been done wrong by two men, and she didn't deserve any of it, if you ask me."

"Two men?"

"You see, Christy has a boy—six years old, now—and he was born when Christy just turned eighteen. It was a farmhand they had—Joe Reader—and he took off and broke her heart. They say he's up in Orleans County somewhere, working on a farm up there. She stayed on the farm with her parents and raised that little boy and then, after a couple years, Rory took a shine to her.

"Now, that was unexpected and I thought, seeing them together, it was the best thing that ever happened for both of them. The rest of the Fremantles—old Benjamin was still alive then—I guess they just thought Rory was 'sowing his wild oats' as the saying goes, but the two of them were in love for sure, and I knew it. I've never seen Rory so happy, or Christy, either. Then that blonde bitch, Tiffany, got it into her head to make Ben jealous by taking someone else. Well, there was no one else around here of the right 'social status' so it had to be Rory.

"She crooked her little finger and wiggled her butt, and Rory fell for it. It didn't last long; it made Ben mad and that's all she wanted. She cried and said she was sorry and Ben took her back."

"But why would Rory do that if he was in love with Christy? It sounds like such a horrible thing to do."

"Well, most people didn't blame Rory, even though they should have. What I heard a lot of people say is that he and Christy had broken up, but she told me it was just a little quarrel and she never expected him to go with somebody else; she was crushed.

"But the Fremantles, and the people who admire them, they all thought that Rory was too good for her; for Christy, the 'farm girl with the illegitimate baby.' Only a few of us really knew her. And Tiffany, with that smile and that figure; who could resist her?"

"Well, it's not exactly what I would have wanted to hear about the man I just met."

"I hear you, Kate. But I know Rory; he's a good man. He and Christy are both victims, if you ask me."

Kate arrived early at the bend in the brook, and she dismounted and walked over to the railing that overlooked the stream. It was a beautiful view, a beautiful scene. Not for the first or the last time, she thought, *This is what I moved here for.*

But while the scene was calm and placid, her mind was not. What she had learned about Rory Fremantle was, as she had just told Linda Norman, not what she would have wanted to hear about the man she was meeting today. But what did it really mean, and did it matter?

It wasn't like she was planning to marry the man or to jump into bed with the man, or both. She wasn't planning anything. He was a good-looking man who seemed open and genuine. He was easy to talk to, interesting, and he obviously was interested in her. The fact that he had abandoned a steady long-term relationship to have a brief affair with his brother's girlfriend was disturbing, but was it the full measure of the man? It couldn't be.

Kate was a mature, experienced woman who considered herself a good judge of character, especially concerning men. She wasn't going to be fooled—not again. It had happened once; Arnold James Stone, Jr. had fooled her and made her life a living hell. But that was then, and this was now; she was going to give Rory Fremantle every chance to show his character. That would be fair to both of them.

In spite of the inner turmoil each of them was feeling, it turned out to be a wonderful time for both of them. Rory's charm and easy-going manner quickly put Kate at ease, and the two rode off together in a laughing and carefree mood.

They rode into Fremantle territory on a trail Kate had ridden before and came to a gate that blocked off another trail that led upward into the woods. Rory quickly dismounted and swung the gate open, and they rode off. It was a rougher trail that rose gradually, and they were in deep woods for about two miles.

They emerged from the woods at the top of a ridge that offered a splendid view of the mountains to the west and north and overlooked a wide valley. There were a couple of benches made of split logs and placed in the best spot for viewing—a majestic overlook reserved for the Fremantles and their friends.

They dismounted and sat together on one of the benches. They each had water bottles, and Rory produced a bag containing two sandwiches.

"I asked Mrs. Mapes, our cook, if she could make us a couple of sandwiches; it's chicken salad."

"Oh, that was thoughtful of you, thanks."

Then he pulled out a bag of potato chips.

"She offered to make a salad, too, but she knew what I really wanted. I've always wanted potato chips, and she knows what I like."

Kate laughed. "So, you have a cook? Your family, I mean?"

"Yeah, Mother couldn't do without Mrs. Mapes. It's a big house, you know, and it takes a few people to manage it, especially with Ben still living there, and me, for now."

"How many?"

"Well, there's Robert; he's sort of a butler, although we don't use formal titles. He serves the meals, drives the car when Mom needs to go out, and manages the house along with the housekeeper, Sandra. Then there's Mrs. Mapes, the cook."

"Does the housekeeper have to clean all twenty-two rooms by herself?"

"Just the rooms we use on a daily basis. Every couple weeks someone comes in to help her go through and clean the rest. Then there's Billy Tourville, who takes care of the horses and the stable."

"Billy Tourville? I've heard that name."

"Really? Who have you been talking to?"

"Maybe it was the man at the hardware store. Ray something?"

"Ray Everett. Coach Everett, as he likes to be called."

"He told me all about your championship soccer team."

"I'm sure he did. He's obsessed with it: 'greatest thing that ever happened in this town' and don't you forget it!"

"Well, yeah, that's pretty much what he said. He's very proud of you."

"Yeah. I suppose that should make me happy. Look, Kate, nothing against Ray Everett. If it makes him happy, that's fine. But that was high school, and I'm not in high school anymore. I don't want to be anybody's hero, and I wasn't really a hero then. I got suspended and couldn't play in the title game. Billy took my place, and he was great; he was the hero, in my book."

"And he works for you now?"

"Yes. He's from a really poor family and he's great with horses, so, when he couldn't find a job, I got him hired for our stable."

Rory set the remaining half of his sandwich down and got up to get something from his saddlebag.

"Kate, you didn't happen to bring binoculars, did you?" he asked.

"No, I didn't."

"Well, you can take a look with mine. You can see some of Wayford from here without them."

Kate stood up and gazed across the broad meadow. In the distance, she could see two church steeples and a few houses in between the trees that lined the far side of the meadow.

"That's Wayford," he said. "It's about twice the size of Merryfield. If you look at that church steeple on the right—that's the Methodist church—and move a little to the right from there, you can see the school."

She took the binoculars, focused them in, and found what she was looking for.

"I see it. I see the screen behind home plate and some bleachers, but I can't see much for the trees. So that was the site of your triumph? Or Ray's triumph?"

"Actually, the title game was played up in Burlington, at the UVM field."

"So, you went to school in Wayford?"

"It's a unified school district: Wayford, Merryfield and Petersford. Three small towns share one high school."

Rory pointed out some of the other features that could be seen from this vantage point, then they finished their sandwiches and chips and resumed their ride.

After about half a mile of a narrow trail through deep woods, they came to a wide clearing where they could ride side by side and they slowed to a walk so they could chat. Rory told Kate some more things about the town and his family and himself.

It seemed that Rory was not particularly ambitious; at least not in the traditional areas one might have expected. He had achieved a degree in Civil Engineering at Northeastern then returned to Vermont and worked at an engineering firm based in White River Junction.

"My cousin's company," he explained. "It was a good job, but it didn't excite me much. Last spring, I told him—my cousin—that is, that I wanted to go and do something else for a while. I wanted to get away from here, so I went south and got a job on an oil rig. Sounds wild and romantic, doesn't it?"

"It does; much more wild and romantic than my story, anyway."

"So, what's your story?"

"My story is kind of cliché, I suppose. I was married to a man with lots of money and power; a man whose entire life was centered on gaining more money and more power. I wanted other things. I tolerated a lot, and the marriage might have lasted longer, but when he started dating an eighteen-year-old bimbo without even bothering to hide it from me, I had had enough. So, I divorced him, bought the house, and moved up here."

"Good move. If you don't mind me asking, are you comfortable? Financially, I mean?"

"Reasonably, but I'm not as rich as most people here in town seem to think. I would have had more money to put into the house, but, just as the divorce was being finalized, I had an opportunity to buy the agency I work for. It was what I had wanted for a long time, and it was a good deal, so I did it. It means I'm a little cash-strapped for a while; I have to live on my commissions and fix up the house a little bit at a time."

They headed back into the woods, single file, and much of the trail they followed was dark and narrow. Another two miles and they emerged into a clearing where they could see the Fremantle house off to the right. They turned left and reached the spot where they had turned off, closed the open gate, then rode back to the bend where they had met.

"That was a nice ride, Rory; thank you," Kate said.

"It was my pleasure, Kate. I enjoy your company very much."

"Likewise."

"Good. Listen, Kate, what would you think about having dinner with me one of these nights? Now, before you answer, I want you to know that I'm not in a rush to get into a romantic relationship right now. I mean, if it happens, it happens, but I'd like to spend some time with you without any obligations, without either of us feeling like... well, you know."

"Yes, I know. I think that would be nice, Rory. How about Saturday?"

"Boss, let me see if I've got this straight. You're twenty-seven years old, single, and you're going out to dinner with a rich, good-looking guy... and it's a 'friendly' date? No sex?"

"It wasn't put in exactly those terms, Millie. He's not in a hurry to get into a relationship, and I understand that."

"Tell me the truth, boss: Is this guy gay?"

"No, Millie, there is not the slightest chance he's gay. It's complicated. He's complicated."

"When a rich hunk takes me out to dinner, it's not complicated at all."

"You don't really understand the situation, Millie."

"No, I don't, obviously. Okay, so are you going to that place again? The Tran-something?"

"The Tranmere? No. Rory thought it would be nice to avoid the 'eyes of the town' for one night, so he's driving us to a place about forty minutes from here; I can't remember the name."

"Alright, I guess you know what you're doing. Are you still driving down Sunday morning?"

"Yes. Not sure what time I'll leave, but I'll call you when I get there."

11 |

"He's taking her to the Woodhouse. They must have wanted to get away from 'prying eyes' for their big date."

Doris Fremantle was having lunch with Tiffany Thompson Saturday afternoon on the veranda at the Fremantle house.

"How did you find out?" Tiffany asked.

"I called the manager at the Tranmere. When he didn't see their names on the reservation list, he called around to the best restaurants within driving distance. They'll be at the Woodhouse at seven."

Tiffany smiled, took a sip of her Chablis, and said, "You're good, Doris."

"Of course I am. I have connections everywhere in southern Vermont, and I use them whenever and wherever I need to. You'll need to do the same thing, Tiffany. Some connections will open up for you as soon as you and Ben are married, and I will hook you up with the rest."

"I wish I knew how long it will be before it happens."

"Not long. I've already written the announcement of your engagement. I'm going to show it to Ben and ask him point blank when he's going to give you that ring. If he doesn't make a decision, I'll make it for him."

"He won't like that."

"He doesn't have to like it. He will accept it because it is the right thing to do and he knows it. You know Ben very well, Tiffany, but not as well as I do. Sometimes he needs to be pushed, and you will have to be the one to push him from now on. When you know what is right for the family, make sure it gets done. Don't give him the opportunity to make the wrong choice."

Tiffany pondered her future mother-in-law's words while Robert cleared away their lunch plates.

"What does Mrs. Mapes have for us today, Robert?" she asked with a big smile.

"We have a vanilla tea loaf with fresh strawberries or those lemon drop cookies you like so much, Miss Tiffany."

"Oh, good. Can we have both?"

"Of course."

Doris lifted her cane and pointed out towards the garden. "You know, Tiffany, that part of the garden will be yours to do with as you please. My prize roses are all over on the west side; the rest is all yours."

"Splendid! I have some ideas."

"Good. We can get someone in, you know. We haven't had a gardener for years, but we can hire someone part-time. It's going to take a lot of work, if you really want to transform it. We need to talk about the east wing, as well. That whole wing of the house will be yours and Ben's. I can call my architect and schedule a time when he and you can do a walk-through and talk about plans."

"Oh, that would be wonderful! But what about Rory? His room is in the east wing, too."

"For now. Before too long, he'll do the right thing and go back to work for my nephew in White River Junction, and he'll live over there."

"You don't think this fling with Mrs. Stone will change anything?"

Doris snorted and shook her head.

"You give her too much credit, Tiffany. My Rory will eat her for breakfast and spit her out."

Over at the high school baseball field in Wayford, a charity softball game was going on, and the Fremantle boys were the stars of the team sponsored by the Lions Club. It was an annual affair, held the first weekend in June to raise money for the non-profit rescue service that served both Wayford and Merryfield.

Over a hundred spectators were on hand, enjoying the game, spending a little money on burgers and soft drinks, and rooting for one or the other—or both—of the ad hoc teams assembled for the event. Hardly anyone cared who won; it was just for charity, after all. But the return to town of Rory Fremantle was an extra attraction for those, like Ray Everett, who lived and died for local sports. Ray was the captain, coach, and pitcher for the Lions Club team, and he was one of those few who actually did care who won.

The brothers were sitting side by side in their dugout, talking while their teammates batted. They were down two runs in the bottom of the sixth inning, and 'Coach Ray' was trying to rouse his team into a rally.

"C'mon guys! Lock and load!"

"Yeah, we're going out to dinner tonight. I'm taking her to the Woodhouse."

"That sounds good; I love that place. And you'll be away from the hometown busybodies."

"Nice hustle, Smitty! Way to go!"

"That's what we wanted. You know, Kate's a really sharp lady, smart and beautiful. She's a winner."

"That's the impression I got, although we've barely spoken."

"Hey, Ben! You're on deck! We've got something going here!"

With two out and a runner on second, Ben drove a long double to right center to drive in one run and Rory followed with a single to tie the game. Ray Everett was ecstatic.

"Hometown! Hometown! Way to go, guys!"

But the team sponsored by the Jaycees scored four in the top of the seventh, and the Lions' team went quietly in their half to end the game.

Coach Ray was disappointed, but he played the good loser and fist-bumped every player on each team—at least the ones who didn't get away quickly enough.

"Great game, guys! Hey, Rory, Ben! You going to join us for a beer? A bunch of us are going to the Overlook Tavern for a couple. How about it?"

Ben looked at Rory, who shook his head.

"I'll have one with you, coach," said Ben, "but I think Rory's got plans."

"Alright, that's okay. Hey Rory, summer league starts up the week after next; we could use you!"

Kate was dressed and ready when the vintage Mustang pulled in a few minutes before six. She waved to Rory from the front porch then walked back through the house and out the kitchen door, locking up as she went. It was another gloriously sunny day—almost hot—and as she went down the steps from the porch, she caught a flash of light reflecting off something up on the ridge. *One of these days,* she thought, *I'll have to go up there and see what shiny thing is up in those trees.*

It was a splendid ride, the day being warm enough to keep the top down. Rory took them on some secondary roads so Kate could see some of the scenery. They went through woods, over rivers, and by a lot of farms.

This was all new to Kate. There were farms in Connecticut, to be sure, but she had seldom ventured out of suburbia. Now she was seeing big dairy barns, grain silos, and lots of crop fields. Many of the fields they passed just looked brown from a distance, but when they got closer she could just see the rows of corn barely poking up out of the ground.

"'Knee high by the Fourth of July' is the old saying here," Rory explained, "and we're right on schedule."

They passed hay fields in abundance and in various stages. Some farmers were mowing as they passed, but many fields had hay on the ground and a few were already baled.

"Everybody's getting their first cut in," Rory said. "It was a bit of a late start this year, but with all this nice weather lately, it's time. And we've got rain coming in a couple days, so now is the time."

"My field was being mowed today."

"Good. They will probably bale it tomorrow or Monday."

They reached the restaurant in plenty of time for their seven o'clock reservation. The Woodhouse was an old Victorian inn that had been restored and converted to a restaurant and catering venue.

"What a beautiful place!" Kate exclaimed. "And it's so busy; the parking lot is packed!"

"I think there's probably a wedding reception going on. You can't see it from here, but there's a big field with a tent out behind the building."

"Well, it's the season for it, I guess."

It was a splendid evening and a wonderful meal. They shared a shrimp appetizer, followed by a *Chateaubriand for two* special that was superb. Kate hadn't had beef like that in a while, and it was just what she wanted.

The conversation was lively and interesting. Rory was one of those people who could, and would, really listen. Kate had been through countless repetitions—with Jim—both when they were dating and after they were married of talking at length while he nodded and smiled and pretended to be interested. It hadn't taken her very long to realize that Jim's interest was completely feigned, but she had kept on trying, if only because she had known that once she stopped talking she would have to listen to him.

It was possible, she knew, that Rory was doing the same thing, but if so, he was the best she had ever known. He understood immediately the position of the literary agent as the "middleman" of the publishing business; the ones who screened thousands of manuscript submissions so the publishing houses wouldn't have to spend their time reading through stuff they would never want to publish.

"It's not perfect, of course," she said. "The tragedy of this business is that hundreds, or probably thousands, of really good manuscripts get rejected, or never get read at all. I'd like to think that we do our best, but it's inevitable."

"But wouldn't the same thing happen if writers sent their stuff directly to the publishers?"

"Well, yes, and that's why we exist; agents, I mean. Most publishers will only accept submissions from agents now."

"Hey, what about movies and television? Do you represent those writers?"

"Yes and no; we don't look at scripts or screenplays. But if our writers' material looks adaptable for film or television, we will negotiate film and television rights for them. I represent a lot of mystery writers, so that's a pretty big part of what we do."

On his part, Rory talked a little bit about working in the Gulf and partying in New Orleans, but he talked more about his hometown. The towns of Merryfield and Wayford had been founded in the late eighteenth century, just before the revolution. Contrary to what most of the townsfolk thought, the Fremantles had not arrived in Merryfield until the 1890s.

"They came up from Massachusetts with lots of money and bought the biggest tract of land in town: almost a thousand acres."

"Wow, and that's where you live now?"

"Yes. There have been a few 'strategic acquisitions' over the years—adjoining farms and plots. It's now eighteen hundred acres."

"What was the family business? Where did the money come from?"

"Well, that's the hazy part of the family history. The last four generations of Fremantles have been lawyers, but the family—especially Mother—have always given the impression that they never really needed to work. As if working for a living was dreadfully vulgar."

"Aah… the 'old money' syndrome."

"Exactly: we simply have it because we deserve it. I suppose I could do some research and find out what the nineteenth century Fremantles actually did to get rich. Maybe I'd discover some horrible crime."

He went on to name some of the other old families in town: the Taylors and the Bennetts, Mudgetts and Perkinses.

"What about the Andrews family? The ones who owned my house?"

"They didn't exactly die out, just drifted away. The old couple—Stanley and Margaret—moved to Florida and none of their grandchildren wanted to live in Vermont, apparently."

Tiffany's family, the Thompsons, were from Petersford, where they owned the valley's biggest employer, Valley Industries. They employed four hundred and although there were other businesses in the three towns, "VI," as they were known, was the economic engine of this part of Vermont.

"Farming is pretty big here, though, isn't it?" Kate asked.

"Oh, yes, farming is very important here. But the small farms are gradually disappearing."

A shadow seemed to come over his face, and he went silent. Just then, their waiter appeared with the dessert cart, displaying a variety of beautifully crafted delights. It was a perfect distraction from what appeared to be an awkward subject for Rory, and his mood was quickly restored.

When they left the restaurant, the air had become a little bit chilly, so they put the top on the Mustang for the ride home. With the mountains behind them to the west, they couldn't actually see the sunset, but when the curving road allowed, they could see the last rays of the sun shining on a couple of distant New Hampshire peaks. It was lovely.

Rory entertained her on the ride home with stories about the sports-obsessed Ray Everett and some of the other colorful characters in town. He mentioned Bitsy Dufresne, and Kate told him she was one of the first people she had met.

"I think she's great; I've learned almost everything I know about Merryfield from Bitsy."

"That was the perfect first contact for you. She knows everyone, she hears everything, and she's really nice. Her mom's the Town Clerk."

"I know. Oh, look, is that my chimney we can see?"

"It sure is. Until we turn the next corner; we're almost there."

They turned into Kate's driveway a few minutes later and pulled up to a stop.

"Rory," Kate said, "I've had a really wonderful time. Would you like to come in for a nightcap?"

"I would love to, Kate."

12

Kate was at the café at eight-thirty Sunday morning when the rush was still on, and she had to wait a few minutes for a seat at the counter. She was not in a great hurry; it would be a three-hour drive to Darien, but there was no pressure to get there early.

As usual, many curious eyes checked her out as she leaned against the stand-up bar where people waited to be seated. She knew that the Fremantles, including Tiffany, would be breakfasting at home this morning, but there would certainly be others who knew she had been out with Rory the night before. It didn't mean an awful lot to her, but she still wondered how long it would be, if ever, before her comings and goings would not be talked about.

Someone finished their breakfast at the counter, and Bitsy waved her over to sit down.

"Thanks, Bitsy," she said as she slid onto the stool.

"Of course, Kate. Here's your coffee."

She looked up at the specials board as she took her first sip of hot coffee. There were two breakfast specials today: pan-fried trout with eggs and home fries or a classic Quiche Lorraine. Both sounded pretty good to her; she'd have to think it over.

Bitsy was too busy to talk, which was okay. The café was full, and the air was filled with chit-chat of the usual sort. Neither of the patrons on either side of her knew her or showed any inclination to talk to her, and that was okay, too. It was almost like being all alone.

Last night was still on her mind, although she had decided long before now that she wasn't disappointed. Rory had been very forthright with her about his reluctance to begin a serious relationship and while a one-nighter with no commitment might have been fun, it wasn't really what either one of them wanted right now. She grimaced thinking about what Millie would have to say about that.

"Do you know what you want, hon?"

"Oh, Bitsy. Sorry, I was miles away. I guess I'll have the quiche."

"Okay; with fruit or homefries?"

"Homefries, please."

"You got it."

They had talked for half an hour or so over a glass of brandy. Kate had shared a little bit about her toxic marriage. She had married money, she explained, but she hadn't married *for* money. At least, that's what she believed, even if others didn't. Would she ever marry again? She wasn't sure. She still wasn't exactly sure what a good marriage was; she only knew what it *wasn't*.

He had chuckled at that and said that it sounded like a very good thing to know, although the price of that knowledge was high.

He asked about children; he knew, or assumed, that she didn't have any. Did she want children? She explained that Jim, her ex, had wanted children; at least one son, anyway. But after the first two years of marriage, she knew with absolute certainty that she did not want to bear a child and watch Jim turn that child into a monster like himself. So, she made sure, without telling him, that it would not happen. As for the future, she would love to have a child with the right man, but she was not in any rush.

Rory had said that he was in no rush, either. He was sure that Ben and Tiffany would have children and carry on the family name; they both wanted the same things and they were perfect for each other.

Ben was hesitating, but that was just because he was Ben. He was the cautious one; Rory was the impetuous one.

Rory had started to say something about his own part in that relationship, but the story broke down in the telling. On an impulse, Kate had said something about Tiffany bearing responsibility for her own actions and, at that, Rory became silent and just kind of stared at the floor. Perhaps, she thought, he hadn't known that she knew about his affair with Tiffany. Was it a mistake to say it?

But Rory had quickly recovered and had even started laughing. "Here we are on our first date," he had said, "and already spilling private stories. I'm not sure what that means for the future, but I would definitely like to see you again, Kate, when you come back."

She had replied that she would like that very much. Then he had finished his drink, they had shared a kiss that was not a lovers' kiss but far from a chaste one, and he had gone.

"Here's your quiche, Kate."

"Oh, thanks, Bitsy."

"More coffee?"

"Yes, thanks."

Kate enjoyed her breakfast slowly, as the café crowd thinned out. One of the benefits of coming in during the later part of the breakfast rush was that she might be able to have a semi-private chat with Bitsy. By the time she finished her meal, the café was quiet enough for a chat without having to shout, even if it wasn't empty.

"So, you're headed home for the week, right, Kate?" Bitsy asked.

"Yes, I'm leaving straight from here. Everything is all set; I've got new locks on all the doors at the house, and Chris or Patty will be there every day, either working or just to check on things."

"Good; they're both dependable. So...how did last night go?"

Kate smiled sardonically. Of course Bitsy knew.

"We had a lovely dinner at the Woodhouse, and then Rory drove me home."

"Uh-huh."

Bitsy was obviously waiting for more.

"Rory is a very interesting man. We plan to see each other again when I get back, but I'm not sure exactly when. It's not what you would call 'serious' yet, but who knows?"

Kate called Millie from her car just after she had crossed the Massachusetts border on I-91 and, as she had expected, Millie was disgusted with her.

"Honestly, Kate, I do not believe you! Are you sure this guy's not gay?"

"Yes, I'm quite sure."

"And you're not gay..."

"No, I'm not."

"So what is the problem? You're a full-grown woman, boss! The 'first-date' thing went out in the sixties, if not sooner. I honestly think you've slipped into the nineteenth century, with all those corny submissions you read."

"Everything's fine, Millie; things will work out, one way or the other."

"Yeah, well, you'd better make sure it's not 'the other,' cause there aren't that many hunks like him out there, you know."

"I know. Listen, Millie, the reason I called is to make sure there haven't been any last-minute changes to my calendar for tomorrow."

"No, everything is set. You've got two zoom meetings in the morning, two phone calls you have to make, and two more that can wait if you don't have time. Staff meeting at one o'clock, and then you're meeting that new client at three."

"Okay, sounds good. I'll be at Gina's tonight if you need me."

Would it work out, she wondered? Rory was so appealing, in so many ways. But there were so many issues.

In the first place, he was reluctant to start a new relationship. If that didn't change, it wasn't going to happen, no matter what. But he was obviously attracted to her, and he might overcome his reluctance. If that was going to happen, then she'd better be sure about her own feelings.

It didn't really matter that he was wealthy, but it made things easier; it meant that he wasn't someone looking for a free ride. He was very good-looking, charming, interesting, a good listener, and surprisingly sensitive and caring. He was also vulnerable; he had been hurt badly. That was where the problem lay, if there was one.

Not only had Rory been hurt badly; he had hurt someone else, and he was carrying a huge load of guilt. It seemed, from what she had heard, that Rory was not showing that vulnerability to others. If he had chosen to show that only to her, that was appealing, but also frightening.

I'm not a psychologist or a mental health counselor; what would I be getting myself into?

Doris Fremantle asked Rory to wait for a minute as Ben and Tiffany went off to dress for church; she wanted a quick word.

"It's all settled; Ben wants to give her the ring this afternoon at their favorite spot on the trails."

"So, Tiffany doesn't know?"

"She probably does, but she'll pretend she doesn't."

"So, you and Ben made the decision."

"The decision was made a long time ago. Ben will officially propose this afternoon, and we'll announce it at my birthday party on Saturday."

“How very special.”

“Don’t be sarcastic, Rory; it doesn’t become you.”

13 ▌

Reggie Plouffe made his usual round of errands after church. The hardware store was first, and he had a long talk with Ray Everett, mostly about the weather.

"Supposed to be a big one," Ray said. "You got your hay in, didn't you?"

"Sure I did. I expect everybody did, unless they was fools."

"You're right about that, Reggie. If this storm is half what they say, it'll be a long time before it's dry again."

"Don't believe it until you see it, Ray."

"How's that grandson of yours, Reg?"

"Oh, he's growing, I can tell you. He'll be starting first grade in September."

"Ain't that something! He didn't go to church with you today?"

"Nah, Christy never cared for church and she don't want Matty going, neither. Nothing I can do about it. Sometimes Peter will go with me, but he didn't want to today."

"Well, times are changing, Reg; can't get the youngsters to care about the things we do. Hey, is Peter playing ball this summer? He looked pretty good at shortstop for the high school team."

"Maybe; American Legion ball starts up in a couple weeks, but Peter ain't decided yet. Can't never get him to make up his mind."

Mary Thurgood was working the register at the IGA as she did every Sunday. She was always happy to see Reggie Plouffe come in for his groceries on Sunday afternoon; she was a widow and he a widower, and although he had never made anything close to a romantic overture, she still held out hope.

"Hell of a storm coming, they say, Reggie. You get your hay in?"

"Of course I did, Mary; had to, you know."

"Sure. How's Christy? And the little one?"

"Oh, she's okay, I guess. She don't mope around as much these days, but she ain't exactly happy."

"Can't blame her. Matty's about six now, ain't he?"

"Sure is; starting school this fall."

"How about that? They sure do grow up fast!"

"Say, Mary, I didn't see none of that coffee I like on the shelf."

"Ran out, Reg; it's coming in on Tuesday. I can run some out to you Tuesday afternoon, if you'd like."

"That's kind of you, Mary, but I gotta go to the Post Office anyway; I'll stop and pick it up."

At the feed store, Harley Ransom was disgusted.

"I know you got yours done, Reg; so did everybody else except that fool Tim Miller. He's mowing today! There's some that's baling today and they should be alright, as long as they get it covered. But Miller ain't got time to cut today and get it in before the rain starts! I told him so! I said 'Tim, you're better off waiting till the storm passes and it's dry again!' But does he listen?"

"He never did listen, Harley."

"He never did!"

"You think it's gonna be as bad as they say?"

"I don't know, Reg; you never can tell. You'll be alright, anyway; your fields are all on high enough ground, except that piece by the brook. But the farms on the north side, close to the river—they're the ones gotta worry."

At the stables on the Fremantle estate, Billy Tourville watched Ben and Tiffany ride away, just like every other Sunday afternoon. It was never going to be any different; he knew that. Unless he could get up the gumption to quit this dead-end job and find something else. There were plenty of places in this state with horses that could use a guy like him, weren't there?

But then, it was easy here. Even if they treated him like a servant—except Rory—the pay wasn't bad, and he got to ride almost as much as he wanted. He wondered how things would change when they got married. Robert had told him that Ben would be popping the question today. So she would be here even more than she was now, and those moments that he lived for, when Tiffany flashed that smile at him and brushed against him as he helped her mount, would continue.

But he knew she smiled that way at all the men, and he wasn't forgetting that she hadn't wanted him hired in the first place; Rory had told him that. Maybe he ought to just quit.

It was their favorite spot to stop and admire the view and maybe have a picnic. They didn't know that it was the same place Rory and Kate had stopped at when they had ridden on the private trail, but that didn't matter anyway. It was the perfect place for a marriage proposal.

Ben did it the old-fashioned way, on one knee and looking up at her. She played her part beautifully, pretending to be surprised when in fact the whole thing had been planned and choreographed by her and Doris.

"Just one thing, my love," he said, after a long kiss. "Please don't spill the beans. Mom wants to announce it at her birthday party on Saturday night. Don't you think we can give her that pleasure?"

"Of course, my darling."

They shared another kiss, and more.

The rain started Monday morning, and it didn't want to stop. It was the kind of slow-moving storm that never became too loud or too violent but never stopped dropping a steady rain. It was raining all over New England.

Down in southern Connecticut, the rain couldn't dampen Kate's mood. She was happy to be back in her office, and everything was going well. Her meetings were productive, her new clients looked promising, and, best of all, one of her established clients had just won an award for her fifth mystery novel. That would mean more sales, and more sales meant more commissions.

Even Millie was happy, although she would not stop badgering Kate about Rory.

"You can't miss out on this one, boss; chances like this don't come along every day."

"Don't worry, Millie. It might still happen, and it might not."

"You've got to make it happen!"

Rory called her Wednesday night.

"How's your week going, Kate?"

"It's going really well, Rory. I'm pleased that you called."

"Well, I wanted to see how you were doing and ask if I could see you on the weekend. You are coming back, aren't you?"

"Of course I am! Did you think I would change my mind and move back to Darien?"

"So, I didn't scare you off, then?"

"No, you're not that scary."

"That's good to know. When are you getting back?"

"Well, I'm pretty busy on Friday, so I think I'll drive up Saturday morning."

"Okay. We have a big family thing Saturday night, but there's a concert in Petersford on Sunday afternoon that might be fun. They have an outdoor venue there that's pretty nice, and they have concerts all summer."

"Who's playing?"

"Two acts: the Milligan Sisters, who just released their second album."

"I've heard of them. Sort of 'folky,' right?"

"Yes, and the other is a local group whose name I can't remember; also sort of 'folk-rocky.'"

"Alright, that sounds fun. Outdoors, you said?"

"Yes, but it's partly roofed over, so half the audience won't get wet if it rains. Should I get us tickets?"

"Okay, I'd like that. What's the big family thing on Saturday night?"

"It's my mom's sixty-fifth birthday, and we're having a big party at the house. All the 'best sort of people' from the valley and nearby will be there."

"Ooh...poor Mrs. Mapes."

"She'll have plenty of help for this one. It's going to be extra special."

"Because she's turning sixty-five?"

"That and more. Ben and Tiffany will be announcing their engagement, finally. It's a secret, so everyone in town knows."

"Of course they do! Well, maybe Tiffany will stop looking daggers at me."

"I wouldn't count on it."

It rained and rained and rained. It was still raining Thursday morning, but it tapered off and stopped around noon. Many people hoped it was over, but the wise old heads—and those who paid attention to the weather forecasters—said it was just a lull.

"It's gonna start up again tomorrow morning," said Ray Everett, who was having lunch at the Maple Leaf Café.

"That's what I heard," John Dusablon answered. "More rain tomorrow."

Chris Doran, sitting between the two, just grunted. He hadn't been able to finish the porch at Kate Stone's house or start painting the shed, either. Cleaning up the old wood stove was about the only thing he'd been able to do.

"I don't know," said Bitsy, as she set Ray's sandwich down in front of him. "Somebody said they saw the sun a few minutes ago."

"Don't matter," John said, "It's just a lull; storm's coming back stronger than ever tomorrow."

"Good thing we've got good drainage on the softball fields," said Ray. "Summer League starts on Monday."

Reggie Plouffe's fields were in good shape; the only field in a flood plain was the small hay field by the bend in Wandering Brook, and that would be a small loss if it ended up under water. But, just as Harley Ransom had predicted, those farms on the north side of town, in the flood plain by the river, were soaked, and they couldn't take much more.

In the early morning hours on Friday, the wind picked up and the rain began again. This time, there was thunder, lightning, hail, and torrents of rain. It went on most of the day, and by noon, every brook and stream was out of its banks. It was a flood like the valley hadn't seen in decades.

Fortunately, the town centers of Merryfield and Wayford were on higher ground and far enough away from any of the streams. But the farms in the northern part of the valley were under water by noon, and many of the dirt roads were washed out and impassable.

Chief Bridger and his eight full-time officers covered Merryfield and Wayford, and they were busy all day, traveling the back roads to check on the farms and isolated homesteads wherever their dispatcher sent them. It was a wonder that nobody needed rescuing, but then, everyone had known what was coming and they were all prepared.

At about three-thirty Friday afternoon, the sun came out. Within a short time, the clouds had all moved off to the east and it had turned into a hot, sunny day. Now, it was a matter of seeing who had lost power, who had no access to clean water, and who needed a car or truck pulled out of the mud.

There would be some losses—mostly corn fields and hay fields flooded—but the valley towns breathed a collective sigh of relief Friday evening that it hadn't been worse and prepared to enjoy a beautiful weekend.

Kate arrived in Merryfield a little after noon on Saturday and drove straight to her house. Chris Doran was there, checking out the porch, but he was just leaving. Chief Bridger had asked him to help pull a couple of vehicles out of deep mud with his heavy-duty pickup truck.

"I'll be back Monday morning; should have that porch finished by Tuesday afternoon."

She had a few things to carry into the house and unpack, then she sat down to eat the sandwich she had brought with her. Looking out from the east end of the porch, she could see the part of the garden that wasn't blocked by the shed. She guessed she'd better go and see how her crops were doing after all that rain, so she went in and changed into jeans and an old shirt to do a little gardening.

Being a novice gardener, she was surprised at how resilient her tiny plants were. Everything had survived the torrents and actually looked better for the rain. Of course, the weeds had loved the rain just as much as her plants, so she spent the next hour or so on her knees with a trowel and a garden fork. When she had made everything look ship-shape, she took a leisurely walk around the outside of the garden plot, only a small part of which she was using. *Maybe some fruit trees would be nice,* she thought. She'd have to ask Patty what she thought would do well here.

When she went back into the house, she was surprised to find that it was past three-thirty. She hadn't decided if she would go out for a meal this evening, but she had a manuscript to read, so she changed out of her gardening clothes, made a cup of tea, and sat out on the porch to read.

With a couple of breaks—for another cup of tea and to call the café to ask about the dinner specials—she was there until after six. It was a long read, but a good one; good enough that she was just about persuaded to offer the writer a representation contract.

At about six-fifteen, she heard a car turn in and looked up to see Patty Doran's car coming toward the house. Patty pulled right up next to Kate's Volvo and quickly got out. Something in Patty's body language alarmed Kate even before she spoke.

"Kate, I've got some really bad news. Rory Fremantle's dead—drowned in Wandering Brook."

14 |

Rory was dead. Kate was stunned and stayed in her chair, speechless, while Patty ran around to the kitchen door and came out onto the porch.

"Patty, I can't believe it. Drowned in the brook?"

"That's the story, as far as I know. I did hear it from one of the police officers who had seen the body, so I'm pretty sure it's true. Some people are saying he jumped in to save a little girl who'd fallen in, but I don't know if that's true or not."

"I don't know what to say, Patty; I don't know what to feel. I've only just met him ten days ago. We weren't lovers, but..."

"Listen, Kate. Why don't you jump in the car and come home with me. I've got a stewing hen in the pressure cooker and there's enough for a dozen. I'm sure you don't want to go downtown tonight."

It was a timely offer; the last thing Kate wanted right now was to be in the café with the whole town talking about it, and she didn't feel like cooking.

Neither of the women spoke a word as Patty drove them to her house. Kate needed to sit and think and Patty knew it.

The Dorans lived about four miles away in a century-old two-story house that sat on a two-acre plot of land. There was a barn behind the house, a shed, a chicken coop, a pigpen, and a huge garden. It looked like every square inch of the plot was either growing something or supporting some kind of livestock. Smoke was drifting lazily out of a chimney and into the still air, and the smell of wood smoke filled the air in the yard.

When they walked into the house, Beth immediately ran up to Kate and shouted, "Hi, Kate!" before throwing her arms around Kate's legs.

"Hi, Beth," Kate replied. She picked the girl up and gave her a big hug. "I'm so glad to see you."

"Good. Mommy said you might be sad, so I should not be... What was it, Mommy?"

"Oh, it's okay, Beth," Kate said. "I think a hug was just what I needed, and you are a great little hugger."

The house smelled intensely of chicken. Patty explained, as Kate followed her through to the kitchen, Beth still in her arms, that old laying hens always ended up in the pot and she liked to stew them in the pressure cooker with lots of vegetables and herbs.

"It smells amazing, Patty. I smell bread, too, don't I?"

"Yes," Patty replied as she lifted a tea towel to show two loaves on the counter next to the pressure cooker. "I baked two loaves of sourdough today; took them out just before I drove over to see you."

"Well, I'm certainly going to enjoy this meal!"

Chris walked into the kitchen just then.

"Hi, Kate," he said. "Really bad news."

"I'll say. Do you know any more about it?"

"I do; I just got off the phone with my cousin, Molly. It was her kids that were involved."

"Oh, no," Patty said. "Are they okay?"

"They're fine. Why don't we sit down and I'll tell what I know so far."

"I'm going to get the supper together, Chris, so you two sit and I can listen while I'm fixing our plates."

Chris and Kate sat at the kitchen table. Beth's highchair was already in place, so she was transferred from Kate's lap to her seat.

"Molly's kids," Chris began, "wanted to see how high the brook had risen. Nothing unusual in that, and Molly told them to be careful. It was all three of them: the two boys, who are twelve and ten, and Rachel, who is just six. They rode their bicycles out to where the brook crosses Tower Road; it's a good view from that bridge. Then the boys decided they wanted to check out that spot where the brook takes that right angle on the Sunrise Farm property."

"On the horse trail?" Kate asked. "Where that big concrete wall is?"

"Yes, right there. Although that wall isn't exactly in place anymore. I haven't been there yet, but I was told the stream was running so strong it eroded the bank behind the wall and pushed it out of place."

"Wow!" Patty said. "It doesn't sound like a safe place for kids right now."

"No, it sure isn't. Molly said she wouldn't have wanted the kids to go there, but she didn't tell them not to; she never thought of it. So they rode their bikes onto the horse trail and out to the bend. Timmy, the oldest one, says he warned the others not to go too close, but he wasn't watching them because he saw someone riding along from the Fremantle property."

"Rory?" Kate asked.

"Yes, it was Rory on that big chesnut gelding of his. He had just reached where the kids were when Timmy heard a scream and turned around. The stream bank had collapsed and slipped into the brook, taking Rachel with it."

"Oh, my God!" Patty said.

"Well, Rory did what any good man would do. He jumped off his horse, shouted to the boys to run downstream, and jumped right in.

Timmy said he couldn't see either Rachel or Rory at first, but then he saw them both on the surface going downstream fast, Rory just behind Rachel. Timmy and the other boy ran as fast as they could on the trail, knowing there was a place not too far downstream where they might be able to reach them.

"Well, sure enough, around the bend there's a place where a rock ledge juts out into the stream, and with the water so high, it was only a foot or so from the surface. They could see Rory, holding Rachel and keeping her head above water while he pulled himself along on some sunken branches. He managed to get just close enough to the ledge and pushed Rachel up to where the boys were reaching for her. The boys managed to grab both her arms, Rory let go, and they pulled her out. When they had her safe on the bank, they looked back and saw Rory just disappearing around the next bend.

"That's the last the kids saw of him. Rachel was still conscious, but she was crying and in a bad way, so Timmy told his brother to ride home as fast as he could to get help, and he stayed with the girl. Well, Molly called the police first thing, of course, then she and the boy headed back to the brook; he was riding and she was running. They got to the bend first, then the cops showed up a few minutes later.

"That's about all I know from Molly, but I heard down at the hardware store that they found Rory's body washed up on the east bank about half a mile down from the bend."

"But Rory was a good swimmer, wasn't he?" Patty asked as she put the bowls of chicken and vegetables in front of Kate and Chris.

"He must have been, to be able to save the girl," Kate said.

"Yes, he was," Chris said. "I don't really know, but folks have been saying they've never seen Wandering Brook so high or so fast."

"Oh, my God!" Kate exclaimed. "I just remembered the birthday party!"

"You knew about that?" Patty asked.

"We talked Wednesday night on the phone, Rory and I. He said it was his mother's sixty-fifth, and they were planning to announce Ben and Tiffany's engagement."

"That's what I heard, too. God, that poor woman. I don't think there's a single person in this town that likes Doris, but nobody deserves that."

At the police station in Wayford, Chief Les Bridger was frustrated and uncertain about what to do. The body had been found a little after four and the news had quickly spread all over Merryfield and Wayford. His eight-man department was already stretched, with calls coming in for assistance from all over the valley, and even though the County Sheriff had sent a few deputies to help—those few he could spare, since the whole county was in the same shape—the last thing he needed was an accidental death to deal with. Worse, the man who had drowned was a prominent citizen and one of Merryfield's best loved.

He had had to tell the dispatcher not to let any calls through to him unless it was someone really, really important. The phone was ringing constantly. The victim's body was on its way to Hanover, where it would be autopsied. Ben Fremantle had come to the station to identify his brother before the ambulance had left and then had gone right back home to be with his mother.

It was his Deputy Chief—Sergeant Meadows—who had found the body. Meadows and one of the Sheriff's deputies had searched the stream bank downstream from the bend, where Rory Fremantle had jumped in to save the little girl. Meadows had called the chief on his cell phone to report that the victim had washed up on the eastern bank in a very rocky stretch of Wandering Brook.

Chief Bridger had been ten miles away, just leaving one of the farms in the northern part of the valley, so he had let Sergeant Meadows handle the situation. They had both been informed of the victim's heroic actions to save Rachel Cote, so the drowning death of Rory Fremantle, though shocking, was not a great surprise. As it was clearly an accidental death, the chief had acquiesced in Sergeant Meadows's decision to carry the body out to where the ambulance was waiting.

The chief had called Ben Fremantle from his car and had told him the dreadful news. The ambulance would stop at the police station in Wayford before heading to the hospital, so the chief asked Ben to meet him there.

He knew, of course, that it was Doris Fremantle's birthday and that it would be a devastating blow to Merryfield's reigning matriarch. Many of the phone calls that were hammering his dispatcher were demanding more information. Some, including Ray Everett, who had called three times, wanted the chief to hold a press conference with all of the local and state media present. The chief did not think that was appropriate, given that no crime had been committed, but he was going to have to issue a statement of some kind, lauding the victim's heroism while bearing in mind the sensitivities of his very important family.

The chief knew what had happened at the bend, having talked to Molly Cote and to the officers who had responded, and he had just finished composing a brief, barebones statement for release to the press and public, but he decided to call Ben Fremantle and run it by him first.

"Thank you for calling, Les. I'm sure your statement will be fine, but if you'd like me to hear it first…"

"Well, here's what I've written: 'Today at four-fifteen P.M., Merryfield and Wayford police officers and County Sheriffs recovered the body of Rory Fremantle, twenty-seven, of Merryfield, on the east bank of Wandering Brook. Mr. Fremantle had jumped into the brook and successfully rescued a local six-year-old child then had been swept downstream by the current of the flooded brook and apparently drowned. This department will release further information when it becomes available.'"

"Apparently drowned?"

"Well, there were injuries to the body, including a head wound. That's not surprising, since that stretch of the brook is extremely rocky. The Medical Examiner will have to determine the sequence of injuries."

"Of course. That sounds fine, Les. I expect you'll get the examiner's report on Monday, right?"

"Yes, we should have it on Monday."

Kate said goodbye to Chris and Beth at nine o'clock and rode home with Patty.

"That was a wonderful meal, Patty; I don't think I've ever had chicken that was so flavorful!"

"That's what a stewing hen is all about; everything gets more flavorful as it gets older; people, too. You just have to be patient cooking them."

"You cook people, too?"

"No, not so far. Sorry we couldn't offer you any alcohol; we both gave that up."

"No problem. I've got a nice bottle of brandy at home. The last time I saw Rory we shared a glass of brandy. You know, Patty, it's a different sort of loss I'm feeling. I didn't know him long enough or well enough for the kind of grief people usually feel. It's just that, I had just begun to realize how deep and complicated he was, and I never got the chance to find out anymore, to explore that depth."

"Hmm...I think you saw a part of Rory that hardly anyone has seen. Nobody else talks about him that way."

They drove the rest of the way in silence. Then, as Patty stopped the car in front of the house, Kate said, "I think I might go to the café tomorrow morning. I know everybody's going to be talking about him, and I don't want people to think I don't care. What do you think?"

"I'm not sure. A lot of people know that you went out with him last Saturday and they're going to talk about you no matter what you do. The thing is, Rory was already a hero to most people, and now he's even more of a hero, so everyone is going to be sad, and they'll expect you to be as sad as everyone else, or more."

"I am sad, very sad."

"I know. If it was me, I think I'd just stock up on groceries and stay home for a while. But I'm not you. Why don't you pour a glass of that brandy and think about it?"

Billy Tourville was having a drink, too.

It had been a long and strange afternoon. First Rory had shown up at the stable unexpectedly and had said he needed to take Jagger out for an hour or so. He had been friendly, as always, but he was a little agitated. Billy had been as helpful as he always was and had watched Rory ride off towards the brook and Sunrise Farm.

Normally, Billy would have been heading home at four on a Saturday, but with Rory out riding, he'd decided he'd better stay until Rory got back, so he'd found some chores to do to keep himself busy. Then, a little after four-thirty, he had heard a door slam up at the house and had seen Ben run to his car and drive quickly off towards town.

There had been no telling what that was about, but a while later, maybe fifteen minutes, Jagger had come trotting back along the same trail he had taken out, with no rider, just Rory's outer shirt hanging from the saddle.

A horse coming back without a rider was always alarming, but something had told Billy to wait, rather than run right up to the house right away. Jagger had been nervous, so Billy had calmed him down, led him into his stall, and took off the saddle. A nice rubdown and a couple of apples had made the horse feel better, and when Billy had walked back out of the stable, Ben had been just parking the car.

Ben had seen Billy standing there and had shouted something to him while holding up a hand with five fingers splayed out, so Billy had waited. It had been more than five minutes, but Ben had walked out of the back door of the house and came over to give him the news.

Now Billy was sitting alone in his apartment, having another beer, and wondering what the hell he was going to do now.

At the Fremantle mansion, Doris was alone in her bedroom, although Ben and Robert were each checking on her periodically.

There was a lot to do. The funeral and all the details that followed any unexpected death would have to be dealt with, but first they had to deal with the party. The lavish birthday party would, of course, not take place. A hundred and twenty people had been invited, from all over southern Vermont, plus a few from New Hampshire.

Most of them were local, so most of them had already heard the news, but they still had to be contacted and asked not to come. Those guests travelling a greater distance needed to be called soonest, so as to cause them as little inconvenience as possible. It was inevitable that some would not be reached, so Ben and Tiffany prepared to meet the guests who would begin arriving at seven and rehearsed exactly what to say to them. Ben, the attorney, was the soul of courtesy and grace, and Tiffany, when dealing with those of her own social class, could be as charming and polite as the situation demanded.

Robert, while on call to answer any summons from Doris instantly, was in charge of deconstructing the elaborate preparations for the party. Much of it could be done in the next few days, but the food would have to be either stored, returned, or donated. The extra cooks and the waiters—those not needed to help with the breakdown—would have to be paid off and sent home.

Mrs. Mapes suggested that since they would certainly be having some kind of reception after the funeral, a lot of the food and wine could be saved for that. Robert agreed and asked Mrs. Mapes to make those decisions herself. But the prepared food would have to go; they would certainly not be serving leftovers.

With so many things to do, it seemed like there was no time to grieve—not for Ben and Tiffany, anyway. Doris had cried out in anguish when Ben had broken the news, and Ben had not been dry-eyed himself. When he had related the whole tragic story, his mother had uttered the same words everyone else in town was saying: *It was so like Rory.*

Chief Bridger had issued the official statement at six o'clock, but that hadn't stopped the phone calls. He told the dispatcher to tell every caller that more information would be released as soon as it became available and say nothing more.

Ray Everett gave up on trying to get more out of the chief; he had moved on. As president of the Boosters Club, he had already decided that they should rename the athletic complex at the South Valley Union High School in honor of their fallen hero. He called several members of the club, and they all agreed it was the right thing to do, although a couple of them urged him to wait a while and let people grieve before rushing ahead with anything.

It would be the School Board who would have to make the decision anyway. Tiffany Thompson was the Chairperson of the Board, and Ray despised her. But he was just about to call her anyway, when his wife put her foot down.

"Are you out of your mind, Ray? She's part of the family and they're in mourning; leave it be!"

Kate went to bed after just one glass of brandy. She thought about calling Millie, but she knew Millie was out on a date with a new prospect, and she didn't want to leave such a gloomy message on voicemail.

Kate very much wanted to fall asleep quickly, but she doubted that was going to happen. Her head was filled with too many thoughts and questions.

Was she sad? Of course she was; a man with so much going for him had lost his life tragically.

Was she heartbroken? No, she barely knew the man. She had wanted very much to know him better, but she didn't love him. How could she?

What were the people in Merryfield expecting of her? Kate wasn't the type who usually cared what other people thought of her, but this was a situation she had never encountered. She was in a new place, a new community, and she had already caused a great deal of gossip through no fault of her own. Now she had met the town's "favorite son," had had a dinner date with him, and he had died a week later.

She couldn't very well go on as if nothing had happened, but she had to go on.

Reggie Plouffe heard it first from his son, Peter; a friend called with the news. Reggie didn't always believe what he heard from teenagers, but one of the Deputy Sheriffs pulled into the yard, knowing the Plouffe family would want to know, and told him the whole story.

"He rescued the little Cote girl?"

"Sure did. She'd have drowned for sure. Then Rory got swept downstream and drowned himself."

"Jesus! Well, thanks for telling me; I'll have to break the news to Christy."

"Yeah, that's what I figured."

He didn't know how she would react. She had been so in love with the man, and then he had gone off with that rich Thompson piece and it had broken her heart. She'd sworn to never have anything to do with him again, or even hear his name. Well, maybe she wouldn't want to hear about it, but he had to tell her, didn't he?

He told her. She listened silently, her face expressionless, then she walked up the stairs to her bedroom and closed the door. A little while later, Matty came down and told his grandpa that his mommy didn't want any supper and to just leave her alone.

16

It was a gloomy Sunday in Merryfield. Most people knew the Cote family, who had come so close to losing their youngest, and everybody knew, or knew about, the Fremantles, who had lost their youngest.

Sorrow didn't keep people from talking about it. Attendance at the three churches in town was a little higher than usual, and all three services featured thanks and praise for the rescue and condolences for the loss. The Cotes were all in attendance at St. Stephen's Catholic Church, and they lingered long after the benediction to talk with friends outside.

Over at St. Thomas Episcopal, Doris and Ben Fremantle, along with Tiffany Thompson, arrived all dressed in mourning black.

Doris Fremantle, just turned sixty-five, was no stranger to grief. She had buried her first son, Matthew, when he was just five and young Ben had not yet been born. She had buried her husband, Benjamin, only four years ago. She knew how to grieve with dignity and propriety; it was what the best families did.

Most of the talking took place at the town's usual gossip centers—the Miss Merryfield Diner and the Maple Leaf Café.

At the Miss Merryfield, Harley Ransom held court, as he often did, at a table with four of his friends. They talked about the Cote family, whom everybody knew and liked.

"Course they shouldn't have been there," Harley was saying, "that goes without saying. But you can't blame Leonard; he was working overtime at the shop in Petersford. God knows they need the money. And Molly, she's as fine a woman as I know and a good mother. Kids are gonna be kids, and God knows I spent many a day standing on the banks watching a spring flood. A mother can't be everywhere!"

"Still," Bill Williams said, "she must have known how high the water was. Why did she let them go there in the first place?"

"She told them to be careful," Lester Potts said. "What more could she do? She was too busy to go with them."

"Bill, you're not listening to what I'm saying," Harley said. "When you were a boy, did you always do what your mom told you to do, when there was some fun to be had? You certainly did not, and don't go saying otherwise, 'cause I was there with you!"

That got a laugh all around the table and a sheepish grin from Bill Williams. After a few minutes, Cedric Shallow spoke up.

"I'm wondering how the Plouffes are taking it."

Heads shook and mouths murmured at that.

"Poor Christy," said Lester. "Ain't nothing but sorrow for that girl."

"Well," Harley said, "that Rory was a rake, alright. But he didn't deserve to die."

"Nobody's saying he did, Harley," said Lester, "But I don't feel half as sorry for the Fremantles as I do for the Plouffes."

At the Maple Leaf Café, Ray Everett was sitting with the manager of the First National Bank and two other members of the Boosters Club.

"I'm not saying he doesn't deserve it, Ray," Walt Drake was saying, "I'm just saying there's no need to move so quickly."

"But why wait? Rory was the biggest hero this town has ever had, and we ought to go ahead and honor him."

"There's heroes and then there's heroes," said Sam Waters, a white-haired man who looked to be in his eighties, at least. "This town has lost men in both World Wars, in Korea, in Vietnam, and in Iraq. You know I'm a big supporter of athletics, Ray, but let's have a little perspective."

"Oh, come on, Sam; the veterans have their monuments already, and it's not taking anything away from them. I'm talking about naming the athletic complex after him. He was one of the finest athletes this town has ever seen..."

"It's a union school district, Ray; don't forget that. Three towns, not just Merryfield."

"That don't matter! He was a hero for the whole district! They'll go along with it, I'm sure."

The waitress came by to refill their coffees.

"You fellows doing alright? Need some more muffins?"

A chorus of "yeses" approved the suggestion, and the waitress went off for another basket of fresh muffins.

"Say, I heard that Rory was romancing that divorcee that bought the old Andrews place," Walt Drake said. "Is that true?"

"It's true," Ray replied. "He took her to the Woodhouse last Saturday for dinner, then drove her home."

"Well, they say she's a looker," said Sam.

"See for yourself, Sam," said Walt. "She's just come in."

All eyes turned towards the entrance, where Kate Stone had just walked in and strode to the end of the counter. Bitsy quickly walked over to greet her.

"Hi, Kate, I think your order's just come up. Let me check."

"Thanks, Bitsy."

Kate had chosen to get a takeout order from the café for breakfast and had stopped at the IGA to stock up on groceries before coming in to get her order. She looked casually around the café, recognizing a few people. Most of the patrons were being discreet, but they were all looking at her and, she was certain, were all talking about her. It would be a long time before that would change.

Bitsy came back from the kitchen with a white bag containing her breakfast and stapled shut with the receipt attached.

"Here you go, hon; credit card this time?"

"Yes, here."

"Wish we had time to talk," Bitsy said as she ran the card. "But I guess you'll want to avoid the crowds for a while."

"Exactly. I'll come in one day soon when it's not too busy."

Kate called Millie at one o'clock Sunday afternoon and told her the news.

"Oh, my God! That's...oh my God! Kate, honey, I don't know what else to say!"

"Well, neither do I. Nothing like this has ever happened to me. I mean, it didn't happen to me, but..."

"He actually jumped into a flooded river and saved a little girl?"

"Yes, he did."

"And drowned."

"Yes. It's the kind of thing you read about, but it never really happens, except, it did."

"Oh, Kate. I was all ready to tell you all about my big date, and now you tell me this."

"Well, I didn't want to, but I had to."

"Of course, of course. Listen, Kate, are you okay?"

"Yes, I'm okay, Millie. I've been thinking about nothing else since, well, since I heard the news. I mean, I've been thinking about how I feel, and how I *should* feel, and what other people are going to think."

"Do a lot of people know that you went out with him?"

"Everybody knows. There are no secrets in Merryfield, Millie. Everybody knows I went out with him, but nobody knows I didn't sleep with him, so I'm sure they all think I did, and now... Well, I don't know. As for me, I'm really sad about it, but I wasn't in love with him, so I don't know how I'm supposed to feel. I can't really be in mourning, you know."

"Of course. You only just met him. I'm sure people won't expect you to wear black or anything."

"Well, it's hard to know what people expect. It's so different here, Millie."

Ben Fremantle's cell phone rang at a quarter to ten. It was Billy Tourville.

"Billy, why are you calling me this time of night? You must know what we're dealing with."

"Yeah, I know, Mr. Fremantle, but I got to tell you that I'm leaving. I mean I'm giving my notice."

"You're giving your notice? Now?"

"That's right. It's time for me to move on."

"Billy, have you been drinking?"

"No, I ain't. I did plenty last night, but not today. I just got to move on, that's all."

"If that's the way you want it. Can you work out two weeks, or are you quitting right now?"

"Two weeks; like I said, I'm giving my notice, like I'm supposed to."

Ben told Tiffany, who was staying the night. She didn't seem surprised and certainly wasn't upset.

"Well, he was Rory's project, wasn't he? I never thought he should have been hired at all."

"I know, but it kind of leaves us in the lurch. Billy's awfully good with horses."

"We've got two weeks to find someone else. You know I've always wanted to upgrade the stables and find a real professional to manage them; we've talked about it."

"Yes, of course. That was going to be one of your projects, but now it's become more of a priority."

"Well, we can talk to that woman at Sunrise Farm…"

"Linda Norman."

"Yes. If we can't find a permanent stable manager within two weeks, maybe she can recommend somebody for the short term."

"That's a good idea. I'll try to find time to call her in the next couple of days."

17

Kate had breakfast at home on Monday morning. She had fresh eggs from Chris and Patty's hens, some of Patty's sourdough bread, toasted, and bacon from the IGA.

She had a busy day ahead, with several submissions to read through, and she was expecting Chris to arrive early to work on the porch. She made herself a second cup of coffee and brought it out to the east end of the porch, along with her laptop and a cinnamon bun.

It was another beautiful day. Ever since the rain had stopped Friday afternoon, there had been nothing but blue skies and mild temperatures in the valley, as if Mother Nature were saying, "Sorry about that, it's alright now."

It was breakfast at home as well for Ben and Doris Fremantle, and Tiffany. Ben had a lot to do at the office, and Tiffany a lot to do at the store, but the first thing the three of them had to do was to make some decisions about the funeral and the reception that would follow.

Ben reminded his mother that the body would have to be officially released after the autopsy, and he did not know for certain when that would be. They had spoken to Father Simpson after the service on Sunday, and he had suggested Wednesday for the funeral service.

"Surely they won't need that long, will they?" she asked.

"I wouldn't think so, Mother. Let's plan on Wednesday, then."

"Fine. I know you both have a lot to do today; I'll call Father Simpson after breakfast, and Robert and I will take care of planning the reception."

Chief Les Bridger was busy, too. So many reports to write, so many officers' reports to read and review—if people only knew! Well, it was what he had signed up for, so no use complaining.

What a weekend! It looked like the weather would stay dry for a while, so maybe things would ease up. The roads that had washed out were being repaired, and nobody was isolated or in any danger. He would have to evaluate everything this afternoon and let the County Sheriff know if he would need continued assistance from his deputies.

The intercom buzzed at ten-thirty.

"It's the Medical Examiner, Chief."

"Thanks, Ginny. Hello, Doc, what have you got for me?"

"Well, first thing, Les, your victim didn't drown. No water in the lungs."

"Okay, so he must have crashed into the rocks. I noticed that big wound over the left temple—was that what did it?"

"Yes, that was what killed him. But the thing is, Les, I found flakes of rust in the wound. He hit, or was hit by, a heavy piece of rusted metal. So, unless you've got old pipes or other metal objects in that brook, you've got yourself a homicide."

A flurry of activity followed. A call to the sheriff first, asking for continued assistance, then a call to all of his officers—on and off duty—to get to the site where the body was found and cordon off the area. Next, the chief called Ben Fremantle.

"Are you serious, chief? Rory might have been murdered? How is that possible?"

"Well, the examiner said there were flakes of rust in the wound that killed him. He was hit by a heavy, rusted metal object. Now, it's possible that there was something in the brook—some old, rusted pipe or some other submerged piece of metal—and that's the first thing we're going to check for, but if we don't find anything like that in the water..."

"Then somebody hit him."

"Right. I'm heading out there right now. I'm going to call Linda Norman and ask her to open up that trail for vehicles; it will be easier to get there."

"Good. I want to go out and have a look myself. I don't want to tell Mom until we know for certain."

"That's probably best. I'll see you out there."

On Saturday, the ambulance had driven across a hay field on a dirt track to get to the site, but with multiple vehicles headed there, it made sense to use the horse trail, which was wide enough for vehicles; it just needed to be accessed from Sunrise Farm. Linda Norman was happy to cooperate, and she moved the vehicle barrier aside with the help of one of the officers. When Ben arrived at the farm, it was already open, and he drove quickly to the site where his brother's body had been found.

Chief Bridger was there with four of his officers and two deputies. Ben parked his car on the trail behind three police cars and hurried to the scene. The chief was directing his men, describing with his arms the area he wanted searched, along the bank and back into the meadow on the other side of the trail. Two officers were in the brook, wearing hip boots and searching for submerged objects that might have caused the injury.

The chief turned toward Ben as he approached.

"Thanks for coming out, Ben. You must know this area pretty well, don't you?"

"Yeah, pretty well. It's really gone down, hasn't it?"

At this section of Wandering Brook, the bank was very shallow on the east side, where they were standing. The shallow slope was covered with rocks of many sizes and shapes: some round, some jagged and sharp. It was fifty feet from where they stood to the water, but two days earlier, the brook would have been lapping against their feet. The chief pointed across the brook to the other bank, which was very steep—almost vertical in some places.

"You see, Ben, the line on the other bank where the flood was highest? It was two feet higher than it is now."

The two men stood there and surveyed the scene, each with his own agenda. Ben was watching the flow of the stream as it was now and trying to imagine what it would have been like on Saturday. Rory would have been carried around the much narrower corner just upstream and through a patch of rocks, some of which jutted more than a foot above the present water level. If he were already dead, or unconscious, the current might have simply carried the body to the point, just below his feet, where it was found. But would the current have been flowing in the same pattern when the water was two feet higher and rushing more quickly?

Chief Bridger was thinking about the opportunities they had missed to gather evidence on Saturday and what they could possibly find by searching the area now. Dozens of booted feet had trodden the area where they were standing, and the slope between where they were standing and the current stream edge would have been under water. No footprints, and precious little else would be found by the water's edge.

Ben was talking, and the chief suddenly heard something that made him stop and listen.

"Sorry, Ben, what did you just say?"

"I was saying, chief, that if Rory hit something in the water and the current washed him up here, the water would have washed anything out of the wound, wouldn't it? If it were any length of time between the impact and his body reaching the bank. You wouldn't be able to tell if he had smashed into something or he'd been hit."

"Hold that thought, Ben. Tell me, what was going on between Rory and that Stone woman? Were they in a relationship?"

"Uhh, they had only met last week, but they went riding together one day and they went out on a dinner date last Saturday."

"A dinner date."

"Yes, they went to the Woodhouse, then Rory drove her home. That's all I know."

"Alright. Listen, Ben, I'm going to leave my sergeant in charge here. I'm going to go talk to Kate Stone."

Kate was sitting on the east end of her porch while Chris Doran worked on the west end, when Chief Bridger pulled up in his police car. She had a glass of lemonade on the table beside her and a manuscript on her lap.

The chief got out of his car and walked up to the porch, stopping to lean against the rail just below where Kate was sitting.

"Good afternoon, Chief, what brings you here today?"

"I'm afraid, Miss Stone, that it is police business this time. I need you to come down to the station and answer some questions."

"Alright. May I know what this is about?"

"It's about the death of Rory Fremantle. He did not drown, as we had thought, and it looks likely that his death was a homicide."

"A homicide? Oh. Well, I'll answer any questions I can. Do you want me to ride with you, or may I drive my own car?"

"You can drive; just follow me to the station."

The interview took place in a little room next to the chief's office. Another officer was present, and the interview was recorded. When the three of them had given their names for the tape, the chief began.

"Miss Stone, what was your relationship with the deceased, Rory Fremantle?"

"We were friends. We had just met a couple days after he returned from the job he had down south. We met at the counter at the Maple Leaf Café, quite by accident. We had lunch together, chatted for about an hour, and decided to go for a ride together the next day. We enjoyed a nice ride, and he asked me if I would like to go out to dinner with him. I said 'Yes.' That was Thursday, and we went out on Saturday.

"We went to the Woodhouse. I don't know exactly where that is; my local geography is still a little sketchy. He drove me home afterwards, and we had a drink at my house. He stayed long enough for one drink, then he left. To be perfectly clear, we did not sleep together and he did not spend the night. As to our relationship, we had every intention of seeing each other again. In fact, he called me on Wednesday night."

"You had gone back to Connecticut for the week, hadn't you?" the chief asked.

"That's right. I drove down to Darien on Sunday. As I was saying, Rory called me Wednesday night and asked if I would go to a concert with him on Sunday. So, we intended to see each other again, but our relationship had not progressed any farther than a kiss. That's about it."

"Thank you. When did you return to Merryfield?"

"I drove up Saturday morning, and I got to the house about twelve-thirty, I think, maybe a little earlier. Chris Doran was there when I arrived, but he was just leaving. I stayed home all day, did some garden work, then sat on the porch and read. I was there until Patty Doran came at just after six and told me about Rory."

"Did you see anyone else that day?"

"No. After Chris left, I was alone all day until Patty showed up."

That was the extent of the recorded interview, but Kate and the chief chatted briefly on the sidewalk in front of the station.

"You've been very cooperative, Miss Stone," the chief said. "You didn't seem the least bit surprised that I wanted to speak with you."

Kate laughed.

"Chief, I live and breathe murder mysteries. Most of my clients are mystery writers. In every story, every book, every television show, and every movie there's at least one character who says something like, 'Officer, you can't honestly think *I* was involved!' or some variation of that. But that's not me. I'm perfectly aware that you need to speak to everyone who might possibly have any information. But there must be many others you need to interview."

"Yes, of course. I'll tell you why I wanted to talk to you first. Remember the day when I went out to your house to talk to Chris?"

"Sure."

"Well, when you went to call him down from the roof, you left a manuscript lying on the table, with a paragraph highlighted. I read it."

"Oh. I shouldn't have left it; it's supposed to be confidential."

"And I shouldn't have read it. But you did leave it, and I did read it."

"Is that the way the murder happened?"

"Not exactly, but close enough that I thought of you immediately."

"Interesting. Well, I don't have an alibi; I could have gone to the brook and back. But I had no motive and you won't find any forensic link. Still, I guess I have to stay on your suspect list for now."

"Exactly. I don't think you did it, but just don't leave town for now."

18

Ben Fremantle parked his car in front of the police station just as Kate was driving away. They made eye contact just for a second, and Kate was struck by the look in his eyes. Every time the two had met previously, he had smiled at her and his smile had betrayed an obvious attraction. But all she could read from his expression today was suspicion.

Well, he had just lost his brother and it was perfectly natural for him to view her as a potential suspect. Still, it was disappointing.

Chief Bridger was still standing on the sidewalk as Ben got out of his car.

"How did that go, Les?"

"It went well, Ben; she was very cooperative. She doesn't seem to have any obvious motive but, as she admits, she doesn't have an alibi for Saturday afternoon, so I've asked her not to leave town. There's clearly no reason to hold her."

"Yeah, I guess you're right. Listen, Les, it may not mean anything, but Billy Tourville called me last night and gave me two weeks' notice. He's quitting."

"Really? That's surprising; it's the only steady job he's ever had, as far as I know. I would have had to question him anyway, since he was probably the last person—other than the three kids—to see Rory alive. Is he working today?"

"Yes, he is."

"Alright. I've got to go check in with Sergeant Maroney at the crime scene, then I'll go talk to Billy. Ben, have you told your mother yet?"

"No. I've got to do that right now. I think I'll pick up Tiffany and we'll tell her together."

Tiffany was in her office at the Tiff-Toff Shoppe, looking over a list of furniture items from a dealer in Ohio when Ben came in. She was expecting him to take her out to lunch, so it was no surprise. But when he told her the news that Rory had been murdered, she was flabbergasted.

"I don't believe it! Everybody loved Rory! Who could possibly... Wait, did the chief say it might be that farm girl he was with? The Plouffe girl?"

"He didn't say, but I'm sure she will be on his list. There's precious little at the scene to connect anyone to the killing. Now, to be clear, Tiff, there's a slim chance that Rory slammed into a submerged metal object, but they haven't found anything like that. The chief is ninety-nine percent sure it was a homicide. He has already questioned Kate Stone."

"Kate Stone? Of course! Ben, she's got to be the prime suspect! He took her out last weekend, drove her home, and who knows what happened? I'll bet it's her, the callous trollop! Has she been arrested?"

"No, no. The chief questioned her, because of the circumstances, and she doesn't have an alibi for her whereabouts, but, as the chief said, there's no obvious motive."

"But there's an obvious situation that could have become a motive."

"Maybe. Les is going to question Billy Tourville today, as well."

"Hmm... He and Rory seemed to be all buddy-buddy, but who knows?"

"Tiff, I need to tell Mom before she hears it from someone else. Will you come with me?"

"Of course I will, hon."

Chief Bridger met Sergeant Maroney back at the crime scene, where the officers were still carefully searching the area on the east side of the riding trail, away from the brook. There was no one in the brook itself.

"There's nothing there, Chief," Maroney explained. "I mean no metal objects in the water that a body could crash into. We haven't searched upstream beyond that rocky section, but what would be the point? If he'd hit something back there..."

"If he'd hit something upstream, the body would have been in the water long enough to wash anything out of the wound before he ended up here."

"Yeah. And besides, the water was two feet higher then. Anything he might have hit his head on would be clearly visible now, wouldn't it?"

"Yes, that's right. At this point, Jim, we're looking for a murder weapon."

"That's what I'm thinking. I sent Watts and Dubrul to get some rakes. The water's still too muddy from the flooding to see the bottom, so we'll need to do some scraping and dredging. Should we call the Staties in?"

"Well, the water's not deep enough to need divers. I think we've got enough equipment to do it ourselves, and I'd just as soon not involve them if we don't have to."

"Okay, Chief; Watts and Dubrul should be back here soon."

"Right. I'm off to question Billy Tourville." He scanned the brook for a few seconds before leaving. "Bert, we'd better search the other bank, too."

The sergeant looked at him quizzically.

"I know, it doesn't seem likely, with that bank being so much higher and steeper, but just to be thorough, let's search it anyway."

"You got it, Chief."

Kate returned home to find Patty Doran standing in front of the porch, holding Beth in her arms and talking to Chris. Before Kate had even stopped the car, the little girl was on the ground and running toward her.

"Hi Kate!" she shouted as the car door opened.

"Hi Beth! I'm so glad to see you!"

Kate picked Beth up and walked over to where Patty was standing and smiling at her.

"You had to talk to the chief, Kate? What's that all about?" Patty asked.

"Well, as it turns out, Rory Fremantle didn't drown. He was murdered."

"Oh, my God!" Patty exclaimed while her husband shook his head sorrowfully. "And the chief questioned you about it?"

"He knew I had dated Rory, and there was something else—a coincidence. Why don't we sit down and I'll tell you what happened."

They sat on the east end of the porch, and Chris joined them. It was still a little early for lunch, but Kate had lemonade in the fridge and cookies in the cupboard; that would keep Beth happy while Kate explained to Chris and Patty about the manuscript the Chief had seen and read.

"But that doesn't mean anything," Patty said. "I mean, it doesn't connect you with the murder; it's just a coincidence."

"Yes, and the chief knows that; it was just enough to trigger the thought that I was one of the people he had to question."

"You don't seem surprised or upset," Chris said.

"No, I'm not. As I told the chief, I live and breathe murder mysteries and I know he has to question everyone who had any connection to Rory."

"And you're not worried," said Patty.

"No. I didn't have a motive, for one thing, although people might think I did. I might have had the opportunity; I was here all alone when it happened, but I can't prove it. As for the means to commit the crime—well, I don't know what the weapon was, but there can't possibly be any forensic link between me and the weapon, because I didn't do it."

Patty frowned, not convinced.

"But can you prove you didn't do it?" she asked.

"I don't have to. It's up to the State to prove I did, and they can't."

"Well, I guess that's the way it's supposed to work," Patty replied. "I'm just not very trusting when it comes to the cops."

"Me neither," Chris added, "but I've got to finish this porch."

Chris went back to what he was doing.

"Can I have another cookie?" Beth asked.

Patty pulled a cookie out of the package and handed it to her daughter.

"Just one more, hon. Kate, where are these cookies from?"

"A bakery in Darien. I got some at the IGA, but they weren't very good. I know the café has good cookies, but I'm not sure I want to go there right now. I might have to break out my baking skills and make my own."

"Beth likes to help me when I'm baking; maybe she could come over one day and help you."

"Yes, yes, yes!"

"That would be fun! Let me figure out what day would be best and I'll let you know. Listen, Patty, do you have a few minutes to talk some more?"

"Sure."

"Thanks. I'm going over in my head what happened to Rory. I know it's not my job to figure it out, but my brain is so wired to mysteries that I can't help myself."

"Yeah, I get it. How can I help?"

"Tell me everything you know about the Plouffe family."

Billy Tourville was trying to be as cooperative as he could, but Chief Bridger had put him on his guard right away by asking him why he had decided to quit.

"Look, Chief, it wasn't my fault Rory drowned, but it does change things for me, you know?"

"Rory didn't drown, Billy; he was murdered."

"What? Murdered? He jumped into the brook to save those kids, didn't he? And they found him washed up on the bank, right?"

"Right, but he didn't drown. He was hit over the head; that's what killed him."

"He crashed into the rocks, then."

The chief shook his head. "Coroner says no. Somebody hit him over the head."

Billy put his hands to his head and groaned. He looked around for his stool and sort of staggered over to it and sat down.

"Man, that's bad news, bad news. Who would do that?"

"It's my job to find out, Billy, so I have to talk to everybody who might have any information for me. Obviously, that includes you."

"Yeah, that makes sense, but you must know I wouldn't kill Rory or do anything to him. He was about the only friend I had in this town, leastways the only 'respectable' one. You know what I mean."

"Yeah, I know what you mean, Billy. Rory got you this job, didn't he?"

"Yup, he did. We always got along, me and Rory, going back to high school. Most of his friends were too snooty to talk to the likes of me, but Rory wasn't like that. He was the one that convinced me to stick it out in soccer; told me I was good and I should just keep working at it and ignore everybody else. He liked me more than the coach did."

"I know all about that. Then you got in some trouble over in Petersford and Rory helped you out and hired you to work here."

"He did. The others didn't want me here: Ben and their mother and Miss Thompson."

"Is that why you're quitting? Because Rory's gone?"

"Sure. They'd probably fire me anyway, so I might as well quit."

"It doesn't look good, though, you quitting right after Rory gets killed."

"But I didn't know he was murdered."

"Unless you did it."

"Yeah, but then I wouldn't give notice, would I? I'd just go."

"But that would be practically admitting you did it. Giving notice makes more sense; it doesn't look like you're guilty."

"Yeah, I guess. But I didn't do it."

"Okay, I'm not saying you did. But you've got to tell me everything that happened that day, from when Rory got here to when his horse came back alone."

"Alright, Chief."

The room they were in was halfway down the north side of the barn. It was a deep space, stretching all the way to the exterior wall, where a door opened directly to the outside. In the back section was a shower and a changing room. The front section had a big utility sink and cleaning equipment on one side, a desk and chairs on the other. There was a pegboard on the wall, with clipboards hanging on hooks and one short filing cabinet, which contained medical records on the horses, as well as miscellaneous paperwork.

Billy had been here, in this room, on Saturday afternoon when he had heard Rory come into the barn.

"What time was that?" the chief asked.

"About quarter to four, I guess; not sure exactly. He went right to number two stall, where Jagger is, and hollered to me to grab a shirt for him."

"He didn't come here and use the changing room?"

"No, he was in a hurry. He keeps a couple of barn shirts here, for when he's just going for a ride—not with company or anything. Keeps his riding boots here, too, but he didn't bother with them, just kept his regular shoes on. I grabbed one of his shirts off a hook in the changing room and brought it to him. He had taken off the shirt he was wearing and hung it on a hook in the stall."

"Is it still there?"

"Yeah, it is. The barn shirt's there, too. He must have took it off while he was riding; it was really hot that day."

"Yes, it was. He was just wearing a tee shirt when we found him. But how did you know that?"

"The barn shirt was hanging from the saddle when Jagger came back."

"Let's walk over to the stall."

They crossed over to number two stall on the other side of the barn, where Rory's horse, Jagger, was standing quietly, as if waiting for them. On one wall of the stall, hanging on hooks, were two long-sleeved men's shirts. One was what Billy had described as a "barn shirt," a tan-colored shirt of a heavy cotton weave, similar to what any workingman would wear. The other was a light blue "sport shirt," of the type that Billy would consider "dressy," while an office manager would consider it appropriate for "casual Friday."

"What else did Rory say to you, besides telling you to grab a shirt for him?"

"Uhh, he just said he needed to take Jagger out for a while; said he'd be back in an hour, or so."

"Nothing else?"

"No, I'm pretty sure that's all he said. I gave him a hand with the saddle, but he didn't say nothing else."

"He was in a hurry; didn't take time to fully change. But he didn't say anything about why he was going out? Even though it seemed very unplanned?"

"Yeah, well, that's all I know, Chief. So, I stuck around to wait for him to come back. Then, about four-thirty, I seen Ben take off in his car and then a while after that, Jagger came walking back along the trail. So I took care of Jagger, and after a while I saw Ben come back. He waved to me and went in the house. I knew he had something to tell me, so I waited, and he come out and told me about Rory."

The chief pondered all that Billy had said while he took the barn shirt down off its hook and looked it over. He put that shirt back on its hook then reached for the sport shirt, but stopped his hand when something caught his eye. There was a piece of paper in the breast pocket.

"Billy, I'm going to grab a pair of gloves and a couple of evidence bags from my car; don't touch that shirt."

His car was parked right outside the barn, so it was a quick trip. The chief slipped a pair of gloves on, then pulled a pair of short tongs from a pocket and pulled out the piece of paper. It looked like a letter. He opened it gingerly, trying to avoid smudging any prints that might be on it. He held the letter by the upper corners, with the tongs and a thumb and forefinger, and he read it.

Billy could see a reaction in Chief Bridger's eyes, but he couldn't tell what it meant.

"What's it say, Chief? Is it important?"

"I can't tell you what it says, Billy, but, yes, it's important."

19

Patty explained what she knew about the Plouffes while Kate sat and listened, Beth moved back and forth between her mom's lap and Kate's lap, and Chris screwed down deck planks in the background.

"Reggie—that's the father—is in his fifties, I guess. Really nice man; everybody likes Reggie Plouffe. He lost his wife about ten or twelve years ago, to cancer. They had an older boy; I can't remember his name. He moved away after high school, out west somewhere. Christy is twenty-four—maybe just twenty-five, now—and the younger boy, Peter, is eighteen or nineteen. He's a 'special needs' kid.

"Peter's still in school. They have a pretty good special ed program at the high school now, but it wasn't always that way. He's two years behind, I think; graduates next year. Anyway, he goes to school and works on the farm, too. He likes the farm work, Christy tells me, but the old man wants him to graduate. But he's likely going to stay on the farm after. Christy works, too, and takes care of her little boy, Matty, who's six.

"I know you've been told the simple version of Christy's story. She got pregnant and had Matty when she was eighteen. The father was Joe Reader, their hired hand at the time. It was a tough situation. Joe and Christy were both minors when it happened, so there wasn't any crime involved. I know most people would tell you Joe just ran off and left her, but it was more complicated than that.

They weren't in love and neither of them wanted to get married. Reggie didn't want them to marry either; he knew it wouldn't be a happy one. But he didn't want Joe around anymore and neither did Christy. So, Joe left and found a job on a dairy farm up near Orleans.

"Christy's been raising the boy on her own since he was born, but she's still at home on the farm, so it's almost like a regular family, with Grampa and Uncle Peter there. Then, when Matty was two—four years ago—Christy met Rory Fremantle. She knew who he was, of course, but had never really met him. It was at the Fourth of July celebration, which they always have at Liberty Park, by the river. Typical small-town thing: a parade that ends at the fairgrounds, a couple of speeches, then it turns into a big picnic. The Lions Club sells burgers and hotdogs, and they have a three-legged race and stuff like that, and later a band plays and there's dancing.

"Anyway, Christy was there with Matty and somehow she and Rory started chatting at the burger stand and sat down together at a picnic table. It was no surprise to find Rory sitting and talking with a young woman, but nobody would have picked out Christy as Rory's type. She grew up milking cows and mucking out stalls; she's a farm girl through and through. Don't get me wrong—Christy is a good-looking woman and smart, too. She just doesn't have any of the outward appearance of someone you'd expect Rory to date: no makeup, no lipstick, and her clothes..."

Patty started laughing.

"What's funny?" Kate asked.

"Well, it's almost like I'm describing myself; she dresses the way I do. But she didn't hook up with a hippie handyman like I did; she snagged the valley's most eligible bachelor. And that took everybody by surprise."

"I bet it did. What did his family think about it?"

"Well, I don't think they gave it much thought, at first. Like everybody else, they just thought he was 'sowing his wild oats,' that phrase they use to excuse upper class boys from behaving badly. Doris certainly didn't expect it to go on for three years. Almost three years."

"So, they were happy together."

"They certainly were. I've been friends with Christy off and on for years, and I've never seen her so happy. As far as I knew, Rory was happy, too. He was working over in White River, and he had an apartment there, but he'd come back on weekends. They were together every weekend. Sometimes he would take her out, but mostly he stayed over at the farm on weekends; Reggie didn't mind.

"Rory got along great with Peter, Christy's brother. I saw them together a few times, and Rory seemed to have a way of being friendly with Peter without being condescending, you know? That's not easy for most people. And Matty, he was just two when Rory came into his life and those two... Well, the way it looked to me, I thought it was a great match and that Rory was going to be Matty's dad and everything would be fine."

She stopped and took a long drink.

"Did something happen between Rory and Christy?" Kate asked.

"Well, there might have been something: a quarrel or a disagreement about something. These things happen in any relationship, you know?"

"Sure."

"But I don't think it was anything serious. It just happened at the worst time. Now, I was friends with Christy, so I know something about that side of the story. But I've never been friends with any of the Fremantles or that Thompson bitch, so I'm in the dark as far as what happened there. All I know is Tiffany got mad about something—probably thought Ben was going to propose and he didn't—so she decided to make him jealous. All I know for sure is that Tiffany stormed out of the café one day—she was having lunch with Ben—and the next day she drove to White River Junction and spent the weekend with Rory."

"And this was at the same time Rory had the quarrel with Christy?"

"Yes. Like I said, I didn't think it was a big deal, whatever the quarrel was, but Rory stayed in White River that weekend, at his apartment. I don't know if he knew Tiffany was coming, but she obviously knew he was there alone. Anyway, they spent the weekend together, and I think she went over at least once during the week."

"How long did it last?"

"Only through the next weekend. I'm sure Doris took a hand at patching things up between Ben and Tiffany, but I'm just speculating. We don't exactly run in the same circles, you know? But everyone in town knew what was going on and the word got around town that Ben had gone to Tiffany and 'laid down the law.' Told her she'd better drop it and come back to him, or else.

"I don't know what really happened; sounds pretty theatrical to me. But, like I said, I'd bet Doris had a hand in it. All of a sudden, Rory was gone. Off to the Gulf of Mexico to work on an oil rig."

"That sounds pretty theatrical, too."

"The whole business was like a play! Or a soap opera. Ben and Tiffany were back together and everything was hunky-dory for the Fremantles. But it left Christy Plouffe alone and heartbroken. And now Rory's dead."

They sat silently with their thoughts for a minute, then Patty spoke.

"I guess I'd better get back, Kate. This girl needs something besides cookies in her belly, and so do I."

Beth was practically asleep on Kate's lap, but she didn't protest when her mom took her back. They walked around through the house to the front yard and said goodbye to Chris. After Beth had been firmly seated in the car seat, Kate asked Patty one more question.

"Do you think Christy, or anyone in her family, was mad enough to want to kill Rory?"

"I just don't know, Kate. I know Christy loved Rory, and I know she was devastated. Mad enough? Maybe. But being mad enough to want somebody dead ain't the same as being crazy enough to kill him. As for Reggie and Peter, well, they both liked Rory so much... I just don't know, Kate."

Chief Bridger was sitting in his office with Sergeant Maroney, both of them staring at the piece of paper on the chief's desk. It was the size of standard stationery, but plain, and apparently torn from a gummed pad. It had been folded to fit inside a letter-sized envelope and then folded again to fit into a shirt pocket.

The intercom buzzed.

"Orleans County Sheriff for you, Chief."

"Thanks. Good afternoon, Lou; thanks for calling back."

"Anytime, Les. What can I do for you?"

"Do you know the whereabouts of Joe Reader? He's a farm hand; used to work here, in Merryfield, and moved up there about six years ago."

"Sure, I know him. He works on the Moreau farm, over in Barton. He's been in trouble two or three times since he moved up here. Nothing too serious."

"Well, we need to question him about a murder. I'm going to send my deputy, Sergeant Maroney, up there tomorrow morning to question him. Can you pick him up for us?"

"Sure I can. Do you have enough to hold him?"

"No, not yet. Do you know if he lives at the farm where he works, or does he have his own place?"

"Last I knew, he boarded at the farm. I can find out for sure."

"I want to get a search warrant to search his premises and vehicle, if he has one."

"I can take care of that; tell me what you've got for probable cause and I'll call my judge up here."

"That would be great, Sheriff. My sergeant will see you in the morning, and let my office know when you've got the warrant."

The note was printed in block letters and said simply:

> Rory,
> Meet me on the horse trail by the bend in Wandering Brook.
> It's about Christy and it's important!
> Joe Reader

Sergeant Maroney shook his head back and forth.

"You don't think this note is enough to hold Reader, Chief?" he asked. "It was obviously what lured the victim to ride out to the brook."

"Yeah, but it doesn't make any sense. Look at the note, Jim; it's printed in a way that's... Well, it looks unnatural. And that's not a signature, it's just a printed name. We dusted it back and front, and the only prints on it are Rory's."

"It was wiped clean."

"Obviously. But why? If Joe Reader actually wrote this note, he wanted Rory to believe it was him, so why not sign it, and why worry about prints?"

"You think somebody else wrote it?"

"That's what it looks like to me; like a clumsy attempt to frame Joe Reader."

"Yeah, maybe. And why would Joe want to kill Rory anyway?"

"I know. Frankly, Jim, it's hard to think of anyone who'd want to kill him, except..."

"Christy Plouffe, or one of her family."

"Right—the last people in the valley I wanted to suspect of murder."

"Sure, they're really nice people, Les, but murder is murder. We've got to consider them suspects."

The chief looked over at the clock on the wall: almost two o'clock. The intercom buzzed again.

"Officer Larose is back, Chief."

"Send him in."

Officer Larose opened the door and came in, holding a clear plastic evidence bag.

"I found the envelope, sir, in the bushes between the house and the barn. Looks like he crumpled it and tossed it on his way to the barn. The only thing on it is 'Rory,' no address or postmark or stamp."

"Did you question the staff?"

"Yes, sir. Robert picked up the mail from the mailbox at about two-thirty, Saturday afternoon, same as always, he says. He puts the mail on a tray and puts the tray on a table in what they call 'the front room.' Same routine every day. Nobody else saw or touched the mail."

"Did Robert say this envelope was with the rest of the mail?"

"He says he can't remember. Usually, he skims through the mail to see if there's anything personal for Mrs. Fremantle that she might want brought right to her room. But they were so busy that day, preparing for the party, that he says he might have forgotten, or he might have done it quickly and not noticed. Either way, he can't remember seeing this envelope."

"Chief, there were a lot of people there that day," Sergeant Maroney said. "A lot of people who could have put that envelope in with the others."

"Right. Stan, did you talk to the other staff and the family?"

"I questioned the cook and the housekeeper while Robert went to ask Mrs. Fremantle about it. Mr. Fremantle was not at home. Robert came back to say that Mrs. Fremantle had not noticed anything unusual and neither had the staff. It seems nobody touched or looked at the mail until Mr. Fremantle—the victim, that is—came home and looked through it."

"Hmm... I'll have Ginny get a list of all the extra staff who were there on Saturday. Stan, I want you to dust that envelope for prints and then I want you to go to the Post Office and find out who delivered on that route on Saturday; we need to figure out if that envelope was in the mailbox or not."

"But they wouldn't deliver it with no address and no postage," said Officer Stan Larose.

"No, but the mail carrier might have noticed if the envelope was already sitting in the mailbox."

After Officer Larose had left, the chief and the sergeant talked about the search at the site where the body was found.

"Nothing at all on the ground, Les. Not only no sign of a murder weapon, but nothing else, either. So many people were there on Saturday that there's no way to separate any tracks or footprints. We searched the brush twenty feet back from the trail on the east side, and all we found was one empty beer can and a couple of candy wrappers. No sign that anybody crossed the field to get to the trail."

"Well, when the killer left the scene, he must have left the trail at some point, or he probably would have been seen. What about that dirt track across the hay field? Where the ambulance crossed on Saturday?"

"I've got two deputies searching there now. The killer might have thrown away the murder weapon into the hay on either side of that track. That's going to take a long time to search."

"Yeah. It's most likely in the brook, though."

"They're still raking it. Nothing so far."

"What about the other side? Any luck there?"

"Well, there's a spot right across from where the body was found where it looks like there's a bit of a trail from the field to the bank. It looks like somebody fishes there, but no way to tell if someone was there on Saturday."

"Okay. You'd better go over the schedule for tonight and tomorrow; make sure we've got coverage while we continue our searches. Then check in at the crime scene. I'm going out to the Plouffe farm."

20 ▌

Chris Doran finished screwing down all of the deck planks around two o'clock and stopped to have a glass of lemonade. Kate offered him the last of the box of cookies, and he generously broke it in half to share.

"If you insist," she said with a laugh.

She looked over the deck and signified her approval.

"That's good work, Chris. So, what's left?"

"Well, the steps are done; I've just got to attach them to the porch. Maybe you can help me haul the steps into place and I can finish it. You see, the steps are a wholly separate unit, with four points of attachment. Easily attached and just as easily detached."

"And why would I want to detach them?"

"The steps are already stained, but when it's time to re-stain them, it will be easy to remove them so you can turn them over to do the bottom."

"Okay, that makes sense."

"Then I'll finish the railing tomorrow morning. If it stays warm and dry, I'll stain the deck and railing tomorrow, too. If not, we'll just wait for the next dry day."

"Alright, then. It will be nice to have my whole porch to use and to be able to use the front door."

As she gazed out across her front yard towards Locust Road, Kate continued to think about the murder. It had been on her mind continuously since Chief Bridger had first informed her that it was a homicide.

"I'm not getting much work done today, Chris," she said with a rueful grin. "I keep thinking about who would want to kill Rory Fremantle and how they did it."

"Well, I'm sure lots of people are wondering the same things, but most of them aren't as analytical as you."

"Oh. That's a nice compliment, thank you. I can't help it; I look at things that happen and I start analyzing. I want to know how and why."

"And who."

"Yes, absolutely. And who. What do you think, Chris? Are there people out there who hated Rory? Is there a motive that's totally unconnected with jealousy or romance?"

"Could be. It seems like most people in this town have a one-dimensional view of the Fremantles; there's that image of the 'first family' who can do no wrong. And whenever Rory did something a little out of line, it was just 'boys will be boys' and it never affected his reputation."

"You mean his romance with the poor farm girl?"

"Actually, that's not what I'm talking about. Tell me, Kate, are you really serious about wanting to figure this out?"

"Yes, I am. Do you know something that nobody else knows?"

"Not nobody. But the places you've got to go, and the people you've got to ask, are places and people Chief Bridger doesn't pay any attention to, unless he has to."

"Well, now you've got me hooked, Chris. Tell me!"

This looked like being a serious conversation, so Kate brought out the jug of lemonade and some ice for Chris and poured herself a white wine with a splash of soda. They sat down at the little table.

"Kate, do you know about Billy Tourville?"

"Well, I heard something about him from the hardware store guy…"

"Ray Everett."

"Yes. He told me about the championship soccer team and how great Ben and Rory were, and how Rory got suspended and couldn't play in the final, and Billy Tourville played instead and they still won."

"Yeah, and Ray and his cronies—the 'boosters'—never gave Billy the credit he deserved; they just lamented the fact that Rory missed out on the big game. Rory was respected by everyone, and Billy was from a poor family with a bad reputation."

"And didn't Rory get Billy the job at the Fremantle house, taking care of the horses?"

"Yes, he did. Ben and their mother and Tiffany didn't want him there, but Rory got his way that time."

"Rory and Billy were friends."

"Yes, they were. That, in itself, was unusual. Most of the 'nicer' people in town—in the valley—didn't associate with people like the Tourvilles. But Rory seemed to take a liking to Billy when they both went out for soccer, and he encouraged him. The coaches weren't as class-conscious as the boosters, but they could be influenced. They didn't mind Billy being on the team—he was a good player—but they listened to stories about kids getting in trouble and some kids got booted off the team. That never happened to Billy, but the fact that he was Rory's friend might have saved him. Anyway, I don't think Billy ever started a game in three years on the varsity until that championship game.

"Now, I could be wrong about that; I was in school at the same time, but I didn't care about sports at all, so what I'm saying is just what I heard. But I knew about a lot of other stuff."

"What 'other stuff'?"

"Well, there was a lot of stuff going on behind the scenes. I'm talking mostly about pot, but there was cocaine, meth, even some heroin being dealt in that high school."

"Really? And you think Rory and Billy were part of that?"

"I'm just saying it was a perfect situation for Rory. Everybody knew he was friends with Billy, but they thought it was just a sports camaraderie thing. Billy had connections with all of the kids who were dealing, but nobody thought Rory did. So, on the surface, it looked like Rory was just as clean and innocent as his brother."

"But he wasn't."

"No, he wasn't. But he kept his skirts clean and his reputation intact. Then he went off to Northeastern for four years. I don't know exactly what went on over those four years; I was working and drinking and living my own life. But it didn't escape my notice that whenever Rory came home for a weekend, he'd get home on a Friday, go out that night, then drive up to Burlington on Saturday. I heard he went up to Montreal a few times, too."

"You think he was running drugs."

"Probably. It was probably mostly pot, which is legal now, but it wasn't then. But there might have been other stuff, as well."

"And the cops never caught on?"

"I don't think they were interested. They made some busts now and then: small time stuff. But Rory was careful and he was lucky. Billy was still his main contact, and nobody ever connected Rory with the people who were 'on their radar' as drug dealers."

"And Billy never got caught, either?"

"Not back then. He got busted in Petersford a few years back, but it was just possession and he got off pretty easy. That's when Rory got him the job."

"I see. So, are you suggesting that somebody might have had a reason to kill Rory that was connected to drugs?"

"It's certainly possible. I don't know anything for sure; I'm just saying that, if you want to find somebody with a motive, you'd better dive into the 'underclass' here in the valley. There could even be somebody in Boston, or Burlington, or even Montreal who had a grudge against him. You see, by treating the Fremantles as if they're above suspicion, the cops are cutting out a whole lot of possibilities."

Chief Les Bridger pulled into the big barnyard at three o'clock. The Plouffe farm was instantly recognizable as a typical Vermont dairy farm. The big red barn that was more than twice the size of the farmhouse, the chicken coop and various sheds that sat haphazardly here and there around the yard, a tractor here and a hay wagon there; all spoke obviously as to what this place was all about. And in case anyone didn't know whose farm it was, a tall old-fashioned silo bore letters on its side that proclaimed: "Plouffe - 1910."

The chief was very familiar with the farm and the family who owned and worked it. As a teenager, Les Bridger had worked a couple of summers for the Plouffes, picking up and throwing hay bales alongside Reggie Plouffe and his brothers. It was tough having to question old friends about a major crime, but it was part of the job. He wished very much that there were someone who had been seen near the crime scene or someone who had openly threatened the victim, but, lacking an obvious suspect, he had to consider anyone with a potential motive, and that certainly included the Plouffes.

Reggie Plouffe was in his kitchen and saw the chief pull into the yard.

"Christy, honey," he called out, "Les Bridger's just pulled in. I expect he'll want to talk to both of us."

"Okay, Dad. I'm reading with Matty; just tell me when."

Reggie walked to the door and waved to the chief as the latter was getting out of the car.

"Afternoon, Les. Sad times."

"That's for sure, Reg. I'm going to need to talk to you and Christy."

"Sure; come on in, Les."

They sat down at the big table in the middle of the big kitchen. The old farmhouse had a separate dining room, but most meals were eaten right here in the kitchen. The chief knew the routine on this farm; a routine that hadn't changed in decades. The Plouffes milked at five-thirty a.m. and five-thirty p.m. They had a big breakfast after milking in the morning, a big dinner in the early afternoon, and supper after the evening milking. Bread and butter were always on the table, and a big pot of something that smelled really good was simmering on the stove.

"Reggie," the chief began, "I got some more news this morning, and you may have heard it already, or not. The coroner says Rory Fremantle didn't drown; he was hit over the head, and that's what killed him. He was murdered."

"Jesus! Are you sure, Les?"

"Well, the coroner is sure, and that's her job."

He heard the footsteps and turned to see Christy Plouffe standing in the doorway, open-mouthed.

"Hi, Christy," the chief said.

"Hi. Did I hear you right, Chief? Rory was murdered?"

"I'm sorry, Christy, but yes, it's true. He was hit over the head."

She looked at her father and at the chief, then said, "Do people think I did it? Is that why you're here?"

"You have to understand, Christy…"

"Oh, I understand, alright. Everybody knows what he did to me. Now, somebody's killed him, and I'm the first one everybody thinks of. Well, I didn't do it."

"I'm sure you didn't, and I'm glad you didn't. But my job requires me to question you and verify your alibi: where you were and what you were doing on Saturday afternoon. It's standard procedure."

"I know, it's standard procedure for anyone who had a motive. I had a motive alright, and I wished him in hell more than once, but I didn't kill him; I couldn't kill him. So, what do you want me to tell you?"

"I just need to know where you were Saturday afternoon. You can tell me now, and when it's convenient for you, you can drive into town to the station and write out a formal statement and sign it."

"Okay. Well, I was here. I usually bake on Saturdays, and I was here all day, mostly right here in the kitchen. I baked four loaves of bread, two pies, and I mixed up batters for muffins for Sunday morning."

"That's right, Les," Reggie said. "She always bakes on Saturday, and she cooked the breakfast and dinner, too. I don't think she ever left the kitchen, except to use the facilities."

"Okay. I'll need both of you to write down where you were and what you remember of where each other was, especially between about three-thirty and five."

"Am I a suspect, too, Les?" Reggie asked.

"I hate to use that word, Reggie, especially knowing you so well. But you could have had a grudge against Rory for what he did, couldn't you?"

"Yeah, I guess you're right, Les. So, it looks like I'm Christy's alibi and she's mine."

"I'll have to speak to Peter, as well, and your man. What's the fellow's name?"

"Walt, Walter Lamb. He and Peter were over on the western edge of the property. You remember that big hayfield we got over there?"

"Oh, I remember, alright."

"Well, the fences got damaged in the storm. They was pretty old and got blown down in the wind. Walt and Peter were mending fences most of the day and didn't get back here until almost milking time."

The chief's cell phone rang, and he excused himself to answer it.

"Larose, sir."

"What have you got, Stan?'

"I've got prints from the envelope. Took me a while to get it flattened out without smudging it, but I ended up with some pretty clear prints. Mr. Fremantle's, of course, the butler's, and Billy Tourville's."

"You're sure?"

"Yes, sir. He's on the database from that bust a few years ago."

"What about the mail carrier?"

"No other readable prints, Chief, just the three I said."

"Did you find out who it was? The mail carrier?"

"Yes, sir. He's off today, but I stopped at his house and asked him; it was right on my way. He said he didn't see that envelope in the box. He's pretty sure."

"Okay, good work, Stan."

The chief put his phone away and turned his attention back to Reggie and Christy Plouffe.

"I'll have to talk to Peter and, uhh..."

"Walt."

"Yes, thanks. Where are they now?"

"They're out manuring the hay fields we just cut. Won't be back here till almost milking time, at least an hour."

"Well, I don't have time to wait right now. Tell them I need to talk to them. I know you're always busy, but I need to see each of them sometime tomorrow. They can come into the station to be interviewed. If we haven't seen them by noon, I'll have to send some-body out, and I'm stretched pretty thin right now."

"No worries, Les. I'll send Walt and Peter in right after breakfast, and Christy and I will drive in when they get back."

Chief Bridger left the Plouffe farm, but he didn't go right back to the station; he drove into Merryfield and back to the Fremantle house. On the way, he called the station.

"Ginny, I need you to call Judge Porter's office and see if he's available. I need a search warrant for Billy Tourville's apartment, and I can give the judge my probable cause over the phone if he can talk to me. Also, get Billy's full name and address for me; it's on Pleasant Street."

21

Billy Tourville saw the police car pull in and park in front of the barn and wished he'd gone home early. *What did they want now?*

Ben Fremantle saw the police car, too, and decided he'd better stroll over to the barn and find out what was going on.

The chief didn't beat around the bush. He exited his car, walked right into the barn and up to Billy, and said, "Did you put that note in the Fremantle's mailbox?"

Billy's jaw dropped. It was the last thing he expected to hear.

"Me? No, of course not! Why would I... no, Chief, no!"

"Billy, we found the envelope the note was in, and your fingerprints are on it."

"What? No, it can't be. It's impossible."

"Look, Billy, fingerprints don't lie. You handled that envelope at some point, and when you put that together with the fact that you gave your notice right after Rory was killed, it doesn't look good."

Ben was approaching, and Billy turned to him.

"Mr. Fremantle, they think I put that note in the mailbox, but I didn't! I wouldn't do that; I couldn't! You know how Rory and I got along!"

Ben was a kind man and naturally sympathetic, but Billy Tourville was not one of his favorite people and Ben's brother had just been murdered, so his reaction was not what Billy would have wanted. He looked questioningly at his employee, then turned to Chief Bridger.

"What's this about, Chief?"

"We have evidence that Mr. Tourville handled the envelope that was placed in your mail on Saturday. It contained the note that lured your brother to his death."

"It wasn't me! I swear, I don't know how it happened! I never saw that envelope!"

"Calm down, Billy," Ben said. "If there's been some kind of mistake, it will work itself out. But, for now, you'd better cooperate with the police and tell them everything you know."

"I don't know anything!"

"Are you arresting Billy today, Chief?" Ben asked.

"No, I just want to question him. But I've requested a warrant to search his apartment. Billy, you can make it easier by giving us permission to search it right now."

Billy looked back and forth between the two men, searching for a hint of sympathy in one of their faces. He didn't find one, so he decided he'd better shut down then and there.

"No. I need a lawyer, and I'm not saying anything until I get one. And no permission—go get your warrant!"

When Billy had seated himself in the back of the police car, Ben spoke to the chief.

"My mom is anxious to speak to you. She's called the station a couple of times and was quite upset that she wasn't put through to you immediately."

"I've been out of the office, and my dispatcher has instructions about what calls to put through to me in the car and which can wait. I'm sorry if Mrs. Fremantle is upset, but..."

"Not to worry, Chief; I understand, even if Mom doesn't."

"Tell you what, Ben. It's probably going to take a while for Billy to get an attorney, so, if there's nothing else pressing, I'll call her right away."

"Thanks, Chief; I appreciate it, and she will, too."

At four o'clock, Kate called the Maple Leaf Café to inquire about their dinner specials and decide if she wanted to get takeout.

"Hi, Kate! It's Bitsy! I'm so glad you called; I've been wondering what was going on."

"Well, you probably know already that Chief Bridger questioned me about Rory's death."

"Yeah, of course I know; the whole town knows! It's kind of scary, actually, 'cause it seems like half the town is convinced you killed him! I know that's crazy, but people believe what they want to."

"I know. I was hoping it wasn't that bad. I'd love to order my dinner from you, but I'm not sure I want to be seen downtown right now. Any chance of getting a delivery?"

"Umm, let me find out. Richie's not here. It was weird; he went all white-faced when somebody told him you were a suspect, and he went home sick. But I'll see if there's anybody who can do it. Listen, we've got a pork tenderloin special, with cider gravy, applesauce, and roasted potatoes."

"Oh, that sounds great!"

"Alright, just give me a minute, Kate."

Chief Bridger closed the door to his office, sat down, and picked up the phone. Billy Tourville was in another room, waiting for the attorney he had called, so the chief figured he'd better call Mrs. Fremantle.

"Fremantle residence."

"Robert, this is Les Bridger, Chief of Police. I'd like to speak to Mrs. Fremantle, if she's available."

"Yes, Chief. I will inform her, and she should be on the line in a minute or two."

He waited for a couple of minutes, wondering what it would be like to live in that gigantic house with servants to do for you; it was a level of luxury he would certainly never know.

"Chief Bridger."

"Yes, ma'am. I understand you wanted to speak with me."

"I did and I do. I am not used to being kept waiting, Chief, and perhaps you should tell your staff about who is important and who is not; they need educating in that regard."

"Yes, ma'am."

"I'll get right to the point. Have you arrested that woman yet? The Stone woman?"

"No, ma'am. At this point, there is not sufficient evidence to arrest anyone. We are pursuing several leads..."

"Chief, you questioned her this morning, and I understand she has no alibi."

"Well, that in itself does not justify an arrest, Mrs. Fremantle. Without a motive..."

"Excuse me, Chief, but the motive is obvious. She threw herself at my boy, which is exactly what you would expect from her kind. He had his way with her and then made it clear that it would go no further. It's a story as old as civilization; he spurned her and she killed him! Well, I want to see her in prison!"

"Mrs. Fremantle, I understand how you feel, but we have no evidence at this point. We will continue to investigate, and she is definitely a person of interest in the case."

"A person of interest? What exactly does that mean? Does that mean she's not a suspect?"

"At this time, ma'am, I would hesitate to call her a suspect since we have no evidence linking her to the crime. But she has been told not to leave the area, and we will continue to investigate anything that might link her, or anyone, to the crime."

"But are you concentrating your investigation on her, Chief? She would seem to be the obvious prime suspect. Isn't that the way you phrase it? Prime suspect?"

"Not necessarily, ma'am. I believe that phrase is used more in movies and television shows than in real-life criminal investigations. All I can really tell you at this point, Mrs. Fremantle, is that Ms. Stone is one of several people we have our eyes on, and her involvement with your son is one of many leads we are following."

"Well, I suppose you know your job, Chief Bridger, but I can assure you that I and my family and the people that matter in this town will be following this process very closely. We want action, and we want results!"

Attorney Clarence Sharp walked into the police station in Wayford, a place he was quite familiar with, at quarter past five. The dispatcher, Ginny, greeted him and buzzed the chief.

"Mr. Sharp is here, sir."

"Thanks, Ginny; he can go right in and have a talk with Billy, and let me know when they're ready."

Sharp knew Billy Tourville as well as he knew the police station. Although Billy only had one conviction—a misdemeanor—he and his siblings had been hauled in for questioning several times over the last decade, and Clare Sharp was the Tourville family's attorney of choice.

Ginny opened the door to the side room where Billy was waiting, and Attorney Sharp walked in.

In less than ten minutes, the door opened again and the lawyer announced that they were ready.

It was a very friendly-looking Billy Tourville who greeted Chief Bridger and Officer Larose. The chief explained what was about to happen; the interview would be recorded. When it was clear that the witness/suspect understood his rights and what was happening, the recording began with each person present identifying himself.

"Chief Bridger," the lawyer said before any questioning had started, "my client intends to cooperate fully in this investigation; he has nothing to hide. In fact, if it will speed things up, Mr. Tourville will allow your officers to search his apartment right now, without a warrant."

The chief looked at Billy.

"Is this your decision, Billy?"

"Yes, it is," he replied, "and here's the key."

He had a key in his hand, and he slid it across the table. The chief picked up the key and handed it to Officer Larose.

"Stan, I want Sergeant Meadows to take whoever is available and go search Mr. Tourville's apartment. It's one-twenty-eight Pleasant Street, right?"

"Yeah, Apartment B. And tell him there's a bag of dope in the top drawer of my dresser; it's less than half an ounce and it's legal and it better still be there when I get home."

When Officer Larose had returned, the questioning began.

"Billy," the chief began, "I want to go through your day on Saturday, the day Mr. Fremantle was killed. What time did you arrive at the Fremantle house that day."

"Eight-thirty."

"Is that your usual starting time?"

"Yeah, usually. Sometimes I only work half a day, 'cause they only have six horses now, but I had a lot to do, and, yeah, that's when I start when I do a full day."

"Did you go straight to the barn, or did you stop at the house first?"

"Straight to the barn. I got no business at the house."

"You don't go to the house at all?"

"Just for lunch. I get one meal when I work a full day, and I go to the kitchen. Mrs. Mapes—that's their cook—she always makes a good lunch for me."

"You eat your lunch in the kitchen?"

"Yeah, or sometimes out back. There's a table, like a picnic table, outside the back door and sometimes I sit there."

"So, you didn't go into the house at all other than the kitchen?"

"Nope. Like I said, I got no business in the house. Can't remember the last time I was in the house, except the kitchen."

"What time did you have your lunch?"

"Twelve-thirty. Always twelve-thirty, and I take a half hour, sometimes a little more."

"Can anyone verify that you never left the kitchen? That you never entered any other part of the house?"

"Mrs. Mapes was there the whole time. She was really busy with getting ready for the party, and she had some people helping her, so I took my plate and went outside and sat there. When I was done, a little after one o'clock, I brought my plate back in and went back to the barn."

"Was anybody else at the barn during the day?"

"Nope. Just me until Rory showed up at quarter to four. I already told you what happened then."

"Right. I'm going to go over all that again, but right now, I want to know how your fingerprints got on the envelope that was used to deliver that note."

"I don't know."

"Do you know Joe Reader?"

"Sure, I know him. He used to work for the Plouffes."

"What about since he moved on? Have you been in contact with him?"

"Couple times, but not lately."

"Has Joe Reader been here, meaning Wayford or Merryfield, recently?"

"I don't know. I ain't seen him in a couple years."

The chief had written a few notes on a legal pad, and he paused for a minute to scan them.

"Billy," the chief said, "I'm going to leave the room for a few minutes. I want you to tell Officer Larose what happened between when Rory showed up at the barn and when you left for the day. I know you've already told me, but we need to have it on tape. When I come back, we'll finish up."

"Chief Bridger," the lawyer, who had been silent the whole time, asked, "will you be arresting my client today?"

"I don't think so, Clare; unless we find something very incriminating at his apartment."

"You won't," was Billy's definitive response.

When the chief had returned to his office with a fresh cup of coffee, he sat down and picked up the phone.

"Hello."

"Reggie? It's Les Bridger."

"Hey, Les. You got more questions for us? Christy and Peter and Walt are all milking right now."

"That's what I figured, Reg. There's something I wanted to ask you about and not bother Christy with it unless I have to."

"Okay, shoot, Les."

"Have you, or anyone in your family, been in touch with Joe Reader recently?"

"Joe? No, Les. I mean, they don't tell me everything, but I sure don't think Christy has had any contact with him. Now, Peter was really fond of Joe; looked up to him, you know. He used to ask now and then about Joe the first couple years after he left, but then, especially after Rory came on the scene, he never mentioned Joe. It was tough on Peter, you know, when my oldest boy, Ricky, went out west for good; Peter sort of latched onto Joe as a substitute big brother, then Rory. Now there's Walt, though I don't think it's quite the same. Peter's nineteen now, and I don't think he needs a hero like he used to."

"What about Walt? Any connection between him and Joe Reader?"

"Well, now that you mention it, Les, he did say when I hired him that it was Joe who told him about the job. I ain't exactly sure how they knew each other; maybe worked together somewhere. But I ain't heard no mention of Joe Reader from him or anyone in this house since then. Why you asking about him?"

"Well, Reggie, I can't give you any details; I'm just following up on a lead. It's probably just coincidence, anyway. Thanks for your help, Reg."

"Anytime, Les."

"Jesus, Boss. You've got the whole town thinking you're a murderer?"

"Well, not the whole town, I hope. I think the Chief of Police actually believes me, but the gossip mill is working overtime."

"So who did kill him? You got any idea?"

"Not yet. As far as I know, there's very little hard evidence to work with. They think they know how he was killed and where, but they don't have the murder weapon. On the surface, it seems almost impossible to find someone with a motive; everyone claims to have liked him. I've had some interesting conversations, though."

"Boss, you're not going to try and figure this out yourself, are you? It's not your job."

"I know, Millie. But it's a mystery, and I'm hooked."

"Of course you are. What about these 'interesting conversations?' What have you learned?"

"I've learned that this community has some distinct layers, and I've learned that this 'picture postcard village' has a lot of dirt under the surface."

22

Kate was up early on Tuesday. She made herself a little breakfast and a pot of coffee then settled on the porch with her laptop to scan some new queries.

Chris Doran arrived at eight-thirty to work on the porch railing. He didn't have much to say on this bright morning, though that was not unusual. He didn't have a helper today, so at one point, he asked Kate to hold a section of the railing in place while he drove some screws. They had just finished that task when Kate's cell phone rang.

"Hello, is that Chief Bridger?"

"Yes, Ms. Stone. Could you drive over to the station, please? You're not in any trouble, but I need you here to clear something up."

"Okay, right now?"

"Yes, ma'am."

As she drove through downtown Merryfield and out towards Wayford, Kate couldn't help but notice people staring and pointing. She had become notorious through no fault of her own.

She parked in front of the police station, right next to a familiar-looking Subaru, and walked in. Chief Bridger was in the outer office, talking to the dispatcher.

"Good morning, Ms. Stone," the chief said with a smile. "Thank you for coming in on such short notice."

"No problem, Chief. Do you need to ask me some more questions?"

"No; in fact, your alibi is here."

"My alibi?"

"It will become clear in a few minutes."

He moved closer to her and spoke softly, so no one could overhear them.

"Ms. Stone, think back to Saturday afternoon, when you spent the day at home."

"Alright."

"Do you remember what you were wearing?"

"Really?"

"Really."

"Okay. After I got my stuff put away and ate a sandwich, I went out to do some gardening, so I changed into jeans and one of my garden shirts. I worked in the garden. It was really hot, so I took off the long-sleeved shirt and worked in my tee shirt and jeans. When I had finished weeding, I walked around the garden for a while, then I came in and changed.

"When I went back out to sit on the porch and read, I was wearing a blouse—it was a yellow blouse, I think—and a light brown pleated skirt."

"Thank you. Now, I'd like you to come into the interview room with me."

Kate followed the chief into the room and was surprised to find Richie Pratt sitting in a chair, looking sheepish and scared, next to a woman who was obviously his mother. She was looking scared, too.

"Ms. Stone," the chief said, "this is Mary Pratt, and I think you know her son, Richie."

"Yes, I've met Richie; pleased to meet you, Mrs. Pratt."

Mary Pratt smiled and nodded; Richie would not look at her.

"Have a seat, please, Ms. Stone," the chief said. "Richie has something to say."

Kate had no idea what this was about. She sat in a chair opposite the boy and his mother, and she noticed for the first time that Mary Pratt had a leather-like case of some sort on her lap. When she and the chief were seated, Chief Bridger spoke.

"Richie, I want you to tell us where you were on Saturday afternoon and what you were doing."

The boy hesitated, cleared his throat, and said, "I was in the woods, up on the ridge by the old Andrews house; Ms. Stone's house, that is."

He stopped, but his mother stuck an elbow in his ribs and said, "Go on, boy."

"I was watching."

"Say it to her, Richie," his mother said.

He raised his head for the first time and looked right at Kate.

"I was watching you, Ms. Stone. With my mom's binoculars."

Mary Pratt opened the case on her lap and pulled out what looked like a very nice pair of birding binoculars.

Kate raised her hands to her face and covered her eyes. Nobody spoke for a minute or so as she sat silently. A chill had gone through her when she had realized what the boy was saying, but it had quickly passed. If it had been a full-grown adult male watching her from the woods, she would have felt differently, but it was a seventeen-year-old adolescent boy. *Just let it go and move on.*

She lowered her hands, looked at the chief and said, "Anything else?"

The chief looked at Richie and asked, "How long were you there?"

"Umm, from two-thirty until five o'clock, then I went home for supper."

"Can you tell us what Ms. Stone was wearing, Richie?"

"Umm, she was wearing blue jeans and a tee shirt in the garden. Then she went in the house and when she came back she was wearing a brown skirt with..." He tried to demonstrate with his hands how the skirt had folds in it.

"Pleats?" his mother offered.

"Yeah, pleats."

"Alright, Richie," the chief said, "I think that's enough. Ms. Stone, I have no doubt that he's telling the truth, so I don't think we need to prolong this. Just one more thing, though."

Chief Bridger hesitated, looking at Mary Pratt who was cringing, and back at Kate.

"Bearing in mind that Richie came forward voluntarily with this information, which gives you an ironclad alibi for the murder, you still could press charges."

"Press charges?"

"Against Richie."

As she looked across at the Pratts, Kate could think of nothing but "deer in the headlights." They both looked terrified.

"Oh, no. Of course not. There's no need. Just...just don't do it again."

The whole room breathed a sigh of relief, and the chief told the Pratts they could leave. Mary told her son to wait in the car and asked to speak to Kate alone. The chief nodded and followed the boy out.

"Ms. Stone, I am so, so sorry about this. He's never been in trouble before, and I was so worried..."

"Mrs. Pratt, I don't really know Richie; we've just met a couple times when he delivered a meal. I don't know if Richie has problems that need to be addressed, but it certainly isn't a crime to be attracted to women. He needs to learn how to be respectful and do things the right way; peeping and stalking are not right. But he's not going to learn any lessons by being arrested."

"Thank you so much; I was so worried."

"Well, let's just move on. I am grateful that Richie came forward; it took courage to do that, and it's a big help to me. Actually, if you could thank him for me... It would have been awkward to say 'thank you'..."

"Of course, I understand."

"But I am grateful; it was a brave thing to do and the right thing to do."

Kate stayed at the station for a while, talking with the chief in his office.

"Mary called me early this morning," he said, "and told me the story. I knew right away it was true; I'd seen her Subaru parked on Livingston Road—that's just on the other side of that ridge—a couple of times, and I thought Mary was up in those woods looking at birds."

"I knew it, too. I've seen, two or three times, something flashing in the woods up there. I thought it was something shiny hanging in a tree, but it must have been the afternoon sun glaring off those binoculars."

"Ah, that makes sense. Well, I'm glad I don't have to consider you a suspect anymore."

"Not as glad as I am! I hope word gets around town quickly, so I don't feel like such an outcast."

"I'll make sure it does."

"Thanks. So, tell me, Chief..."

"Why don't you call me Les?"

"Sure, and you must call me Kate. I know you can't tell me much, but..."

"You want to know how the investigation is going."

"Of course I do!"

"Well, it's difficult. We've got leads we're following, but without a murder weapon..."

"That makes it tough. It's the same with any murder; link the victim to the weapon and the weapon to the killer. Without those links, it's hard to prove anything."

"It sure is. All we know from the post-mortem is that the blow to the head killed him and there were flakes of rust in the wound. So, we're looking for a rusted metal object."

"But if the object was thrown back into the brook..."

"The current would have washed away all of the blood, just like in that story. So, even if we find the weapon in the brook—which we haven't yet—it will probably be impossible to prove it was the murder weapon."

The intercom buzzed.

"Chief?"

"Yes, Ginny?"

"The State's Attorney is on the line."

Kate stopped at the IGA on her way back through Merryfield. She felt more confident about meeting people now that she knew she had an alibi, although she was aware that very few people knew that yet.

Mary Thurgood was a little startled to see Kate come in; she had heard all about "Kate and Rory" and the rumors that "that divorcee from Connecticut" must have been involved in Rory's murder. But she was a veteran of the gossip trail and didn't jump to conclusions too quickly.

As she watched Kate going up and down the aisles with her shopping basket, Mary thought Kate seemed awfully confident for someone suspected of murdering the town's favorite son. *Well, maybe everyone's wrong. Or maybe she's such a brazen cold-hearted bitch that she's able to put on a face and bluff her way through it.*

Kate picked up a few necessities then stopped in front of the cookies. She almost grabbed a box of a well-known brand then had a better idea.

"Good morning!" Kate said cheerily as Mary rang up her purchases. "Beautiful day, isn't it?"

"It sure is, Ms. Stone," Mary replied, trying to keep her face from asking questions. "Thank you, and have a nice day."

Kate walked into the Maple Leaf Café a couple minutes later. Bitsy greeted her with a surprised smile.

"Hi, Kate, so good to see you!"

"Hi, Bitsy! I'm feeling good today."

There were two men sitting at the counter and a dozen or so at the tables; all of them were looking right at Kate.

"Well, that's good, hon; what's up?"

"I talked to Chief Bridger this morning, and he's perfectly satisfied with my alibi; I am in the clear."

"Oh, that's awesome! I'm so glad! Are you gonna sit down and have something?"

"Not this morning; I've had breakfast, and it's too early for lunch. I was wondering if you have any of those great cookies?"

"Yeah, sure; you want a dozen to go?"

"Yes, please."

State's Attorney Ned Raymond was familiar with Chief Les Bridger and with the community. Though he was a native of a different part of the county, he had spent a lot of time in the valley and had worked with the chief many times.

"What's going on over there, Les?"

"Well, as I'm sure you know, Ned, I've got a high-profile murder case here."

"I know more today than I did yesterday. Maybe I should say I've *heard* more. Doris Fremantle called me at home last night and bent my ear for half an hour."

"Oh, brother."

"Yeah. You know me pretty well, Les. You know I'm not going to be influenced by the social status of a murder victim."

"I know that, Ned. But try explaining that to Doris Fremantle."

"Exactly. So, tell me what the status is, Les. Is 'that woman' a valid suspect?"

"Meaning Kate Stone? No, Ned, she isn't. I had questioned her because of her relationship with the victim, but just this morning, a witness came forward with an alibi for her. A very strong alibi. I never believed she had a motive, in spite of what Doris thinks, and now I consider her in the clear."

"Okay. What else have you got?"

"We still don't have the murder weapon, and we may never have it. We're following up on a lead that involves two possible suspects. The victim was apparently lured to the place where he was killed by a handwritten note found in his pocket. My deputy is up in Orleans today, questioning the man who allegedly wrote the note. His name was on the note but printed in block letters."

"That won't fool a handwriting expert."

"Right, that's our next step. Now, the note itself had no fingerprints other than the victim's. But the envelope it was delivered in had prints from the man who works for the Fremantles in the barn. We searched his apartment last night and found envelopes and note paper that match, but that could easily be a coincidence; you could buy both at the drugstore or a dollar store. He obviously handled that envelope at some point, but that doesn't prove he delivered it or knew of its contents."

"Anything else to connect him to the crime?"

"He was the last person to have any contact with the victim, other than the three kids at the brook, and he gave his notice as soon as he found out the victim was dead."

"Really?"

"He did. He told me it was because Rory—that's the victim—was the only one in the family who liked him, and he was certain they'd get rid of him anyway. The two of them had been friends since high school. Frankly, Ned, I was very surprised to find his prints on that envelope; his reaction to the murder seemed genuine and there didn't seem to be any motive."

"Sounds like you've got a lot of work to do. Well, I was really hoping we could charge someone quickly, but it looks like that's not going to happen, so the two of us are going to be under some pressure. Have you got enough help?"

"Yes, I do, Ned. The sheriff has been very cooperative, and I've got four of his deputies helping with the ground search on both sides of the brook. I'm still hoping to find a murder weapon."

"Alright, Les, keep in touch."

"Thanks, Ned, I will."

The chief spent the next half hour going over the list of items found at Billy Tourville's apartment. There was nothing that seemed incriminating or even relevant to the case. Then Sergeant Meadows rapped on the door and came in, carrying a laptop.

"Chief, wait till you see what we found on Billy's computer."

23

It was a really busy Tuesday lunch at the café. Each of the fifteen people who had been in the café when Kate had stopped in for cookies had told someone the news that 'the Stone woman' was no longer a suspect in the murder of Rory Fremantle. Some did not want to believe it, but they all wanted to talk about it, so word spread rapidly around the village.

Bitsy was working the counter, as usual. Kate had not told her the details of her alibi, only that someone could prove she was at home all afternoon. Bitsy told everyone who would listen that Kate was in the clear—not a suspect at all. A few people were delighted to hear the news, a few were indifferent, and a lot were unbelieving.

"Somebody's lying" was a frequently heard response, along with "sounds like a coverup."

At Ray Everett's table, Walt Drake was shaking his head in disbelief.

"Maybe she was at home all afternoon, but I don't believe she had nothing to do with it. They spent the night together the Saturday before, didn't they?"

"That's what I heard," Ray replied, "but I don't know the truth of it."

"It sure sounds like a lovers' quarrel to me," said Luke Drake, Walt's brother. "Rory's broken more than one heart in this town. It wouldn't be any surprise if he broke another."

"Or just maybe," said Sam Waters, "she broke his. Maybe she turned him down and he dove onto the rocks to end it all."

The other three all shook their heads.

"No," Ray declared. "Not Rory!"

Over at the Miss Merryfield Diner, Harley Ransom was disgusted.

"Rich folks are the same everywhere; they get away with murder!"

"What are you saying, Harley?" Bill Williams asked. "I heard she's got an ironclad alibi. That's the word they said: 'ironclad'."

"What I'm saying, Bill, is that when someone from downcountry comes into our town with a lot of money, they can throw that money around and do whatever, or get whatever, they want. Not like you and me."

Cedric Shallow said, "Harley, are you saying the Stone woman bought herself an alibi?"

"Who knows? She certainly could have, with all that money. For that matter, she could have hired someone to bump off Rory!"

"You're just speculating, Harley," said Lester Potts.

"I got a right to, don't I? I seen it over and over! Now, you just wait and see; they'll try to pin it on some poor slob who ain't got a dime! Mark my words!"

"There's truth in what you say, Harley," Bill Williams said, "but I ain't sure that woman is as rich as you say. Chris Doran told my boy that the work he's doing is on a tight budget; says she ain't got nothing to spare. And Chris don't tell no lies, not since he quit drinking."

Harley shook his head and muttered, "Damn hippies!"

Tiffany heard the news and called Ben immediately.

"They're saying she's got an alibi; she was home all afternoon, and she can prove it!"

"Really? I haven't been out of the office, so I haven't heard anything."

"Well, I don't know if it's true; it could be just a false rumor. Have you talked to Chief Bridger today?"

"Not yet. I'll call him."

"Your mother's going to be upset; she was really hoping to get this over with."

"Well, don't say anything to her yet. I'll find out what's going on, and I'll get back to you."

Chief Bridger was on the phone with Sergeant Maroney when Ginny buzzed him.

"Ben Fremantle is calling, Chief."

"Oh, good. Hold on a second, Jim. Ginny, would you ask Ben if he can drive over here right now? It's important."

"Sure thing, boss."

"So what have you got, Jim?"

"Not a lot, I'm afraid. Joe Reader insists that he hasn't been in Merryfield or Wayford for two years and he hasn't spoken to Billy Tourville in at least that long. He says he hasn't been in contact with Christy Plouffe or her family since he left their farm and moved here. I asked him if he had written anything to Rory Fremantle and he just laughed. Said, 'Why would I do that? Never spoke to him in my life.'"

"Well, I wouldn't expect him to admit it, if he did write that note. Did you search his place?"

"Yes. Nothing incriminating. Found a little bit of pot, but nothing illegal. He doesn't have a vehicle right now. We dusted for prints in his room, just so we can compare with what we get from Billy's place."

"Good; did you get a handwriting sample?"

"Sure did."

"Alright, guess you'd better head home. Thanks, Jim."

While he waited for Ben Fremantle, the chief looked over what he had on Billy Tourville.

His fingerprints were on the envelope, so he had handled it at some point. The obvious assumption was that he had delivered the envelope with the note inside. But maybe not. Maybe someone—someone who had been at Billy's apartment—had picked up an envelope from Billy's desk, or bureau, or wherever he kept envelopes. Entirely possible, but that would still suggest that Billy was involved or knew somebody who was involved.

He had given his notice the day after the murder. If he had disappeared, that would be one thing, but he had given two weeks' notice. It made perfect sense that he would want to leave the job, given that Rory was the one who had hired him against the wishes of the other members of the family. As Billy had said to the chief, they would probably get rid of him anyway. But the timing, if not suspicious, was damned awkward.

Other than the three kids at the brook, Billy was the last one to see the victim. Other than the murderer, of course, if it wasn't him. That didn't necessarily mean anything, but there was no one to verify Billy's words or actions at the barn. Maybe Rory had showed him the note or discussed it with him. Maybe Billy had urged Rory to go and meet this person who had something important to tell him. But that was just speculation.

All of that didn't add up to enough to charge Billy with anything. The fingerprints were the only thing that amounted to real evidence, but they didn't prove anything, only suggested several possibilities.

He turned to look at Billy's laptop again and clicked to open the file.

Now this. But what did it mean? The chief wasn't even sure it was a crime, and even if it were, what did it have to do with the murder?

Chris finished up in mid-afternoon. The new decking, the steps, and the railing were all in place and had one coat of stain.

"Looks like the sunshine is going to last another day, Kate. I'll come back in the morning to give it all another coat."

"That's great, Chris! Do you need some money?"

"Yeah, if I could get a check tomorrow, that would be good. I've gotta get some receipts together; bits and pieces from the hardware store, mostly. We're under budget, though."

"Oh, that's nice; you don't hear that very often. Hey, tomorrow's Wednesday, right? Do they have that same special at the diner every Wednesday?"

"They sure do."

"Well, then, I'll take you to lunch tomorrow. We can settle up for what you've done and talk about the next project."

"Sounds good, Kate."

Ben sat down beside Chief Bridger at the chief's desk. Whatever the chief wanted to show him was on the laptop in front of them.

"This is Billy Tourville's computer, Ben, and this is what we found."

He clicked the file open and watched Ben's face turn an angry shade of red.

"I don't believe it! Why, that little..."

"Now, Ben, you've got to stay calm."

"Stay calm? He's got photographs of my fiancée!"

"Right. Now Ben, you're an attorney, so you obviously know what is criminal and what isn't..."

"How many?"

"There are twenty-seven in all. Almost all of them are of Tiffany in her riding habit, usually getting on or off her horse."

"Of course, those are the times he would see her. You said, 'almost all'?"

The Chief clicked to the last three photos. The first was of Tiffany climbing out of the swimming pool, then there were two photos of Tiffany lying on a deck chair in her bikini.

"He's finished! Chief, I'm going to make him wish..."

"Hold on, Ben, let me explain a couple things before you go rushing off. This is important."

Ben's usually calm patrician face was screwed up in rage, but he was no fool.

"Okay, Chief, I'm listening."

"First, these last three give you a pretty solid case for a misdemeanor criminal charge, but the others..."

"Yeah, I get it. Definitely an 'expectation of privacy' at the pool, but not necessarily in front of the barn or on the trail."

"And she was fully clothed."

"Right. I could probably make it stick, but the pool shots are a lock."

"Okay. Now, as much as these photos are disturbing and probably criminal, there's no obvious connection to Rory's murder."

"No, there isn't."

"But Billy is still a suspect in the murder. If you intend to fire him..."

"Oh, he's gone, Chief, today!"

"Alright, that's what I expected. The thing is, Ben, I've requested another warrant to seize and search his phone; it wasn't covered in the warrant I got yesterday."

"The photos would have been taken with his phone, and there could be more."

"Possibly. But I don't want him scared off before I get the warrant; he might destroy the phone. I should have it within the hour, and then the two of us can go pay him a visit. As soon as I've got his phone, you can go ahead and fire him. Then you can charge him or wait to see what's on his phone."

Billy Tourville was not terribly surprised to see Chief Bridger pull in and stop in front of the barn, but he certainly didn't expect to see Ben pull in right beside him rather than park up by the house. What could this be about?

Officer Dubrul was with the chief. The two policemen looked grim and business-like as they walked into the barn; Ben looked furious. Billy smiled in what he hoped was a disarming way and asked, "What now, chief?" He knew there was nothing illegal or incriminating in his apartment, and if there had been, they would have arrested him last night.

The chief pulled the warrant out of his pocket.

"I've got a warrant to seize and search your phone, Billy; let's have it."

That was a surprise, but, no big deal, right? He pulled his cell phone out and handed it to Dubrul.

"What's it about?" he asked. "I ain't done nothing, and I know you didn't find nothing at my place, 'cause there ain't nothing there."

"I've seen the photographs, Billy," Ben said. "You're fired, as of right now, and maybe more! Get your stuff, and get out of here!"

The photographs. He'd forgotten, but still...

"Hey, I didn't break no law. There's nothing criminal about taking pictures! There wasn't nothing dirty about it!"

Ben was keeping control, but the strain was showing.

"You took photos of Tiffany without her knowledge or permission. I could have you arrested right now, but I'm going to wait. She and I will discuss the matter and decide what to do. For now, you need to get off this property!"

"Billy," the chief added, "I'd advise you to go home and stay there. If you leave town, you will be pursued and brought back, and you will be in a lot more trouble."

Ben had wanted to wait until after dinner to tell his mother and Tiffany the news, but the anger showed so clearly on his face and in his body language that both the women insisted he tell them what was wrong. Doris told Robert to bring them cocktails on the back terrace and to tell Mrs. Mapes to delay serving dinner for fifteen minutes.

"What is it, darling?" Tiffany asked. "You're furious about something. Is it that woman?"

"No, it's not her; it's something else. But I have to tell you, Mother, that Ms. Stone has an alibi, and Chief Bridger no longer considers her a suspect."

"Oh, I know that; Robert told me earlier. Just tell us what's upset you, dear."

"Alright. It's not very pleasant. Chief Bridger had Billy's apartment searched last night..."

"Is he a suspect now?" Tiffany asked. "We should have gotten rid of him!"

"Actually, I have gotten rid of him; I fired him less than an hour ago. But the reason has nothing to do with Rory's murder. At least, it doesn't seem to." He looked right at his fiancée. "Les Bridger showed me what he found on Billy's computer this afternoon. Billy has taken twenty-seven photographs of you, Tiff, and uploaded them onto his computer."

"What! Photos of me?"

"Yes. Most of them were taken when you were in your riding habit, getting on and off your horse."

"Most of them?"

"There were three taken at the pool."

"Oh, my God!"

"In your red bikini."

Tiffany got up from her chair and stormed around the terrace, shouting things like "the pervert!" and "we'll destroy him!" but Doris remained still and calm, saying nothing.

Ben waited a bit, letting Tiffany blow off some steam.

"What are we going to do, Ben?" she asked. "Has he been arrested?"

"No, not yet."

"Why not?"

Doris, who didn't seem the least bit surprised, murmured something and took a sip of her drink. Ben and Tiffany both looked at her, knowing she had something to say.

"It would be a misdemeanor at worst, right, Ben?"

"Right."

"We have other ways—at least I do—of punishing the fool without dragging the family name through the court system."

"I definitely want him punished," Tiffany exclaimed. "What about a lawsuit? Surely we could do that!"

Doris shook her head. "Same thing, dear. We don't want any more gossip if we can avoid it. Besides, there's no point in suing someone who has no money. Ben, what other evidence did Les find? Can he link the man to the murder?"

"Not yet, not definitively. His fingerprints were on the envelope that the note was delivered in; the note that lured Rory to the brook."

"That sounds pretty definitive to me!" Tiffany said.

"But it's not proof. There were envelopes of the same kind at Billy's apartment. It strongly suggests that someone—not necessarily Billy—used an envelope that they picked up at Billy's apartment, an envelope that Billy had handled. It's not enough to charge Billy with murder, but the chief has his cell phone now, and there could be other evidence on the phone. We should know more tomorrow."

24

The quiche was excellent, as always, and Kate was glad she had decided to have an early breakfast at the café.

"The crust is just flaky enough," she explained to Dan Howarth, a man she had seen and greeted several times before but hadn't spoken to. "It doesn't shatter into flakes that fall on your plate, like a croissant."

Dan Howarth smiled and looked pointedly down at her plate. She followed his gaze and laughed when she saw the flakes on her plate.

"Okay, a few flakes. Anyway, I love this pastry. I can never get mine just right."

"Heck, if you even try you're doing better than most. My wife gave up years ago, just buys the ready-made ones."

Bitsy stopped to refill their coffees.

"Hey, Dan," she said, "my mom needs a new car."

"Really? She hasn't called me. She usually lets me know and tells me what she wants."

"Well, she needs a little push. See, she's gonna give me the one she's driving now as soon as she gets a new one."

"Oh, I get it—it's really you that wants a new car."

"Yeah, but she's been driving that Camry for almost three years and she usually trades in about that time. Like I said, she just needs a little push."

Kate laughed.

"I didn't realize you were such a schemer, Bitsy."

"Well, a girl has to be, doesn't she?"

She went off to serve another customer, and Kate turned to Dan.

"Are you a car dealer, then?"

"Yes. Dan's Toyota, on New Farm Road, right between Wayford and Petersford. Used cars, too. Best deals in the valley."

"That's good to know. I'm hoping to get a couple more years out of my Volvo."

"I've seen your car. Good resale value; I can give you a hefty trade-in on that car when you decide to buy."

"Well, that's good to know, too."

Bitsy stopped again to clear Kate's plate.

"Something sweet today, Kate? We've got banana chocolate chip muffins."

"Ooh! Sold!"

"I'll have one, too," Dan chimed in.

Chief Bridger was at his desk early on Wednesday morning, reviewing witness statements from the Plouffe family. He had interviewed Reggie and Christy himself, and there was nothing new or different in the statements they had signed at the station the day before. But Sergeant Meadows had been the one to interview Peter Plouffe and the hired hand, Walter Lamb.

No surprises; the two had sworn that they were doing exactly what Reggie had said—mending fences on the western edge of the property. Meadows had asked them both questions about their relationship with Rory Fremantle. The hired hand claimed to have had a cordial, but not close, relationship with the deceased, up until the time Rory had dropped Christy for a fling with Tiffany Thompson. Rory had been a frequent visitor at the farm, and everyone had gotten along.

"He was like one of the family for a while," Walt had said. "None of us knew then that he was no good."

Peter Plouffe had been very nervous when interviewed, which was no surprise. Sergeant Meadows knew as well as anyone that Peter was "a little slow," so he was very patient in his questioning.

"I looked up to Rory like a brother," Peter had said. "He was my mentor."

Sergeant Meadows came in at nine and sat down with the chief. He set Billy Tourville's cell phone down on the desk.

"Chief," he said, "I've got all I can out of this phone. Spent a couple hours with it last night and another hour this morning."

"And what have you found?"

"He's got some photos on here, but none of Miss Thompson. There are a few what you might call 'risqué' photos—all of a former girlfriend. But he must have deleted the ones of Miss Thompson after he uploaded them. Nothing suspicious and certainly nothing illegal as far as photographs are concerned. But he's definitely lying about not being in contact with Joe Reader. There are dozens of text messages between the two of them; the most recent just ten days ago."

"Really? What are the messages about?"

"It's hard to tell, because they're all very short; two or three words, like 'go ahead' and 'not ready.' It's like they're some kind of code. Some of them are just a 'thumbs up' emoji."

"They're doing something illegal, probably drugs, and they don't want anything incriminating on their phones. What about calls?"

"No calls to or from Reader, just texts. There are a lot of local calls and a few to and from a Boston number. That number looks like a landline; all the local calls are cells."

"Any voicemails?"

"None. I should be able to identify all of these numbers this morning."

"Okay, work on that and get back to me."

Kate arrived at Sunrise Farm just before nine o'clock, and Linda Norman was out in the yard to greet her.

"Good morning, Kate," Linda said, a big smile on her face. "I'm glad to hear you're not a suspect."

"Not as glad as I am. How's Dolly?"

"Oh, she's looking fine. Like I said on the phone, I think she's about six weeks out. Hard to tell with an unplanned pregnancy, but I've been through this plenty of times, and I'm pretty sure."

"Then no more riding until she births the foal. Let's have a visit with Dolly, and then who have you got for me?"

"I've got a nice black gelding named Brutus for you."

Half an hour later, Kate was on the trail with her 'loaner' horse. A few minutes' ride brought her to the crime scene, where the yellow police tape blocked off access to the brook on one side and the meadow on the other. A lane had been left open for riders to get by. She stopped right at the place where, about thirty feet to her right, Rory Fremantle's body had been found washed up on the stony shallow slope.

It was the first time she had actually seen the crime scene. She had ridden past this spot several times, but had never stopped to notice the details of the terrain. It was easy to see how the body had washed up at this spot; the stream bank was broad and shallow on the eastern side. Looking over toward the western bank, she could see that that bank was much steeper—almost vertical for a stretch of twenty feet or so.

"Ma'am?"

She hadn't noticed anyone about. A police officer was standing a few yards away, on the side away from the brook.

"Oh, good morning, officer. I'm alright here, aren't I?"

"Yes, ma'am, as long as you don't cross the tape."

"I won't. Are you still searching?"

"We've searched the meadow on this side thoroughly for about fifty yards back from the trail. We've got three men on the other side of the brook right now, doing the same over there."

"Have you found anything?"

"Uhh, ma'am, I'm not really..."

"Oh, of course. Sorry. Well, I just stopped out of curiosity. I'll be on my way."

"Yes, ma'am. Enjoy your ride."

Kate rode along the trail slowly. Trees lined the opposite bank across from where the body had been found, but there were openings further along, where she could see the fields on the western side. She saw one of the sheriff's deputies searching methodically in the high grass; what a tedious task! But necessary—the murder weapon might be anywhere.

She stopped at a spot where a long rocky ridge poked out from the eastern bank into the stream, isolating a quiet pool of nearly still water. This must be the place where Rory had managed to lift the little girl up high enough for her brothers to grab her. It was easy to visualize how it had happened, imagining the water at least two feet higher than it was now.

Just around the bend, less than fifty yards, was the big bend where Rachel Cote had fallen in. Kate had stopped here before, where the big concrete wall was supposed to protect the bank from erosion. It looked very different now.

The massive rectangle of concrete was still in the brook, but its position had changed. The power of the flood had pushed it out

of alignment, and it was no longer quite vertical. The rushing water had gotten around behind it, and there was a large pool of water between the barrier and the crumbling bank. Orange traffic cones
had been placed to warn people from getting too close, although the
brook seemed neither powerful nor dangerous at the moment.

From this vantage point, Kate could see along the western bank
and across the hay field. Three deputy sheriffs were now visible,
moving slowly through the hay and scrutinizing the ground as they
went. The field had looked flat from where she had been a few minutes before, but she could see now that there were ridges running
north and south. Not steep ridges, but gently sloped ones.

After a few minutes, she continued along the trail. She crossed a
couple of meadows and a narrow brook and came to the place where
the private Fremantle trail led up into the woods. She stopped and
thought about it for a minute. The gate was closed, but there was no
lock; all she had to do was dismount and swing the gate open. Why
not?

This was the trail she and Rory had ridden; the trail that led to
that lovely overlook where they had stopped for lunch. But this time,
Kate noticed a narrow trail that led downward and off to the right.
She decided to take it. After half a mile or so, she came out of the
woods and was facing a big hay field to the north. She could see Wandering Brook a few hundred yards away, meandering west to east before it turned north at the big bend.

This time, she had remembered to bring a pair of binoculars. After adjusting the focus, she could follow the line of the brook and
could just see the bend and the orange traffic cones on the bank. But
she couldn't see any more of the brook, only the tops of the trees
along the western bank. The ground was higher between the brook
and her vantage point.

This is the Plouffe farm, she thought, as she traversed to the left. Then she stopped; she could see something peculiar. She adjusted the focus again, and it became clearer. She realized what she was seeing and pulled her cell phone out of her pocket.

Chief Bridger was filling out one of the endless daily and weekly reports his job required when the intercom buzzed. *Good,* he thought, *maybe that's the handwriting expert.*

"Yes, Ginny."

"It's Kate Stone, Chief."

"Okay, Gin, thanks. Kate, what can I do for you?"

"Les, I'm looking north across the Plouffe's big hay field."

"What are you doing out there?"

"I'm on horseback. I took a different trail, and this is where I ended up. I'm seeing something that might interest you. I see an old tractor, an old truck, a couple of broken-down hay wagons... It looks like a 'farm machinery graveyard.'"

"A junkyard; every old farm has one."

"Well, it's hard to tell exactly, but it looks like it's only about two hundred yards from the brook. But the men who are searching can't see it; the ground in between is too high. It would be a good place to find a heavy piece of rusted metal, wouldn't it?"

"It sure would, Kate. I'll be there in twenty minutes."

25

It took a while for Kate to reach the junkyard on horseback as there was no trail to follow and Brutus had to maneuver around some hillocks and a couple of very muddy patches that still remained from the heavy rain of the previous week. She was trespassing, of course, but she felt that Chief Bridger had, at least implicitly, wanted her to meet him there, so it must be alright.

About halfway between the starting point and the goal, she came to the brook. It was about twenty feet wide at this point and quite shallow. An old wagon track that looked like it hadn't been used in a while ran along the near bank to her right, crossed the brook, and continued to the north, heading roughly towards her destination. The bottom looked solid, so she urged Brutus into the stream and across.

A voice called out to her, and she turned to see the officer she had spoken to earlier waving at her from about a hundred feet away to her right. He must have crossed somewhere between the bend and the ford she had just used.

Kate stopped and waited for the policeman to reach her.

"Ms. Stone?"

"Yes, officer."

"Hello, ma'am. I'm Larry Watts. The chief called me and told me to meet you over here. I'm not sure exactly where we're going…"

The young policeman seemed to be very pleasant and eager.

"It's a pleasure to meet you, Larry. I'm Kate Stone, but I guess you knew that."

"Yes, ma'am."

She pointed to the north.

"Can you see that? Just over that knoll, you can see the top of a truck cab and a hay wagon."

He squinted and said, "Yeah, I can just barely see something."

"Oh, of course, it's easier for me to see it from the back of a horse. It'll be obvious when we get closer."

They walked towards their destination; Watts on foot and Kate on Brutus. Before long, they could see the whole collection.

"Wow!" said Watts. "It's a lot of old machinery! A tractor, an old mower, a tedder…"

"I called the chief and told him about it. It's not very far from the brook, and if the murder weapon was a piece of rusted metal…"

"Yeah, that's good thinking."

A shout came from the right. Two of the sheriff's deputies were just cresting a ridge and walking towards them. Watts waved to them and beckoned them to come along.

In a few minutes, the four of them were gathered around the junkyard, checking out their find.

"The chief's on his way, guys," Watts said to the deputies. "Don't touch anything until he gets here."

Les Bridger was a little grumpy as he drove the police cruiser over the rutted dirt farm road that crossed the big hay field. Reggie Plouffe was sitting beside him; the chief had stopped to pick him up since he would know the quickest route to the site.

Reggie was chatting about some of the old vehicles and other equipment that now resided at his "machinery graveyard," but the chief wasn't really concentrating on the chatter. He had gotten a call in the car just before reaching the farm, informing him that the handwriting expert had determined that neither Joe Reader nor Billy Tourville had written the note that had apparently lured Rory Fremantle to his death.

Of course it was better to know the truth, he told himself. But it would have been so much easier if one of those two had written it. He felt like he'd taken two steps backward. Now this rusted machinery find. Would it mean anything? It might be the source of the murder weapon, but that wasn't like finding the weapon itself. How he wished there were a real detective on his little eight-man police force!

Reggie Plouffe was getting excited as they approached the scene.

"Les, you see that old truck frame over to the left?"

"I see it, Reg."

"That was my dad's 1956 GMC truck. Oh, that was a truck, Les! In-line six engine, you know. Dad used to tell me how he drove Mom over to the hospital in Hanover in 1960, the both of them thinking I was gonna be born before they got there! They made it, though, just in time. Dad drove that truck until the day he died. I finally parked it here in '88, or maybe '89."

On another day, the chief might have loved a story like that, but he had other things on his mind. First, what were they looking for? And how would they find it?

He parked the cruiser and got out to take charge. Kate and the three men were standing back a good distance from the junk, expecting the chief would not want them disturbing anything.

"First thing," he said, "I want to thank you, Kate. It was a good observation, and it might help us a lot."

She smiled and nodded but didn't say anything.

"Now, gentlemen, we want to determine, if we can, if anyone has been here recently and if anything has been disturbed. It may not be easy or obvious, so take your time and move slowly around the area before you walk in among the wrecks."

Officer Watts and the two deputies spread out around the site and began to study the ground.

Kate walked over to stand beside the chief.

"Les," she said, "I've got to leave pretty soon; I'm meeting Chris for lunch. But I was thinking something, and I want to share it with you."

"Okay, go ahead, Kate."

"Well, I crossed the brook at the ford straight back that way." She pointed due south, the way she had come. "And Officer Watts crossed somewhere between there and the bend."

"Right, there's another ford closer to the bend."

"Are there other places you can get across upstream from the bend?"

The Chief beckoned to Reggie Plouffe, who had been admiring his old vehicles from a distance.

"Reggie," he asked, "how many places can the brook be crossed above the bend?"

"Oh, there's two fords we use pretty regular, right over there." He pointed toward the same places Kate and the chief had mentioned. "There's another about a quarter mile upstream. But you know, Les, you can cross just about anywhere if you don't mind getting wet. Just about anywhere upstream from the big bend."

"But what about Saturday, when the brook was so high?" Kate asked.

Reggie chuckled and said, "Ain't no way anybody could've crossed on Saturday. Nowhere all the way down to the bridge at Tower Road."

"That's what I thought," she said. She frowned and looked back and forth between the chief and the farmer. "Well, I've got to mount up and get going."

Something in her expression told the chief she had something more to say.

"Excuse us, Reggie," he said and walked over towards Brutus alongside Kate. "What is it, Kate?"

"I didn't want to say it in front of Mr. Plouffe, but..."

"I understand."

"Well, if the weapon did come from here, on Saturday, then whoever picked it up couldn't have gotten across the brook with it. So, doesn't that mean Rory was hit on this side of the brook? Not where the body washed up?"

"Damn. You're right, Kate; it has to be. If the weapon did come from here, that is. But the bank is so high and steep on this side..."

"But the water was much higher, and maybe Rory was trying to scramble up the bank to save himself."

"Damn. That's good thinking, Kate. And that would mean it was somebody who was on the Plouffe farm that day."

"That's what I was thinking."

The Miss Merryfield Diner was busy at noon when Kate walked in, but there was a noticeable decrease in the volume of noise as she strode toward the table where Chris was waiting for her. You could almost call it a hush. Everybody in town had heard by now that she had been cleared as a suspect in Rory's murder, but that didn't make her any less notorious. She was still the "rich divorcee from Connecticut," and she was still the most attractive woman in any room she walked into.

"Am I late?" she asked as she sat down opposite the handyman.

"Not even close. It's only three minutes past twelve, and that's on time in my book."

"Good. I've had a busy morning, and I'm hungry."

"Me, too."

Their waitress appeared quickly with water and menus, but rather than hand the menus to them, she just looked questioningly at Chris.

"Yes, Dottie, we'll have the special—both of us."

Dottie walked away grinning.

"Well, Chris," Kate said, "you've done a great job so far. What have you got for me?"

He reached down to a satchel that sat on the floor beside his feet and pulled out a small bundle of papers.

"I've attached some receipts, mostly from the hardware store, and the totals are right here on the front."

Kate took the papers from him and quickly looked through the stapled receipts.

"Looks good, Chris. We're about three hundred under budget."

"Right. The two big jobs are done. What I'm thinking is, since it's going to rain tonight and for the next few days, I'll go and work on some other little jobs I've got lined up—indoor work, mostly—and we'll wait for a stretch of sunny days to paint that shed."

"Sounds reasonable. That just leaves the wood stove."

"I've ordered the new grates; no telling how long that will take. But there's no hurry. I'll have your firewood delivered the same day as mine—probably in a couple weeks. When it gets here, my brother and I can stack it for you."

"I can help with that, too. I'm pretty strong, you know."

"That's fine. Ain't much better exercise than stacking wood."

Kate had her checkbook out already, and she happily filled out a check and handed it to Chris, just as Dottie arrived with the overflowing plates of ham, beans, and mac & cheese.

"Oh, that looks great!" Kate said.

Dottie grinned and said, "I'll have your takeout container all ready, Miss Stone."

Nothing was said for the next ten minutes or so as Chris devoured the entirety of his lunch and Kate ate half of hers. Coffee and banana cream pie followed, and they sat and talked while slowly eating dessert.

"The funeral's this afternoon, I hear," Chris said.

"Oh. Well, I don't think I'd be welcome."

"No, probably not. They're having a reception at the house later—probably the same people who were invited to the birthday party, mostly."

"God, what a horrible time for this to happen. Not that there would be a good time..."

"No."

Chris was silent for a minute while he finished his pie. Then he took a sip of coffee and looked thoughtfully at Kate.

"You know, Kate, if you wanted to find out more about some connections, there's a place to find out."

Kate glanced around, making sure no one could hear her, and said, "You mean connections between Rory and Billy Tourville?"

"Yes, and some others you don't know. There's a bar called Bucky's, on New Farm Road. It's right on the town line; the bar's in Wayford and the parking lot's in Merryfield. It's kind of a redneck bar; they have bands on the weekend. I used to see Rory there almost every weekend, usually with Billy and Joe Reader."

"Joe Reader? The farmhand who..."

"Yeah, you know about that. Well, he kept up his connections in the valley after he left and he'd come down some weekends and meet up with his old cronies at Bucky's."

"Well, redneck bars aren't exactly my thing."

"No, and I'm not suggesting you go there. But there's someone who could help you. Someone who likes and admires you."

The image of young Richie Pratt came into her head, and she shuddered. Chris caught her expression and said, "Not that kind of admiration, Kate."

"Good. So who do you mean?"

"Bitsy Dufresne."

26

The Merryfield/Wayford Police Department was comprised of nine officers: the chief, two sergeants, and six patrolmen. Except for the two officers who would be working the night shift, the whole department was gathered around the conference table Wednesday afternoon.

The table was littered with paper—stapled witness statements, file folders, reports—and each officer had a notepad in front of him and a coffee cup. The officers were chatting with each other and sipping their coffees when Chief Bridger raised a hand for silence.

"Alright, guys, let's focus. You've all read the reports and the witness statements. Now, Sergeant Maroney, I want you to summarize what we've got and what we haven't got."

The sergeant cleared his throat and began.

"We know that the victim was killed shortly before four p.m. He had been in the brook, carried along with the current and presumably trying to find his way to safety; he was known to be a good swimmer, but the current in the brook that day was very strong. His body was found at four-fifteen p.m., washed up on the east bank of the brook, with a catastrophic head wound just above the left temple. The wound was inflicted with a piece of rusted metal. He must have been hit either as he was trying to get to the bank on the eastern side or as he was scrambling to climb out on the western bank. There were flakes of rust found in his wound, so he couldn't have been in the water very long after he was hit.

"We do not have the murder weapon. If it was thrown into the brook, we might still find it, but it would be difficult to positively identify it because the water will have washed it clean of any blood. Extensive searching on both sides of the brook has not found such a weapon. We do have a possible source for the weapon: the junkyard on the Plouffe property. Someone had been there recently. We know that from examining the ground, but we cannot tell if some piece of metal had been picked up or removed from one of the old vehicles. There are certainly plenty of potential weapons there—axles, drive-shafts, etc.

"If the weapon was picked up at the junkyard that afternoon, the assault likely took place on the western bank, because no one could have crossed the brook that day unless he went all the way down to the bridge on Tower Road."

The chief raised his hand.

"Just a second, Sergeant. Now, this is theoretical. I mean, the possibility that he was struck trying to climb up the western bank. It would mean that his body had to have been carried back across the stream to the other side but quickly enough that the wound wasn't washed clean. We can't tell now just exactly what the flow of the stream was like that day, when the water was more than two feet higher than it is now. Go ahead, Sergeant."

"We know why the victim was at the brook that day. He received a note, which was among other pieces of mail at the Fremantle house. The note asked him to meet Joe Reader at the bend in the brook and said it was about Christy and it was important. Christy would refer to Christine Plouffe, the victim's former girlfriend. The note was signed 'Joe Reader,' but the writing was in printed block letters, as if to disguise the handwriting, and we now know that Joe Reader did not write it.

"The victim picked up the note in an envelope that was among other pieces of mail on a table in the house. The note itself had been wiped clean; no fingerprints except the victim's. However, the envelope had prints from three individuals: the victim; Robert, the butler at the Fremantle house; and Billy Tourville, the groom who handles the family's horses."

Officer Dubrul made a noticeable noise in his throat, and all eyes turned to him. The chief gestured to him to speak.

"It's gotta be Billy, doesn't it? I mean, his prints are on the envelope, he lied about not being in contact with Joe Reader; he could easily have followed Rory to the brook and waited. Plus, he's got those photos of Miss Thompson on his computer. Why don't we just bring him?"

"Those are all valid points, Darren," the chief said. "And Sergeant Meadows is going to bring Mr. Tourville in again as soon as we've finished here for further questioning. But we know from the handwriting analysis that Billy did not write that note. Neither did Joe Reader. That doesn't mean that either, or both of them, weren't involved somehow, but there has to be someone else who wrote that note and we have to find out who. Furthermore, it is hard to see any direct link between the photographs on Bill's computer and the murder. Being a peeping Tom or a stalker doesn't make one a murderer."

"And they were friends," Sergeant Maroney added. "Friends since they were kids in school. If Billy had a motive to kill Rory Fremantle, it's something we know nothing about."

"Right," the chief said, "and something that would go against everything we know about the two of them." He paused and drummed his fingers on the table for several seconds. "Alright, officers, here's what we're going to do. Sergeant Meadows is going to bring Billy back in and interrogate him. He definitely lied about Joe

Reader, and we need to get the truth out of him, especially why he was frequently in contact with Reader. What was that about? Was it drugs? Did it have any connection with Mr. Fremantle?

"I have a call in to the sheriff up in Orleans County, to pick up Reader again. I'm hoping they can bring him down here tomorrow; if they can't, we'll have to go get him. Sergeant Maroney, you will go up there again, if necessary; we'll know this afternoon. If not, I want you to interview Walter Lamb and Peter Plouffe again tomorrow, separately, and get down their movements on Saturday, as exact as we can get. And find out when was the last time anyone on that farm visited that junk pile. I will interview Reggie and the girl myself.

"Now, we have more searching to do. I know it's tedious work, but we've got to search the ground farther up and down that trail and keep raking the stream bed farther along downstream. Sergeant Maroney has been in charge of the searching; he will hand out the assignments. Now, let's get this file put back together in some kind of order, then we get back to work."

Kate stopped at the cafe on her way back home. Bitsy was surprised to see her.

"I thought you were going to the diner today."

"I was; I mean, I did. I mean, I just came from there. I just wanted to ask you something."

She looked around to see if anyone was close enough to hear her, and Bitsy took the hint and walked to the end of the counter where the register was.

"Sure, what is it, Kate?"

"Well, I need to ask you a big favor, but I can't ask you here. What time do you finish today?"

"Oh, about three o'clock, more or less."

"Okay. How about coming over to my place for supper tonight? I'll throw some burgers on the barbecue, and I'll make my killer potato salad."

"Oh, wow! That would be awesome! What time?"

"About six?'

"Sure. Can I bring some beers?"

"Absolutely."

Sergeant Meadows and the chief were interrogating Billy Tourville when the phone call from the Orleans County Sheriff came in, and the chief stepped out to take the call.

"Thanks for calling back, Lou."

"No problem, Les. I can have one of my deputies drive Joe Reader down there tomorrow."

"That'll be a big help, Lou; I'm pretty stretched right now. Have you picked him up?"

"Not yet; he's not on the farm right now, but he's probably just out running errands. We know where he goes, so it shouldn't be too hard to find him. We'll let you know."

"Okay, okay, so I lied. Look, Joe's a friend of mine and I didn't want to get him in trouble."

"Get him in trouble?" Sergeant Meadows replied, "Billy, this is a murder investigation, and you and Joe are both suspects. You're both in more trouble already than you've ever been before. Don't give me that crap, and start telling the truth. When is the last time you saw Joe Reader?"

Attorney Sharp leaned over and whispered something to Billy, who nodded.

"Last week. He came down one day—just for the day, 'cause he works on a farm, you know—and he was at my place for a couple hours."

"What day was this?"

"Thursday, I think. Yeah, it was Thursday."

"Did he stay the night?"

"No, he had to work in the morning. I mean, that's what he told me."

"What time of day?"

"Well, he was at my place from about seven, or maybe seven-thirty, until nine or a little after. Then he had to leave, 'cause, like I said, he had to drive all the way back to Barton and work in the morning. So they left."

"They? Who else was there?"

Chief Bridger re-entered the room at this point, sat down, and quickly scanned the sergeant's notes.

"Uh, a couple of his friends: a guy and a chick."

"What were their names?"

"Can't remember."

"He came to your place with two strangers and didn't introduce them?"

"Well, he did, I guess, but I just don't remember."

"Billy," the Chief asked, "why were they at your place? Why did Joe Reader come to visit you with two people you didn't know?"

"Like I said, he's my friend."

"What did you talk about?" the sergeant asked.

"I don't know, just stuff. Like I said, he's my friend and he comes by when he's in town."

The chief asked, "Did they take anything with them when they left?"

"Uh, no. I mean, why would they?"

"Are you dealing drugs, Billy?"

"No, I ain't! You can't bust me for having some weed; it's legal now!"

"It's legal to possess it, but not to sell it."

"I ain't dealing nothing!"

"What about Joe? Is he dealing?"

"No. I mean, how would I know?"

The chief flipped a page of his notebook and the sergeant leaned over to point at something. The chief nodded and asked, "Billy, can you explain these text messages between you and Joe Reader?"

"What do you mean? They're just messages."

"They're almost all one- or two-word messages. It looks like you're arranging or confirming something you don't want to put in writing."

Billy shrugged and said, "If that's what you want to think. I ain't saying nothing more."

Chief Bridger called Sergeant Maroney after finishing with Billy Tourville.

"Jim, they're going to bring Joe Reader down for us tomorrow, so you're free to go and interview Peter Plouffe and Walt Lamb first thing in the morning. If you get there at seven, they'll be through milking and they'll be having breakfast. I'll call Reggie and tell him to make sure they don't head out before you get there. I don't want them talking to each other and coordinating a story."

"Well, I'm sure they know we were at the junkyard; we didn't exactly make a secret of it."

"True, they might have figured out what we're after..."

"Especially if one of them did it."

"Right. But we'll do it this way anyway and hope for the best."

Then the Sheriff from Orleans County called back.

"Les, I've got bad news. Joe Reader's gone. He hasn't been seen since seven this morning and he's got one of Claude Moreau's trucks. Probably in Canada by now."

27

Kate had some work to do reading some new queries, but she was able to get her potatoes boiled and her dressing made in between; she was a master at multitasking. By the time Bitsy arrived, a few minutes after six, the killer potato salad was finished and the charcoal was heating up.

Bitsy pulled into the yard in a rather sorry-looking eight-year-old Toyota and waved to Kate as she parked beside the Volvo. She got out and walked to the porch steps, a six-pack in her hand and a big grin on her face.

"Kate, it looks great! Chris did a nice job on the porch, didn't he?"

"He sure did! Come on up, Bitsy. Have you been here before?"

"Well, just once. I mean, I've seen the place a million times and heard a lot about it, but I've only been inside once."

She stopped, looking a little embarrassed.

"Okay. Is it something you don't want to tell me?"

"Uh, well, it was when the house was empty, after the old Andrews couple moved away. My boyfriend—I mean he was then, not now—he brought me here one night, and we climbed in through one of the windows in back."

"Oh, a little nighttime adventure."

"Yeah, we had had a few beers, you know, and we thought it would be fun."

"Yeah, I know. I had a few nighttime adventures when I was younger, although I never broke into a house."

"Well, the window wasn't locked, so we didn't actually 'break in.'"

Kate laughed and said, "I doubt that the police would have seen the distinction."

"Well, that's all in the past, anyway. Hey, can you show me around?"

Kate gave the charcoal a look, then they went into the kitchen, poured two beers and put the rest in the fridge, then went on a ten-minute tour of the house. Bitsy oohed and ahhed over everything; her memory of the interior was as hazy as her head had been on that long ago night. When they had finished the tour, Bitsy helped Kate carry the burgers, buns and potato salad out to the porch.

"I think the coals are ready," Kate said.

"Yeah, it looks like."

While Kate laid four burger patties on the grate over the charcoal, Bitsy looked out over the lawn and the garden.

"Your garden looks great, Kate. Where'd you get the plants?"

"Oh, Patty gave me some—Patty Doran, Chris's wife."

"Oh. Yeah, she knows a lot about gardening, I guess. I haven't seen her for a long time. Chris comes in, but she doesn't."

"Well, she's got the little girl to take care of, and their yard is like a farm all crammed into two acres. It's got to be a lot of work to tend it all."

"Yeah, it must be. Kate, I'm so glad you invited me over; I was hoping we could be friends."

"Of course we can. You're one of the first people I met here, and I need a friend. I did have an ulterior motive in asking you over, though. I hope you won't be upset."

"Why would I be? You said you wanted to ask me a favor. What's wrong with that?"

"You haven't heard what the favor is yet."

The burgers were well started, and Kate looked over the stuff on the table.

"Let's see, we need plates and forks, napkins; what else?"

"Do you have any relish?"

"Oh, yes, I do—in the fridge. Mustard, ketchup and relish; is that good?"

"Perfect. I'll help carry."

When everything had been fetched from the kitchen, Kate gave the burgers a turn and the two of them sat down to talk.

"So, what's the favor?" Bitsy asked.

"Okay, let me give you some background first. You know that I'm a literary agent."

"Right. Which means you read stuff that authors write and decide if it's good enough to publish."

"Right. Well, I decide if it's good enough for me to submit to a publisher. I'm the go-between, the middleman. Ultimately, it's the publisher who decides."

"Okay. And you get a percentage of what the publisher pays to the author."

"Yes. And if the book sells, I get a percentage of the author's royalties."

"That sounds good. If it's a bestseller, you could get rich."

"Well, one bestseller isn't likely to make me rich, but if I represent an author who keeps writing bestsellers over and over..."

"Ahh, I see. Do you have any of those?"

"I've got one, and a few others who are at least moderately successful with everything they write. It adds up, but that doesn't mean it's easy. Anyway, what I wanted to explain is that I specialize—most agents do. I represent mystery writers."

"Oh, that must be fun! Like murder mysteries?"

"Yes, mostly. So, as I told Chief Bridger, I live and breathe murder mysteries; it's what I do."

"You told the chief that?"

"Yes. He interviewed me. Well, you know that; I was a suspect for a while."

"Yeah, everybody in town thought you killed Rory. Then, all of a sudden, you had an alibi. How did that happen?"

"Well, I don't think I should tell you, exactly. It would hurt somebody."

Bitsy frowned and looked puzzled.

"I don't get it."

"Let's just say somebody proved I was home that afternoon, but I can't tell you who."

Now Bitsy grinned mischievously.

"Oh, so you had a visitor you don't want to talk about. A male visitor, maybe?"

Kate couldn't quite keep the grimace off her face, thinking about Richie Pratt watching her from the woods. She certainly wasn't going to tell Bitsy about that.

"Maybe. Anyway, the chief was surprised that I didn't react with shock or anger when he started to question me, and I told him that I knew he had to question everyone with any connection to the victim. I explained that murder mysteries are my bread and butter and I know what he has to do."

"Yeah, that makes sense."

"Anyway, as the investigation has progressed, I've gotten more and more intrigued by the case."

"You want to solve it, don't you? You want to play detective."

"Well, yes, I kind of do. But I need help."

"My help?" she asked eagerly.

"If you're willing."

"Well, sure! I'd love to help! What do you want me to do?"

"Hold on a minute, and I'll explain."

She flipped the four burgers over and moved them around, holding her right hand palm-down to check for the hotter spots on the grill.

"Alright," Kate said, "they'll need a couple minutes. Do you need another beer before we sit down and talk?"

"Oh, I'll get them, Kate! Just a sec!"

Bitsy raced into the kitchen, barely containing her excitement. She returned in a minute with two open bottles of beer and sat down.

"Okay, I'm ready!"

"Good. First thing—tell me about Bucky's."

Chief Bridger had to do some scrambling to deal with the bad news. He decided to have Sergeant Meadows question Walt Lamb and Peter Plouffe in the morning and send Sergeant Maroney back up to Barton.

"Now, Jim," he said, "they'll be dealing with Joe Reader themselves. He crossed the border into Quebec at eight-fourteen this morning with a stolen truck, so that's grand theft auto, to start with. I want you to question Claude Moreau and everybody else at the farm about Reader. We need more details about his activities and movements as it affects our case."

"The staties will be involved now, too. Are we calling Joe Reader a murder suspect now?"

"Yeah, we have to. The whole thing doesn't make sense yet, but the fact that he's on the run certainly points the finger at him."

The chief sat alone in his office, nibbling the sandwich he had ordered for his supper and riffling through the witness statements in the case file. How to make sense of all this?

An idea had been in his head for a while now. It was unusual and irregular, but he was getting nowhere, so why not? He picked up his phone and dialed the number.

"Yeah, I guess you would call it a redneck bar, but it changes on the weekend. They usually have a rock and roll band on Friday and Saturday, so the atmosphere changes and the crowd changes. But it's always a fun place; I go there quite a bit. I mean, just because it's a redneck bar doesn't mean there's people throwing bottles and beating up hippies. It's a town bar, and all sorts go there."

"Okay. If I wanted to find out more about Billy Tourville and Joe Reader, would Bucky's be the place to go?"

"Yeah, for sure. They were both there last weekend."

"Really? Both of them?"

"Yeah, I saw Joe come in Thursday night with Alan Brooks and Carol Tetreault. They were still there when I left. I didn't see Billy that night, but they were both there Friday night."

"Friday night? Are you sure?"

"Sure I'm sure. They were sitting at a table way in the back, about as far from the stage as you can get."

"I don't think the police know that."

"Well, they wouldn't. The cops never go in there, 'cause no will talk to them anyway. If they went in plainclothes, it wouldn't make any difference, 'cause everybody knows who they are."

"That's very interesting. These burgers are ready. Let's eat, and then we'll talk some more."

They assembled their burgers with condiments spread on toasted buns, and Vermont cheddar cheese added. Kate's killer potato salad made the meal complete, and a nice craft brew washed everything down.

"Mmm, this is good, Kate," Bitsy said between bites. "Love the salad."

Kate's cell phone rang.

"Excuse me, Bitsy. Oh, hello, Les. What's up?"

Bitsy continued to eat while watching Kate, who was listening and occasionally nodding. After a couple of minutes, she said, "Yes, I'd love to. Sure, I can do eight o'clock. I'll see you then."

She sat down, a satisfied smile on her face.

"What is it, Kate?"

"Bitsy, you must keep a secret for me. I'm sure people will find out eventually, but it must be secret for now."

"Okay. What is it?"

"That was Chief Bridger. He wants me to help with the investigation. He says I have a more analytical mind than anyone on the police force and he thinks I could be a big help. I'm meeting him tomorrow morning to read all the witness statements and review all the evidence."

"Oh, my God! That's awesome! Detective Kate!"

They had a celebratory toast and happily finished their meal, both smiling all the while. When they were finished, Bitsy asked, "So what's the favor you wanted to ask?"

"Well, you've already done some of it by telling me about Bucky's and Billy and Joe being there last weekend. But I need to find out more, and I don't think I would exactly fit in at Bucky's."

"So you want me to do some snooping for you at Bucky's?"

"I know it's asking a lot, and I don't want you to do anything dangerous..."

"Oh, I know how to be careful. Hey, wait a minute, wait a minute. Kate, I have just got the greatest idea ever! Stand up."

"Stand up? Why?"

"I'll explain."

The two women stood up, and Bitsy edged herself right next to Kate.

"Look, we're almost the same size. Close enough, anyway. I don't suppose you have a pair of jeans with holes or tears in them…"

"Uh, no."

"Well, I've got three pairs, so you can wear one of mine."

"What do you mean?"

"Look, you are as classy a lady as this town has ever seen, but I can dress you down so you'll fit right in. I've got the clothes, I've got the shoes…"

"Bitsy, that's crazy. I'm still going to look the same."

"No, no, no. Listen, my mom's got a whole drawer full of wigs. I'll put a blonde wig on you, and I'll make you up so you'll look totally different. You'll be the hottest chick at Bucky's, and you won't look anything like Kate Stone. We'll go there together tomorrow night."

"I don't know about this, Bitsy."

"Believe me, Kate; we can do this!"

28

At the Maple Leaf Café, Ben and Tiffany sat at their favored window seat for breakfast Thursday morning. A few of the other customers had been at Rory's funeral, and they all had words of sympathy and condolence. Most just smiled sadly at them as they walked in. It had been a dignified Episcopal service at the nearly full St. Thomas's, followed by a brief graveside ceremony.

The reception at the big Fremantle house had been attended by most of the people who had been invited to the birthday party that had been tragically canceled. They were the well-to-do of the valley towns; the "right sort of people." Doris Fremantle had, naturally, been brave, composed, and dignified.

"She's amazing," Tiffany said. "I don't know anyone else who could have carried it off without breaking down."

"Well, that's Mom. She does everything the right way, no matter the circumstances. She's had so much tragedy in her life."

"But tragedy isn't something you can get used to, even for someone like Doris. It has to hurt so much."

"Of course it does. But she is always determined to present the right face—the proper face—to the outside world. People of my mother's class show their dignity to the world, not their grief."

They sat silently for a while, sipping their coffee, then Tiffany spoke again.

"She's amazing. We talked about setting the date for the wedding, and she managed, without actually saying it, to make it clear that she wants a grandchild as soon as possible."

They exchanged questioning looks before Ben asked, "Are you okay with that?"

"Sure. I'm ready to throw out my pills today. Is it what you want?"

Ben smiled and said, "It is, honey, very much."

Their server approached with breakfast and broke up their reverie. When they had finished most of their meal, Tiffany asked what Ben knew about the murder investigation.

"Well, I haven't talked to the chief for a couple of days, but the word around town is that both Billy Tourville and Joe Reader are being looked at as suspects."

"Who's Joe Reader?"

"He used to work for the Plouffes on their farm. He was the father of Christine Plouffe's baby, and he left after she got pregnant. Works up north somewhere now. I'm not sure how he figures in it, but that's what I heard. The cops aren't very good at keeping secrets, so everybody seems to know he's a suspect, but I haven't heard any details."

"But they haven't arrested anyone, yet?"

"No. They obviously don't have enough evidence, yet."

Kate arrived at the police station promptly at eight o'clock. Ginny greeted her with a smile and asked if she'd had breakfast.

"I had a little something at home."

"Well, the chief told me to ask you. He's in the conference room and there's coffee and muffins, but we can send out if you want anything else."

"Oh, thank you, I'm sure I'll be fine with coffee and muffins."

She walked into the conference room to find the chief standing by the table, a typed sheet of paper in one hand and a muffin in the other.

"Good morning, Kate. Help yourself to coffee. I had Ginny pick up these muffins at the Maple Leaf, so they're better than the ones at the IGA."

"Oh, good, I love their muffins."

"I'm going to want you to read all of these witness statements, but first I need to update you on the latest bad news. You know who Joe Reader is, don't you?"

"Yes. He was the farmhand for the Plouffes, and he's the father of Christy Plouffe's son."

"Right. He was also involved, we believe, in luring Rory Fremantle to the brook before he was killed. He denied being in town anytime in the last two years, but we know that's a lie. Now he's gone. He stole his boss's pickup truck and crossed the border into Quebec yesterday morning."

"Oh. Well, that's pretty incriminating. I've got more on him. I've been told that he was seen at Bucky's both Thursday night and Friday night."

"Friday night? Are you sure?"

"That's what my contact said. He was sitting with Billy Tourville."

The chief uttered an expletive.

"He just won't stop lying! Look, I've got to make a couple of phone calls. Why don't you start reading these witness statements, and I'll be back."

Kate began with Billy Tourville's initial statement, followed by the transcripts of his subsequent interviews. It didn't take too long to read them, and it was obvious that he had been lying at first and was still lying. Whether he was trying to protect someone else or himself wasn't exactly clear. Next, she read the statements of the members of the Plouffe family and their hired hand, Walter Lamb.

She was just picking up the statements from the people who were at the Fremantle house that Saturday—four servers and two extra cooks, plus the regular staff—when Chief Bridger re-entered the room.

"Well," he said with a sigh, "I called Jim Maroney in his car to give him an update on Joe Reader and I called the sheriff up there, too. He's going to question Claude Moreau about Reader's whereabouts last weekend."

"He's still missing?"

"Yes. There was a possible sighting at a gas station on a route that would take him to Montreal, so he's probably in the city. If he ditches that truck somewhere, it will be pretty easy for him to disappear in the city."

"Especially if he's got contacts there."

"Right. And if he's been dealing drugs, he probably does. Anyway, the D.A. called while I was on the phone, so I've got to call him back, and we've got to pull Billy in again."

"Les, I've noticed something interesting."

"Okay, let me have it."

"Well, Billy said he didn't know, or remember, the names of the two people who were with Joe Reader at his apartment."

"Right."

"According to the information I got from my contact, Joe Reader entered Bucky's at about nine-thirty Thursday night, and he was with a man and a woman. Their names were Alan Brooks and Carol Tetrault."

"They're both locals. We know them, and Billy certainly knows them. Another lie."

"And I just noticed something else. I haven't read through these yet, but Carol Tetrault was one of the servers for the Fremantle birthday party. She was at the house that day."

"Okay, okay, we're making some connections."

"Les, do you think Billy Tourville is a risk to flee?"

"Probably not, but we've got enough to hold him."

"I was just thinking: The information I got was basically hearsay, nothing confirmed. But I have a plan to get some more information—and confirmation—tonight. It might be worthwhile to have Billy free to associate with his friends."

"You mean free to go to Bucky's tonight?"

"Yes."

The chief frowned, but the frown turned into a grin.

"Do you want to tell me your plan?"

"No, because you might tell me not to do it."

The chief drummed his fingers on the table while he thought about it. Bucky's Tavern was the focal point of a local subculture; a subculture that was practically impossible for the police to penetrate without informants or undercover operatives, neither of which they could afford. Whatever Kate Stone had planned, it might be their best chance to get the information they needed to solve this case. He stood up and smiled at her.

"I've got to go and make that call to the D.A. Just don't put yourself in any danger, Kate."

Danger? She hadn't actually thought of it in those terms. Embarrassment, yes, if somebody recognized her. But yes, considering it was a brutal murder she was investigating, there might very well be some danger. Maybe it wasn't such a good idea.

She picked up the next witness statement and started reading it.

Sergeant Meadows returned to the station a little after nine o'clock to find the chief on the phone and Kate Stone alone in the conference room, going through the case file.

"Don't ask me," Ginny said. "The chief brought her in and told me to get coffee and muffins and leave her alone."

The sergeant wasn't entirely sure what to do. He had new testimony from two witnesses; was he supposed to deliver it to the chief, or to this woman who was apparently reading all of the other evidence?

Then the chief hung up the phone and waved Meadows into his office.

The sergeant sat down across from his boss and set his notes down on the desk, but before he said anything, he pointed a finger towards the conference room. His puzzled expression betrayed the question he was about to ask, but the chief preempted it.

"It's alright, Sergeant; Ms. Stone is here at my request. She's a very intelligent woman with a lot of experience with cases like this. Now, what have you got?"

The chief clearly wasn't leaving any room for objections.

"Okay. I interviewed Walt Lamb first. He was very confident, spoke clearly and without any hesitation. He gave me a full, detailed report of everything he and Peter Plouffe did that day."

"You interviewed them separately, right?"

"Yes. But Lamb said that the boy was with him the whole time; they were doing all the same things. They were over on the western boundary of the property, mending fences that had been blown down in the storm. Those fences were pretty old, so they had to bring a lot of new posts and wire to replace the old stuff. He said they went back to the house for lunch and to get some more materials, then they went back to the same area and worked there all afternoon."

"They never left that area any other time?"

"That's what he said. They got back just in time for milking."

"What about the junkyard?"

"I asked him when was the last time he or anyone else on the farm visited the collection of abandoned vehicles and equipment and he said he and Peter had gone there one day last week to look for a spare part for his truck, but he couldn't remember which day it was."

"A spare part? What part?"

"He couldn't remember."

"Couldn't remember? That's pretty unlikely, don't you think?"

"Yeah, it sounds that way. Anyway, he said they didn't find anything useful. He said that's the only time he or Peter has been there in months."

"Alright. Anything else?"

"He suggested that I 'take it easy' on Peter. Said the boy gets really nervous when he's talking to people he doesn't know, especially authority figures. Sort of gave the impression that he thinks of Peter as a 'little brother.' It was like he was trying to say that Peter is pretty helpless on his own and needs to be protected by somebody older and smarter."

"Hmm. You talked to Peter next?"

"Yes. He didn't say much. At first he asked if Walt could sit with him during the interview and I said 'No.' I told him he didn't have to talk to me if he didn't want to, and he could have a lawyer present if he wanted one, but that he wasn't considered a suspect and we weren't going to arrest him. That relaxed him a little, but he didn't offer anything new—pretty much repeated what Lamb had said."

"Did it sound rehearsed? Like Lamb told him what to say?"

"It wasn't word for word, but it was the same information."

When Kate had finished reading all of the witness statements, she paused to think things over then went back and re-read one of them just as chief Bridger was reentering the room.

"Les," she asked, "is there a copy of the fingerprint analysis in the file? I haven't looked at that stuff yet."

"Yes, of course."

He sat down and opened the case file and quickly found what he was looking for and handed it to Kate.

She looked over the fingerprint report then set it back down on the table and smiled.

"Robert," she said.

"Robert Parsons, the butler? "You're not saying 'the butler did it,' are you?"

"No, that would be a little too 'cliché.' But Robert has some explaining to do. He said that he didn't notice the note when he went through the mail. He either forgot to go through the mail or simply didn't notice the note for Rory because he was in a hurry and he was only looking for letters addressed to Mrs. Fremantle."

"Right. So, it's reasonable that his prints would be on that envelope if he shuffled through them."

"But look, Les. Both left and right thumb prints on the envelope and right index on the back. There's a smudged print on the left side back that's probably the left index." She held her hands up in front of her, as if holding a letter. "Robert held that envelope with both hands. There's no way he didn't notice it."

29

It was still mid-morning and Chief Bridger wanted to drive out to the Plouffe farm to interview Reggie Plouffe again, so he called the Fremantle house and asked Robert to come to the station after serving lunch, around one or one-thirty. Then Kate and the chief did a little brainstorming about how to proceed. Knowing Robert fairly well, the chief doubted that he could be involved in the murder—not intentionally, at least. But he clearly had some explaining to do.

"If the note didn't originate from Robert, then someone gave it to him and asked him to put it in with the mail," he said.

"Right," Kate replied. "Probably someone working at the house that day. We'll need to get handwriting samples from everyone. Maybe we can get them from employment documents. That way we wouldn't be tipping anyone off."

"Good idea, Kate. Robert will know about that, but... Well, just in case, I'll phone Ben Fremantle. Those employees will have to have signed documents, either with an employment agency, or a payroll service, or with the family. Ben will know."

"Les, how many people know that Joe Reader has fled the country?"

"Good question. I asked the sheriff up in Orleans County to delay announcing it, but every law enforcement agency knows, so it won't be secret for long."

"I was going to call you, Chief," said Ben Fremantle. "How is the investigation going?"

"Well, Ben, we've got some interesting leads. I can't tell you much, as I'm sure you understand."

"Of course, Les. I do hear things, though. The word around town is that both Billy and Joe Reader are suspects."

"Well, they're both on our radar, but we are pretty sure somebody else is deeply involved, and we need to pinpoint who that was. You can help me out, Ben."

"Sure, Les. What do you need from me?"

"I need handwriting samples from everyone who was working at your house on that Saturday. The regular staff as well as the extras who were there for the party. Would you happen to have any employment documents on hand, or do I need to go to an employment agency?"

"Oh, I have them, Les. The extra employees technically work for the caterer, but we have always insisted that they sign a waiver of liability. I have those right here in my office, plus the original employment agreements for each of the regular staff. Do you need the originals, or will copies do?"

"Originals would be best, Ben; we'll need to fax them to the handwriting analyst, so the clearer the better. Can you bring them to the station?"

"Sure. I can have them there in fifteen minutes."

"That would be great, Ben. I have to leave in a couple minutes, but if you bring them to Ginny, she can fax them right away and return them to you."

"Will do."

Kate stopped at the cafe for lunch before heading home. There was one seat open at the counter, on the far end, right next to Ray Everett, who greeted her cautiously.

"Good day, Mrs. Stone."

"Mr. Everett, nice to see you."

Kate's smile was charming, as always, and Ray had heard, as had everyone, that she was off the hook, but there was still a little doubt. She had, after all, dated Rory Fremantle shortly before he was killed.

"Shocking times, don't you think?" he asked.

"Yes, indeed. It will take a long time for everyone to get over this."

Bitsy approached, a big grin on her face.

"Hi, Kate. How's things today?"

"Very well, Bitsy. What do you recommend today?"

"Well, we've got what Paul calls a 'Polish Reuben'; it's like a reuben only with kielbasa instead of corned beef—that's what Ray's having..."

Kate glanced over at the remaining half of Ray's lunch; it was a big, hearty sandwich with fries on the side.

"It's a winner, Mrs. Stone," he said with a grin.

"Please call me Kate," she said. "It does look good, but it's maybe too much for me.'

"Well," Bitsy continued, "we also have a salmon salad. Poached salmon on fresh greens with a citrus dressing."

"Oh, that sounds just right; I'll have that, Bitsy."

Kate sipped her coffee while Ray slowly worked on his sandwich. After a couple of bites, he turned to her and asked, "Have you heard the latest on the investigation?"

"Well," she replied, "I'm not sure what the latest is. I've heard that Bill Tourville is a suspect and somebody else who used to work around here. Joe something?"

"Joe Reader. Yeah, that's the rumor: Billy and Joe. But neither one's been arrested; nobody has. It's damned frustrating."

She nodded in agreement.

"Does anybody know," she asked, "how it actually happened? I mean, why was he there in the first place?"

"I don't know, Mrs. Stone—Kate, I mean—but I have to think Billy had something to do with it. They're no good, those Tourvilles, the lot of them."

"But I heard that he and Rory were friends. Didn't Rory kind of take him under his wing and look out for him?"

"He sure did, and he never should have. He was too kind for his own good, if you ask me." He paused briefly and shook his head back and forth. "One of the finest young men this town has ever produced. It's a shame he ever got mixed up with Billy or any of that crowd. They're no good."

Reggie Plouffe was happy to see the chief again; he was the kind of man who always seemed to find a reason to be happy, no matter what was happening. He offered Chief Bridger some fresh coffee and put a plate of doughnuts on the kitchen table in front of him.

"Christy made these this morning. The boys ate most of them, but there's a few left."

The chief never said "no" to fresh doughnuts and fresh coffee, no matter how much he had already had that morning. After a few minutes of talking about the weather and such, the chief got to the point.

"Reggie," he said, "I know you've already told me what you remember about Saturday, but we have to go over it again."

"That's okay, Les. That's your job, ain't it?"

"It sure is. Now, you told me that Peter and Walt spent the whole day out mending fences over on the west side."

"That's right."

"From after breakfast until almost milking time."

"That's right. Course, they come in for lunch, but they went right back out."

"Okay. They must have had one of the trucks, right?"

"Sure they did. They had Walt's Ford. That's his own truck that he brought with him when I hired him. Me and Christy, we drive the GMC; I've always liked GMCs, you know."

"I know that, Reggie. I didn't know that Walt owned the Ford, though."

"Yes, he does, that's his own truck."

"Do you recall that they—meaning Walt and Peter—needed to get more supplies anytime during the day? Did they come back here, or maybe go to the hardware store anytime?"

"Uhh, well, I can't be certain. I don't recall that they came back to the house except for lunch, but I don't know if they ever went to the hardware store. Walt would go ahead and do that on his own; he wouldn't have to tell me. You'd better ask him."

"I will. Another thing, Reg. When's the last time you went to that junkyard of yours to look for spare parts?"

"Spare parts? That's a laugh. Les, when we park an old vehicle or a piece of machinery out there, we've pretty much stripped it already. I'm not saying it's never happened, but I can't recall a time in years I've gone out there looking for anything useful. If there was anything useful, it wouldn't be there!"

Footsteps on the stairs were heard, and Christy walked into the kitchen.

"Hi, Chief," she said with a smile. "I see you found the doughnuts."

"They're wonderful, Christy; wish my wife could bake like this!"

"Thanks. Am I interrupting?"

"No, no. I'm just about finished with your dad."

"Well, I wondered if I could have a word with you." She looked at her father, and he realized that she wanted to speak privately.

"Well, I've got some things to do in the barn, so if you're finished with me, Les, I'll just leave you two alone."

When Reggie had ambled out the door and towards the barn, Christy sat down at the table. She looked worried.

"What is it, Christy?"

"Well, I'm worried about Peter."

"Okay. Is he in trouble?"

"Maybe. I don't know. How well do you know Peter?"

"Not well at all, really. You know I've known the whole family my whole life, but it's not like I spend a lot of time out here. I know Peter's got 'special needs,' as they say."

"Right. Do you remember Ricky? My older brother?"

"Sure. He left about fifteen years ago, didn't he?"

"Yes. He's ten years older than me and fifteen years older than Peter. So, when he left, I was only nine and Peter was only four. Ever since then, it's like Peter's been searching for an older brother. He looked up to Joe, and he was really hurt when Joe had to leave. He kind of resented Walter when he first came on here and then, when I met Rory... Well, he loved Rory and Rory loved him. And then, well, you know what happened..."

"Yes, I know."

"Since Rory and I broke up, Peter's become more and more attached to Walt. I suppose that's natural. Peter still needs a role model that's not as old as Dad. But I'm worried that he's too attached. Walt's a good hired hand, but I'm not sure he's the kind of man to be looked up to."

"What is it about Walt that you don't like?"

"I just don't think he's as honest as Dad thinks he is. Dad trusts him, but I don't. He came from over in Petersford, and we didn't know anything about him, but Joe recommended him. Dad didn't want Joe here anymore, but he trusted him enough as a reference for Walt. But the people Walt hangs out with when he's not working, well, they're into a lot of bad stuff."

"What kind of 'bad stuff?'"

"Drugs, for one thing, and I don't mean pot. Also some B&Es, and stuff like that. I don't think Walt has a record..."

"No, he doesn't."

"But a lot of his friends do."

"Okay. Are you suggesting that this has anything to do with the murder?"

"No, I'm not. I wouldn't have any way of knowing that. What worries me, though, is that... Well, I know Sergeant Meadows interviewed both Walt and Peter yesterday."

"Yes, he did."

"Well, I don't really trust Walt at all and, I hate to say it, but I'm not sure you can believe anything Peter says right now. I think he'll say whatever Walt tells him to say."

Robert Parsons was a sixty-year-old man with grey hair, a trim build, and a demeanor that shouted "butler" to anyone who had ever seen *Downton Abbey* or *Upstairs, Downstairs* or any number of classic films about upper class households. He had been serving the Fremantle family for forty-two years, beginning as a chauffeur when the household staff was larger and progressing through the ranks to his present position.

Chief Bridger had called him shortly after meeting with Kate and had agreed to allow Robert to serve luncheon to Mrs. Fremantle before reporting to the police station. When he sat down across from

Chief Bridger's desk, he looked as calm and unruffled as he always did.

"I appreciate your coming in, Robert," the chief said.

"Of course, Chief. If I can help in any way, I am more than happy to do so."

"Well, here's the thing, Robert. You told us when you were first interviewed that you didn't remember seeing the envelope addressed to Rory among the other pieces of mail. You were very busy that day, had a lot of things on your mind, and just couldn't remember."

"That's right, Chief."

"But the pattern of your fingerprints on that envelope indicates that you held it in both hands, like this."

He held up both hands to demonstrate.

There was a subtle change in the butler's facial expression, as if he were realizing for the first time that he might be in some trouble.

"You must understand, Chief Bridger, that my job requires a lot of discretion; confidentiality is vital in protecting the family I serve. Frankly, I can't count the number of times that I have been asked to deliver messages to Master Rory from some young female regarding a potential assignation. I simply assumed this to be another 'love letter,' as you might call it."

"It wasn't a love letter, Robert. The note enclosed in that envelope asked Rory to meet someone by the brook, and we believe that someone killed him."

Robert bowed his head and closed his eyes. Now the guilt and sorrow were plain to see.

"Who was it who gave you that note to deliver?" the chief asked.

"It was one of the servers from the catering outfit: a Miss Tetrault. But surely her fingerprints were on the envelope, weren't they?"

"No, they weren't. Was she wearing gloves, by any chance?"

Robert's expression changed, as if he had just remembered something.

"Yes, she was, Chief. That's most unusual. The kitchen help always wear gloves, of course, but the servers who were setting up the dining room weren't required to. But Miss Tetrault was wearing gloves that day; the only one of the servers who was."

Shortly after Robert left, Chief Bridger got a call from Sergeant Meadows.

"We finally got something, Chief. We raked up a piece of pipe about two feet long from the brook."

"Great! Where was it?"

"I haven't measured exactly yet, but I'd say at least sixty yards downstream from where we found the body. It was caught up on some reeds and partially submerged, but it looks like it wasn't there very long, or it would have been deeper in the mud."

"What does it look like?"

"It's been washed pretty clean by the water, but there's still some rust on it, and it's pitted where the rust was washed off. No chance of blood stains or fingerprints, I'm afraid, but it's definitely heavy enough to kill somebody."

"Okay. Bring it in so I can have a look at it, then we'll send it off to the lab. Even if we don't get anything from it, I want Paula's opinion about it as a possible murder weapon."

30 |

Kate put her phone down after talking to the chief. They had a possible murder weapon, but not one that could be positively linked to either the victim or the killer. That's the way it seemed, at least. And they had another suspect—Carol Tetrault, who had handed the envelope to the butler to be placed in among the mail.

A lot to think about before making her appearance at Bucky's. According to Bitsy, there was a very good chance that Carol Tetrault would be at the bar tonight; she didn't miss many nights. The chief still didn't know if she was the one who had written the note; they would get the handwriting analysis results tomorrow.

It was early afternoon, and Kate had some actual work to do before Bitsy came over for the "makeover." First, she had to call the office.

"Hey, boss! How's it going up there?"

"It's going well, Millie."

"Did they find the murderer yet?"

"Not yet, but we're working on it."

"We? *We* are working on it?"

"You're not going to believe this, Millie. The Chief of Police has actually asked me to help him with the investigation."

"Wow! How did that happen?"

"Well, I guess some of the things I said and did convinced him that I know a lot about murders and murder mysteries, and he needed help, so he asked me."

"That's awesome! Kate Stone, amateur detective! You must be excited!"

"Sure I am. Listen, there's not a lot I can tell you right now, but there's going to be some excitement tonight, I think."

"What's going on? Tell me!"

"I can't right now. Maybe I can call you after I get home tonight, but it might be too late."

"Too late to call me? Who do you think you're talking to? And what is going on? You've got something planned, and I want to know!"

"Millie, I probably shouldn't have even mentioned it."

"But you did, and now you've got me on the hook! Listen, boss, you have got to tell me what's going on! If not now, then you absolutely must call me tonight!"

"Okay, okay. I promise. But right now we have some work to do. I've got the individual reports from each agent, but I need the financial report..."

"I'll have it to you in ten minutes."

"Okay. Then I need to speak to Jack first."

"Okay, I think he's ready for you."

Chief Bridger and Sergeant Meadows went back to the "machinery graveyard" on the Plouffe property, but by way of the horse trail this time so as not to alert anyone on the farm that they were there. The piece of pipe was on the way to the lab, but the chief wanted to have a look again to see how likely it was that it had come from this place.

Wandering Brook looked pretty tame right now, but the banks still showed clearly the evidence of the flood. They parked the cruiser near the bend in the brook, where two men were standing on the bank, pointing and gesturing toward the big concrete slab that now sat at an angle in the brook, with water flowing around it on both sides. The chief knew who they were and why they were there.

"Afternoon, Chief," one of them said as the two police officers approached.

"Afternoon, Brian," the chief responded. "What do you think?"

"Well, it's going to be a hell of a job to do it right, and we definitely don't have that kind of money in the budget this year. Jim and I were just talking about some kind of temporary fix. We might be able to shift it back to approximately its original position."

The other man nodded and said, "The bank's all washed out behind it, but it will be better than nothing. I mean, if we have another flood this year, which is pretty likely, we'll need something there, or this whole bank we're standing on could wash right into the brook, trail and all."

"Meanwhile," Brian added, "we design a permanent solution and hope we can get it done next year."

The two police officers walked upstream to the nearest ford, which wasn't far, and reached the junkyard in just a few minutes. They glanced around at all of the old, rusty equipment, checking out an old mower, a broken-down tedder, a tractor, and then Meadows raised his right arm and pointed right at Reggie Plouffe's beloved old truck.

"Look at that, Les. In the back."

They walked up to the old GMC pickup. The sides of the bed had the remains of a frame that had been used to extend the height so the truck could hold more material, probably hay. All that remained now were a couple of rotten planks still attached to a piece of pipe sticking out of the side of the truck bed.

"He made a frame," Chief Bridger said, "with six pieces of pipe and some two-by-six planks. I remember what it looked like. I threw plenty of bales into this truck myself."

There was only one pipe still attached, but looking on the ground nearby, they quickly found four more.

"There were six," Meadows said, "and now there's only five. And they're exactly the same as the pipe we raked out of the brook."

Sergeant Maroney called a little after seven and just minutes after the chief had promised his wife he'd be home soon.

"What have you got so far, Jim?"

"Well, like you said, Les, the locals and the staties are all over it, so I had to wait my turn. But as far as physical evidence goes, it's pretty sparse. Joe Reader hardly owned anything himself, and what he did own he was able to fit into the truck he stole. Looks like a man who was prepared to go at the drop of a hat."

"Like a typical drug dealer."

"Exactly what I was thinking. I finally got a chance to sit down and interview Claude Moreau; it's a pretty sad story. He says Joe Reader was the best hand he had, and he doesn't know how to replace him. But he's beginning to realize what was going on. He said he bent over backwards to give Joe time off whenever he wanted it because the guy had done such good work for him for six years. Reader would get every other weekend off to go over to Burlington. That's where he said he was going, anyway."

"How did he get there? Or here, or wherever?"

"Moreau would let him use one of his trucks. Reader would use his own money for gas, most of the time."

"Did he say why he was going to Burlington?"

"He told Moreau he had a sister in Burlington who had a handicapped son that Reader would help. Like a 'mentor' thing. But we've already checked out his family, and I told Mr. Moreau that Joe Reader had no siblings and no living relatives outside of some cousins in California. When I told him that, he realized he'd been had. Joe Reader's been lying to him for years, and now he's run off to Canada with one of his trucks."

"I don't suppose there's any chance Mr. Moreau knows anything about Reader possibly dealing drugs."

"No, he appears to be pretty naive about things like that. But I'm hoping to get more information out of some of the other people on the farm."

"Good. We've received information that places Reader here in Merryfield and Wayford both Thursday and Friday last week. I'm hoping to get confirmation of that tonight. See what you can get from his co-workers and call me tomorrow."

"Will do."

Bitsy Dufresne was in her glory. Makeup first, then the wig, and finally the clothes. That's what she had declared, and Kate had agreed, not without some trepidation.

"Don't argue, Kitty; I know exactly what I'm doing."

"Kitty?"

"That's what I've decided to call you. Just for tonight."

"Okay. Actually, it's perfect. My grandmother used to call me Kitty, so I'm used to it."

"Great!"

The light seemed to be best in the kitchen, so Kate sat at the dining room table while Bitsy started applying a foundation to her face.

"It already feels like too much, Bitsy."

"I know, I know, but listen. You're not a waitress."

"What's that supposed to mean?"

"It means you're not used to having to look your best in places that are really different. I mean the lighting, mostly. Like my friend, Mary Ann. You met her, didn't you? She works tables on some day shifts at the café, and she works weekend nights at the Tranmere."

"Oh, right."

"Well, the face she wears to work a night shift at the Tranmere would look hideous on a day shift at the café. You have to know what the lighting is going to be, and I know exactly what it will be. And we want you to look different, too."

"How different am I going to look?"

"Well, for one thing, I'm doing your coloring to go with a blonde wig. I brought two, and we'll decide which is better. But besides that, we don't want you to look chic and sophisticated, like you normally do; we want you to look saucy and hot!"

"Uh, remember, Bitsy, I'm not looking to take anyone home with me; I just want to talk to some people."

"I know, but if you want guys to talk to you, you gotta look like someone they want to take home. Don't worry, the bartenders and the bouncer like me—especially the bouncer. As long as you're with me, you're as safe as you could be."

31

Mikey Paris was standing outside the front door of Bucky's Tavern when he saw Bitsy's Toyota roll into the gravel parking lot. Thursday nights at Bucky's were pretty regular for Bitsy, so he wasn't surprised to see her, but when another chick got out of the passenger seat, that was a surprise indeed. Who could this be?

The newcomer was taller than Bitsy and very good-looking in her tight-fitting jeans and loose denim shirt over a white tank top. A very cute blonde, and someone obviously new in town. The two women were both smiling as they approached the front door, and Bitsy threw out her arms for the big hug she always received from her favorite doorman.

Mikey was well over six feet, very powerful-looking, and very black. He picked up Bitsy as easily as lifting a cup of coffee and engulfed her in a massive embrace.

"My favorite!" Mikey exclaimed. "I thought you weren't gonna show up; it's almost ten."

"Oh, I wouldn't miss my Thursday night! Hey, Mikey, this is my friend, Kitty. We were together in school, at Castleton, and she's visiting for a couple days."

"Kitty," the big man said very graciously, "it is my pleasure to meet you. Friends of Bitsy's are always welcome."

"Thank you, Mikey; a pleasure to meet you, as well."

They walked into the bar, and Kate knew immediately that Bitsy was right about the makeup; the lighting was quite dim in the rustic old tavern. As her eyes became adjusted, she could see that there were maybe sixty people in the place, which looked like it could hold a hundred. On one side of the big room was a small stage, unoccupied, and on the other side were two coin-operated pool tables. The juke-box was against the wall right between the two.

Bitsy nudged Kate's arm and pointed towards the long bar.

"There's a couple of seats open; let's sit at the bar and you can meet Eddie. Maybe we can sit at a table later."

The open seats were toward one end of the curved bar, which was convenient. When they were seated, the stage was almost behind them and they could see practically the whole room. The bartender approached with a big grin on his face.

"Hey, Bits. Who's your friend?"

"Hey, Eddie. This is Kitty. She's an old friend from Castleton, just visiting."

"Great! Is this your first time in the valley, Kitty?"

"Yes, it is. I've been meaning to visit for years, and I've finally made it."

"Well, Bucky's is the place to be. What can I get you, Kitty?"

"I'll have a Bud, please."

"Same here, Eddie," Bitsy said.

Eddie looked to be in his thirties, maybe forty. He had a mous-tache that should have been trimmed a little better; it hung over his upper lip too much. His brown hair was starting to thin, and though his arms looked well-muscled, his loose, short-sleeved shirt couldn't hide a noticeable beer gut. He went to get their beers and Kate looked slowly around the barroom. Some of the patrons were looking curiously at her, which was no surprise. It was obviously a "hometown" bar, and strangers were few and far between. Strange females, especially good-looking ones, were bound to excite interest.

"You both want glasses?" Eddie asked as he set their bottles on the bar.

"Yes, please."

When the bartender had left to serve someone else, Kate spoke.

"Great seats, Bitsy; I can see almost the whole room."

"Yeah, and almost the whole room is looking at you."

"Well, first things first. Tell me about Mikey."

Bitsy laughed.

"Every woman's first question the first time they come in here! Mikey's great; he's the best doorman ever! But he's true blue—has a steady girlfriend and he never strays. She doesn't come in when he's working, so he could haul a lot of action if he wanted but, like I said, he never strays. Are you disappointed?"

"Well, I'm not looking for any action; that's not why I'm here. But if I were..."

"Yeah, I know. Mikey's a hunk, alright. He's a really nice guy, too—always tries to keep the peace. That's the best kind of bouncer; the kind that tries to stop trouble before it starts."

"He looks like he can handle himself pretty well if trouble does start, though."

"Oh, you'd better believe it. Everyone in the valley knows not to mess with him, but every once in a while someone from somewhere else will come in and start trouble, and they always end up sorry."

"Well, I won't start any, then. So who's here that I should know about?"

"Um, it looks like you're about to meet Carol Tetrault."

A good-looking brunette was walking towards them carrying a bottle of Budweiser. She was very thin, dressed in ripped jeans and a blue crop top that showed off her belly button ring and flattered her bosom. Her face was pretty, but she didn't have Bitsy's expertise with her makeup, and she looked a little sallow.

"Hey, Bitsy. Who's your friend?" the woman asked, trying to sound neutral and non-threatening.

"Hey, Carol. This is Kitty. She's an old friend from school—from Castleton. She's just visiting for a couple days."

"Nice to meet you, Kitty. Are you looking for some fun tonight?"

"Well, my plan was to just have a couple of beers and listen to the jukebox. But then I met Mikey..."

Carol's face lit up.

"Ha! Good luck with that!"

"Where's Alan tonight?" Bitsy asked.

"I think he's over at Billy's; they should be here soon. Hey, you guys wanna shoot some pool?"

Bitsy looked at Kate with raised eyebrows, and Kate said, "Yeah, sure."

"Let me settle up with Eddie," Bitsy said, "then we'll be right over."

When Carol was out of earshot, Bitsy asked, "What was that? I mean, about Mikey?"

"Well, I got the feeling that Carol doesn't like competition, so I figured I'd pretend I'm after Mikey. She might be more talkative if she's not worried about me stealing her boyfriend."

"Ooh, smart move! Hey, when I get a chance, I'll have a word with Mikey. This might work even better if he's in on it. I mean, if he knows you're not really serious, he might play along."

"Good idea, Bits!"

They played pool for about half an hour—"Kitty" and Bitsy against Carol and her friend, Daisy. None of them were great players, but they were competitive and each team won a couple of games. They chattered in a friendly way, about the music and about the guys in the bar. A few men stopped to watch them play and check out the new "talent," but moved on when Kate showed no interest in them.

Kate had plenty of opportunities, while waiting for the others to play, to check the place out and soak up the atmosphere. She had been expecting something like the roadhouse in *The Blues Brothers*, but there was no screen in front of the stage and no one in the place looked like they were about to start throwing beer bottles around. All in all, it wasn't that much different than some of the bars she used to visit in her college days, although the crowd was older here and definitely dressed more casually.

When Mikey came in to get a soda from the bar, Bitsy took the opportunity to get two more beers and grab a quick word with the doorman. A few minutes later, Mikey wandered over to the jukebox and stood there looking over the selections. It was Kate's shot, but she flubbed an easy one and handed the cue over to Daisy then sauntered over to the jukebox and stood beside him.

"Hey, Mikey. What do you like?"

She gave him a big, bright smile, clearly suggesting that it wasn't the music she was talking about.

Carol looked at Bitsy and said quietly, "She's not wasting any time, is she? I don't think she's got any hope, but more power to her."

Mikey smiled back at "Kitty," and he was about to say something when the front door opened and two men walked in. Recognizing them immediately, Mikey just waved at them.

"Regulars, I take it?" she said.

"Yeah, they're here all the time. Billy Tourville and Alan Brooks. Alan is Carol's boyfriend."

The two men walked directly over to the pool table where Carol stood with Daisy and Bitsy, not even noticing the hot new blonde who was talking to Mikey. Carol sidled right up to the taller, red-headed guy—that must be Alan. The other guy was Billy Tourville then. Kate had not met or seen him, although she had heard his name several times.

Alan Brooks was about six feet tall, and nearly as thin as his girlfriend. Billy was a couple of inches shorter and more stoutly built. He would have to be, Kate thought, if his work was handling horses. They both looked nervous—agitated—although Kate would learn that Billy always seemed to look nervous.

Alan whispered something to Carol, who responded by shaking her head. Then Billy said something, and Carol made a gesture with her arms out and palms up, as if to say, "I don't know anything."

Then Alan jerked his head toward the other side of the room, and he and Billy started walking away. They both noticed Kate for the first time as they walked by. Neither stopped walking, but Billy almost tripped over a chair as he was checking out the new chick.

Carol and Daisy were right behind them having said something to Bitsy about abandoning their game.

"Well, I guess it's a two-girl game now," 'Kitty' said to Mikey.

"Yeah, it looks like they've got something to talk about—not unusual. Hey, Kitty, I've got to get back to the door. Pick a couple of tunes, and we'll talk later."

"Yeah, I'd like that. Thanks, Mikey."

The doorman had put in enough coins for four songs and only chosen two, so Kate picked a current Taylor Swift hit and an old Johnny Cash tune then rejoined Bitsy by the pool table.

The others were well out of earshot, so Bitsy asked, "Did Mikey tell you who they are?"

"Yes, I was hoping they'd come in. It's the first time I've seen either of them."

"Well, when they came over, the first thing Alan asked Carol was 'Have you heard from Joe?'"

"Hey, let's keep playing. We don't want them to think we're talking about them." Kate picked up a cue and started looking over the table. "Meaning Joe Reader?"

"I guess so. He didn't say a last name, but they're all friends, and, like I told you, they were all together last weekend."

Kate put in an easy shot then walked to the other side of the table. "And what did Billy say?"

"He said something like, 'He knows better than to call me.' He seemed really upset."

"Hmm... Well, that tells me something." She tried a difficult angle shot and missed. "Is Daisy part of their crowd, too?"

"Right now she is. She's really quiet and doesn't drink much and doesn't get involved in anything dangerous, but she's always had a thing for Billy." Bitsy was lining up her shots and looked like she might be able to win the game. The seven ball went in, followed quickly by the three, and Bitsy took her time lining up the eight ball. "She's the kind that needs to be needed, you know? And lately it seems like Billy's needed a shoulder to cry on, and Daisy's been there for him." She coolly stroked the eight ball in. "That's game, Kitty; rack 'em up!"

Kate racked the balls for another game while she tried to think of ways of getting to talk to any of them. No good rushing it, though; she needed to seem uninterested.

In the midst of the next game, Kate walked up to the bar to get two more Buds. As she was waiting for Eddie to bring them, she heard the door open and a heavy-set man walked in. The man looked immediately over to where Billy and Alan and the women were sitting and waved to them then walked up to the bar.

The man was brazenly checking out Kate's figure, and she turned her face away. He reached the bar just as Eddie set the beers down.

"Hey, Walt, be right with you," the bartender said.

"Sure, Eddie," the man replied while looking right at Kate.

She grabbed the two bottles and turned to walk away, but the man was in her way.

"Excuse me," she said, with a friendly smile.

"Yeah, sure. I haven't seen you in here before."

"I'm just visiting; I'm playing pool with my friend, Bitsy."

"Great, maybe we can talk a little later. You look like someone I'd like to meet."

"Well, I'll be right over there."

She walked away with the beers and heard the man order a Jim Beam for himself and a round for his friends at the table.

When she reached the pool table, she asked Bitsy, "Eddie called him Walt; is that Walter Lamb?"

"It sure is. Looks like he's interested in you."

"Well, I'm interested in him, but not the same way. What do you know about him?

"He's a jerk. I mean, I guess he's a good farmhand, but he's pretty nasty to women. You know the old saying, 'He thinks he's God's gift to women?'"

"Of course."

"Well, that's Walt in a nutshell. Be careful."

"Oh, I will. Does he always hang out with those guys?"

"Yeah, when he's here. He doesn't come in as often, because most morning's he's up too early. But some mornings he doesn't have to milk, I guess, so he comes in here the night before. I'm not sure if it's always the same, but last week he was here Thursday night but not Friday."

"Was he hanging out with Billy and Joe Reader?"

"Yeah, and Alan and Carol. They're always together, especially when Joe is in town. Listen, Kate, I don't know exactly what they do, because they don't talk to me about it, but it's generally known that if you're looking for anything, they can get it for you."

"Meaning drugs?"

"Coke, smack, meth, ecstasy—you name it."

"And everybody knows about it?"

"Pretty much. I'm sure the cops know it, too, but they'd have to catch them in the act, wouldn't they?"

"Yeah. It must be tough for a small-town police force—not enough manpower or resources."

There was a whoop of joy from the other side of the room, and Kate and Bitsy both turned around to see Walt, Billy, Carol, Alan, and Daisy lifting their glasses in a happy toast.

"I wonder what that was about?" Kate said. "It looks like they're celebrating."

It didn't take long to find out. Walt had told Eddie before heading to the table and now everyone had heard the news—Joe Reader was on the run, had stolen a truck, and was headed for Montreal.

When Carol came over to play the jukebox a few minutes later, she was beaming.

"What's up, Carol?" Bitsy asked her. "You guys are all happy about something."

"Well, it's good news for Billy, isn't it? With Joe on the run, it's practically a confession. I mean, everybody knows Billy didn't do it anyway, but now the cops will be after Joe and leave Billy alone."

"Yeah, that makes sense. Well, good for him."

Now Walt Lamb was approaching.

"Hey, Carol, did you play something I like?" he asked.

"Nah, if you want to hear that old country crap, use your own money."

She sauntered away, grinning, and the Plouffe's farmhand put some money in and picked his tunes then walked right over to stand beside Kate.

By this time, there were some serious players on the other table, but Bitsy and Kate were still playing by themselves.

"What's your name, honey?"

"Kitty. I'm just in town visiting Bitsy. Are you a pool player?"

"Yeah, I'm pretty good. My name's Walt, by the way."

"I know. I asked."

He seemed pleased to hear that, which was just what she intended.

Just then they heard someone call Walt's name. Billy, Alan, Carol, and Daisy were heading out the front door, and Alan was gesturing to Walt.

"Hey, ladies," Walt said, "those guys are going out to smoke up. You wanna get high?"

Bitsy and Kate looked at each other, and they both shook their heads.

"Maybe later," Bitsy said.

Walt waved a hand towards the others.

"Well, maybe I'll stay here and shoot some pool with you two. You don't mind a threesome, do you?"

Bitsy rolled her eyes, and Kate chuckled and said, "Rack 'em up."

They played three-way eightball for a while, Walt flirting almost continuously while Kate tried to think of a way to turn the conversation to her advantage.

"Hey, Walt," Bitsy asked, "that's interesting news about Joe Reader, isn't it?"

He chuckled. "It sure is. I'm the one that brought the news. The cops were trying to keep it under wraps, but they can't hide nothing from me; I've got contacts all over this valley. You ladies wouldn't believe the things I know."

Kate smiled at him and asked, "Are you in some kind of position of power, Walt?"

"Well, I'll tell you what, Kitty. I'm just a farmhand, as far as anyone knows. But nothing happens in this town, or the whole valley, without me knowing about it. I've got my fingers in a lot of pies, I can get anybody anything they want, and the cops are clueless. I've got a contact inside the department, and they don't do nothing without me knowing about it. Hey, one of my songs is playing. You like it?"

Kate listened.

"A waltz? A country waltz?"

"Yeah, it's 'The Last Cheater's Waltz.' You like it?"

"Oh, I've heard this at an Emmy Lou Harris concert, I think."

"Yeah, she did it, but this is the Johnny Duncan version. You wanna dance, Kitty?"

"No, let's just shoot pool, Walt. I do like the song, though."

"Do you like it because you like to cheat?"

"No. I'm single and unattached, so there's no cheating. Is that why you like it?"

He laughed. "No, I'm as unattached as you are—divorced."

"Hey, Walt," Kate said, "I'm curious about something. I just got in town this morning, and I've heard, like, six or eight people talking about this guy that got murdered."

"Rory Fremantle."

"Yeah, that's the name. Was he a big man in town?"

"He was, for most people. Rich boy. His family is old and wealthy, and he was the fair-haired boy. But he played around with the wrong crowd, and he got what was coming to him."

32

Kate and Bitsy walked out the front door of Bucky's Tavern at quarter to twelve, brushing past Billy Tourville, who was headed back in. Kate wished she could have learned more, but the information she had picked up was important, and she had no wish to have another beer or to drink a shot of whiskey with Walt Lamb. The amorous farmhand was getting too suggestive and too physical, and she had no wish to pay the price it might take to learn any more.

They stopped to say goodnight to Mikey and to ask one more favor.

"Mikey," Bitsy said, "I don't think Walt's going to follow us out, but if he does…"

The big man smiled and said, "Understood, Bits. He won't get farther than where I stand. Kitty, it was a pleasure to meet you, and both of you get home safe, please."

They walked quickly towards Bitsy's car, and a figure came out of the shadows.

"Bits? Can you help me?"

It was Daisy, the girl who had been with Billy.

"Daisy, what's up? We just saw Billy going back in."

"Yeah, but I don't want to go back in. Can you give me a ride home, Bits? Please?"

"Uhh, sure, Daisy. You live on Pleasant Street, right?"

"Yes. It's right on your way, isn't it? I don't want to be any trouble."

"No trouble, girl. Hop in."

Daisy got in the back, and, in the dim glow of the overhead light, it was clear that she had been crying.

When they were all seated, Bitsy started up the car and asked, "Daisy, what's up? Are you okay?"

"Yeah, I guess. We just had a bit of a fight, that's all. He won't listen to me, you know?"

"Yeah, I know. That's men for you."

"I mean, it seemed like good news, right? Joe being on the run? It means the cops will think Joe killed Rory, and they'll leave Billy alone now. Not that Billy could ever have done it. He loved Rory, and he trusted him."

"Oh, I know he did," Bitsy said as she left the parking lot and headed into Merryfield. "Everybody knows that, except the bitches in the big house. They're the ones that have it in for Billy."

"You're so right, Bits! But the thing is, with Rory gone, I think Billy's going to fall in with Walt and Al and that crowd even more than he was. He's lost his job, he's lost the friend he looked up to more than any other, and he doesn't have any idea what he's going to do next."

"Has he started looking for another job?" Bitsy asked.

"Not really. I mean, it's only been a couple days. I told him he should call that woman at Sunrise Farm. If anybody knows where he should look for a job with horses, it would be her. But he thinks it's a waste of time."

Kate was itching to ask some questions, but she knew she'd better not. She was supposed to be the out-of-towner who knew nothing. But Bitsy knew how to keep the conversation going.

"That Walt Lamb gives me the creeps, Daisy," Bitsy said.

"Yeah, I know. Most of the girls feel the same way about him, but he usually hooks up with someone. He didn't waste any time getting next to you, Kitty."

"Yeah, well, he's not the kind that impresses me. He seems to think a lot of himself, doesn't he?"

Daisy sort of snorted. "He sure does. He likes to control other people and keep his own hands clean. He never gets caught and never gets blamed."

"Then why does he brag so much?" Kate asked. "That seems kind of careless."

"Yeah, it does. He'll shoot his mouth off when he's looking for some action, and you're not from around here, so he probably figured it didn't matter. Still, I bet he didn't actually admit to anything, did he?"

"Not exactly, but he did tell me he could get me anything I wanted."

"Yeah, that's what he always says, but when it comes down to delivering, it's always someone else doing it for him, isn't it? Bitsy, you remember when Billy got busted, over in Petersford?"

"Yeah, I remember."

"Well, it should have been Walt. He set the whole thing up then disappeared when it got hot and let Billy take the blame."

"I kind of remember that," Bitsy said. "Though I never knew for sure what happened."

"Well, I was hoping, after Rory helped him out and gave him a job, that Billy wouldn't do any more jobs for Walt. He's got Alan working for him, and he'll do just about anything, and Carol, too."

"I thought Carol was just hanging out with them because she's with Alan," Bitsy said.

"Well, I don't really know. I want to be with Billy, you know, but I try to stay away from the things they're getting up to."

There was silence for a couple minutes as Bitsy turned onto Pleasant Street.

"It's the one on the left, with the maple tree, right, Daisy?"

"Yeah, that's it. You know, Bits, I don't know why the cops haven't gone after Carol about the murder. I mean, she hated Rory more than anyone, didn't she? She was the one Rory threw over when he started seeing Christy Plouffe."

"I'd forgotten that, Kate—that Carol was going with Rory that summer before he met Christy. I would have told you that if I'd remembered."

They had just dropped Daisy off and were approaching Kate's house just at midnight.

"Do you think the police would know that?"

"Probably not. I mean, it wasn't like a long-term romance that the whole town would know about. Rory was wild that spring; he was like a honeybee in a field of clover! Carol just happened to be the one he'd been seeing for a couple weeks when he met Christy. Probably nobody remembers that."

"Except Carol."

"Right! She remembers, for sure! And she would certainly hold a grudge!"

Bitsy pulled up right in front of Kate's porch and stopped the car. They looked at each other, and Bitsy started grinning.

"This has been a lot of fun, Kate, hasn't it?"

"It certainly has, Bitsy. I've learned a lot, and, yeah, it was fun. I hope you don't get in any trouble over this."

"Why would I get in trouble?"

"Well, after I tell the chief everything I've learned, it won't be long before things start happening. Every one of that crowd will be pulled in for more questioning and could even be arrested. There's a chance that some of them might connect the dots and realize that I was there digging for information."

Bitsy shook her head vigorously.

"I don't think so. The only one smart enough to realize it is Walt, and he was into his third beer and third shot when we left. No one is ever going to see 'Kitty' again, and there's no way they will make that connection. Don't worry about it. Hey, do you want some help getting all that makeup off?"

"No thanks, Bitsy. I promised I'd call Millie, and I think I'll pour myself a brandy. Do you want one?"

"Oh, no. I've got to be in work at eight. Say hi to Millie for me; she's gonna love this!"

"Oh, my God, boss! I can't believe you did that!"

"I almost can't believe it myself. But it really happened. I went to a redneck bar made up as a hot blonde, and now I'm sitting here with a glass of brandy and working on scraping this face off while I talk to you."

"Did you take pictures? Tell me you took pictures!"

"Sorry, Millie. I just want to get this face off as quickly as I can. I didn't want to have any pictures or messages left on my phone any-way. Nothing that could connect 'Kitty' with me."

"'Kitty?' Is that what you called yourself?"

"Yes. It was Bitsy's idea, but it worked perfectly because my grammy used to call me that, so I was used to it."

"Well, I don't really get what you're worried about with the phone…"

"Just being ultra-cautious, Millie."

"Okay, I'm disappointed that I can't see 'Kitty,' though. God, that must have been fun!"

"Yeah, it was fun. There were some awkward moments with a lecherous farmhand, but it went well overall, and I learned a lot."

"So, do you know who did it?"

"No. I mean, there's a group of people who I believe were responsible, and I think we're close to being able to make an arrest, but I still can't figure out who is the one who actually struck the blow. There's still a lot of work to do, but no more 'undercover;' I'm putting 'Kitty' back in a box, never to appear again."

Daisy Millette was still up at two-thirty when she saw the car drive by and stop three doors down, where Billy Tourville lived. It was Alan's car, and Carol was in the front seat beside her boyfriend. Billy got out of the back seat and said something to Alan then walked straight to his door.

Daisy breathed a sigh of relief when the driver said something in reply then drove off. She was still dressed, so she hurried out her door and across the street. Billy's entrance was up a staircase on the right side of the house, and he was at the top of the stairs, still fumbling with his keys, when he heard Daisy call out to him. A few minutes later, they were seated on Billy's couch, he with a beer and she with a glass of water.

"Tell me what happened, hon," Daisy said.

"Nothing much. Walt has something planned; something he says will be very lucrative, but he's keeping it quiet for now."

"Billy, do you really want to get involved with it? Whatever it is, it will be dangerous. More so for you than for Walt—you know that."

"I'm gonna need money, Daisy; I haven't got a job anymore, remember?"

"But you can get one; why won't you call that woman at the farm and see if she can help you?"

"Daisy, nobody's gonna help me! That Thompson bitch and the Fremantles have probably already told everyone in the valley and across the state about me, and no one is going to hire me!"

"You don't know that for sure, Billy."

"Don't I? You're just too naive, Daisy."

He took a swig of his beer and picked up the pipe he had been filling while they talked. He handed Daisy the pipe and lit a match for her. They each took a hit before speaking again.

"Did Walt say anything more about Joe Reader?" Daisy asked.

"Well, like you heard him say earlier, he's certain that the cops are convinced that Joe killed Rory and they'll focus on him and leave me alone."

"Did he do it? Was it Joe?"

"I don't know, Daisy. It's all a nightmare! Joe told me he had to be back in Barton before noon on Saturday, so I don't think he could have done it. But I can't swear that he actually went; that's just what he told me. The others won't say anything about it. They know how much I liked Rory."

"But they didn't."

"No. Walt is still pissed about Rory undercutting him on a big deal years ago—claims it cost him ten thousand dollars. That's probably not true, but he still hated him. And you know how Carol felt about him."

"So, do you think those guys did it? Walt and Carol and Alan?"

He shook his head back and forth and picked up the pipe again.

"I don't know, Daisy, and I don't want to know."

33

Kate had told the chief that she would be at the station at nine o'clock. She hadn't actually gotten to bed until almost two, because she had wanted to write some notes while everything was still fresh. With five hours sleep, a hurried shower, and a quick review of her notes behind her, she walked into the Maple Leaf Café at ten past eight.

Mary Ann had the early shift on this Friday and was behind the counter while Bitsy, who had just started at eight, had a section of tables. She and Kate waved at each other, and Kate took an empty seat at the counter next to Ray Everett.

"Good morning, Ms. Stone," the hardware man said with a smile. "How are you this fine morning?"

"I am well, Mr. Everett; thank you for asking. How about you?"

"Oh, I'm doing pretty well. Whenever Paul does his 'Trout and Eggs' special, it's hard not to feel good about the day."

"Ooh, that looks good. Local trout?"

"Absolutely! Pan-fried with salt pork and served with home fries and eggs! Can't beat it!"

Mary Ann poured a coffee for Kate and asked, "Would you like the special, Ms. Stone?"

"Yes, I think I will have it, Mary Ann—eggs over easy, please."

"You got it!"

The hardware man was perusing a list of names on a legal pad, and when he noticed Kate glancing at it, he asked, "Are you a baseball fan, Ms. Stone?"

"Well, I used to be. Maybe I could be again."

"That's a funny answer."

"It has a lot to do with my marriage. My ex-husband was not very tolerant of opinions he did not share, so I had to suppress my love of the Yankees as long as I was married."

"Oh, I get it; he was a Sox fan, and you were Yankees."

"Exactly."

"It's what we call a 'mixed marriage' in these parts. There's a few of those here in the valley."

"And do people make it work?"

"Most do; I figure if it were a deal-breaker, they wouldn't have got hitched in the first place!"

Ray laughed at his witty answer.

"Well, that's the way it should have been with us, but my ex was a 'special case,' in more ways than one."

"I see. Well, the reason I asked is I'm planning our annual trip to Fenway Park. I always organize a trip for a Saturday or Sunday in July. Sometimes, if we get enough people, we can afford to charter a bus, but I need four or five more people."

"Oh, well, I'm not sure. It'll probably be mostly men, won't it?"

"Mostly, but there'll be at least four women—maybe more. Linda Norman, from Sunrise Farm, always goes."

"Oh, I'll bet she's fun. I like Linda."

"Well, you think about it; it's gonna be a blast! I've got a couple more regulars I haven't got to yet, so there's a good chance we'll have enough for a bus, and that means there'll be room for another ten or twelve."

Ray's face seemed to change, as if he'd just remembered something sad.

"Of course, Rory loved the Sox, too."

"Oh, that's sad. Did he used to go on these trips?"

"When the boys were younger, they would both go. The old man didn't care much about baseball, but he'd let Ben and Rory go along with us, after they'd reached ten or eleven. But after they were all grown up, not so much. Rory would go sometimes with his buddies from college. Last time he went on one of my trips was two years ago. Rory was going with the Plouffe girl then, and he brought Christy, Peter, and Christy's little boy along. They had a great time!

"Peter really wants to go this year, but they're not sure yet. He was in the store with Walt Lamb, their hired hand, on Saturday afternoon, picking up a few odds and ends, and we talked about it. Walt don't seem to care about baseball, and Reggie and Christy don't care to go. I told Walt I'd look after Peter if he wants to come along. I mean the boy's nineteen, for Pete's sake. He may be a little slow in the head, but there's no reason he can't go to a ballgame with a bunch of people from his hometown."

"Sounds reasonable to me. Did this hired hand seem to think it would be a problem?"

"Oh, he just hemmed and hawed about the milking schedule and this and that. I'll just give Reggie a call and tell him I'll be responsible for the boy, and I'm sure it will work out."

"This was Saturday afternoon when you talked to them?"

"Oh, yes. Every other week I take Friday off and work all day Saturday. That's been my schedule for years now."

Kate walked into the police station right at nine o'clock, and Ginny greeted her with a smile.

"Good morning, the chief's in his office and he said for you to go right in."

"Okay, thanks, Ginny."

The door was open, and the chief was sitting at his desk, writing some notes.

"Come on in, Kate; we've got a lot to talk about this morning," the chief said. "I've got some information to share, and I hope you do, too."

"Oh, I certainly do, Les!" she replied as she closed the door behind her. She was carrying a notebook, which she set down on the chief's desk. There was a chair waiting for her, and she quickly sat, eager to get started.

"Kate, wouldn't you like a coffee before we start?" the chief asked, apparently bemused at her eagerness.

"Oh, sure."

A pot of coffee sat on a hot plate at one end of the desk beside a plate of doughnuts. She poured a cup for herself, looked inquiringly at the Chief, whose cup was full, and grabbed herself a doughnut.

"Alright then," she said. "Les, before we say anything else, I have to tell you something I learned last night that may be a surprise to you; I don't know for sure."

"Okay, what is it?"

"Well, when Walt Lamb walked into Bucky's last night, he told everyone that Joe Reader was on the run. Before he got there, nobody knew about it. Later, he told me himself—Walt, that is—that he has a contact in the police department and he knows everything that goes on."

The chief grimaced, but he didn't look surprised.

"Kate, thank you for telling me that first thing. I have known for a while that information leaks out of here sometimes, and I know who it is. So far, there has been no reason to... Well, let me put it this way: The man is otherwise a good officer, and nothing he has said outside the department has caused any harm, up to now. I have been holding off confronting him about it."

He leaned back in his chair and looked up at the ceiling.

"You may wonder about this, Kate, and it's entirely possible that I am wrong. It's not just that I consider the officer in question to be a good cop; it's more than that. He has connections to some small-time criminals all around the valley, and there have been occasions when that has been useful to us. I want to keep that pipeline open as long as I can."

"Because the information pipeline works both ways?"

"Exactly. I don't want to close it until I have no choice."

"Okay, that makes sense. But I did wonder: Does this officer know that I'm helping with the investigation?"

"Probably, almost certainly. The only one I actually told was Sergeant Meadows, but Ginny has seen you reading the statements and going through the evidence, so she knows. Yeah, I'm sure the whole department knows by now. But you didn't go to Bucky's as 'Kate Stone,' did you?"

"No, I was pretty well disguised, and I don't believe anyone was there who had seen me before. I am more concerned that someone might figure it out afterward—after they have been arrested and charged, for instance—and I don't want my friend to be implicated because she brought me there."

"I see. That is a possibility, although I think it's a remote one. But I am sure, Kate, that both you and your friend were aware of the risk before you decided to do this."

"Yes, of course we were. But maybe I didn't consider the risk to Bitsy as much as I should have. I couldn't have done it without her, though."

The chief raised his eyebrows just slightly, and Kate realized it was the first time she had named her accomplice. But Chief Bridger either already knew or didn't care who it was; he went on as if she hadn't said it.

"Kate," he said, "let me fill you in on some news I've gotten this morning before you start."

"Sure."

"I've already talked to Sergeant Maroney, who's up in Barton. He talked to a couple of people who work for Claude Moreau last night and another first thing this morning. According to all of them, Joe Reader was there as usual on Saturday. He helped with the milking both in the morning and the evening."

"So, he was never here on Saturday."

"That's right. This came from three people, interviewed separately, and Moreau said the same thing. We already knew that Reader didn't write that note, and now it looks pretty certain that he was not the killer. That doesn't mean he wasn't involved, though."

"Right. Although the others could have used his name on that note without his knowledge."

"True. And by 'the others', you mean…"

"Walt Lamb, Carol Tetrault, Alan Brooks, and possibly Billy Tourville."

"'Possibly?' It sounds like you don't think Billy was in on it."

"Well, everything I have heard so far tells me that Billy really looked up to Rory. I don't know much about Alan Brooks, except that he apparently does things for Walt; things like drug deals and B&Es. As for Walt and Carol Tetrault, they both had strong motives; Billy didn't seem to have any motive."

"But they met at Billy's apartment, and that's where the envelope and note paper came from."

"Right," Kate said. "But I think—and this is just a theory at this point—that they may have duped Billy into helping them set it up. He might never have known what they were planning."

"That's an interesting theory. It certainly fits with what we know about Billy; he's definitely a 'follower,' not a leader."

"And Walt Lamb is a leader. That's the strongest impression I came away with; that group of people are Walt Lamb's followers, his crew."

The chief nodded his head and said, "I think that's right, Kate. Now we have to put together what we know and figure out how this went down. Why don't you tell me all about last night and everything you learned."

About forty-five minutes later, Officer Stan Larose walked into the police station in his street clothes.

"Hey, Ginny," he said nervously. "Do you know what this is about?"

"No, I don't, Stan; the chief just told me to call you in. Like I told you when I called, he just said it's still your day off, but he needs to talk to you."

"Okay. Who's in there with him?"

"That Stone woman."

He frowned and looked puzzled.

"Well, tell him I'm here and waiting."

Ginny buzzed the chief and told him.

"He says go right in, Stan."

"Uh, is she leaving?"

"He just said go right in."

Larose walked over to the chief's office and opened the door. Kate Stone was sitting in a chair across from the chief, a notebook and pen on her lap, and an empty chair sat next to her.

"Sit down, Stan," the chief said.

He sat down in the empty chair, looking suspiciously at the woman next to him.

"What's this about, Chief?" he asked. "I don't mind being called in on my day off, if it's important, but..."

"It's important, Stan. First thing, I'm sure you know by now that Ms. Stone is helping us with the murder investigation."

"Uh, yeah."

"Well, in the course of this meeting, you are to answer her questions as if they were mine. Do you have your cell phone on you?"

"Yeah, sure I do."

"Put it on the desk, please."

The puzzled officer took his phone out and placed it in front of him on the desk.

"Now tell me, Stan," the chief said. "Did you call Walter Lamb yesterday?"

Stan Larose was starting to feel like the walls were closing in, and his face showed it.

"Uh, I talked to him yesterday, yeah, but it was him that called me."

"Have you talked to him this morning?"

"No."

"Show me."

He turned on his cell phone, went to his phone log, and slid the phone over to the chief. He pulled out a handkerchief and wiped his brow.

"That number you see this morning; that was my mom."

"The New Hampshire number?"

"Yeah, that's her. Walt's number shows up yesterday."

"I see it. Now, Stan, let me explain a couple things. Ms. Stone and I are interviewing you right now as part of the investigation into the murder of Rory Fremantle. You can have a lawyer present if you wish.”

“But I didn’t... Look, Chief, you know that Walt’s a friend of mine...”

“I know that, Stan. He is also now our number one suspect in the murder. Now, do you want a lawyer?”

“No, no. I’m sorry, Chief. I never thought he would do anything like that. I’ll tell you anything you want to know.”

“Two questions first, Officer Larose,” Kate said. “Did you tell Walt Lamb about Joe Reader fleeing the country?”

“Yes, I did.”

“Did you tell him that I’m assisting in the investigation?”

“Uh, no. I didn’t know that until later.”

“You didn’t try to contact him after you found out?” the chief asked.

“No. Like I said, I had no idea Walt would be involved in that. He’s had a lot of dealings with Joe Reader, so I told him about that, but that’s all.”

Kate and the chief exchanged a look—a look of relief, perhaps tempered by suspicion.

“Here’s what we’re looking at, Stan,” the chief said. “We believe that a group of people, led by Walt Lamb, conspired to murder Rory Fremantle. You have been involved in the investigation, so you know some of what happened. A note was slipped to Rory on Saturday afternoon; a note that asked him to meet the writer at the bend in the brook. After the incident in which Rory jumped into the brook to save a little girl, he was carried downstream and was then hit with a blunt object, presumably as he tried to get out to safety.

“We know that Joe Reader did not write that note, although his name was used. We believe that the note—referring to Christy Plouffe and allegedly signed by Joe Reader—was deliberately designed to lure him to his murder. We still have not reconstructed exactly how it happened, but we know that Walt Lamb and Carol Tetrault both had strong motives. Alan Brooks and Billy Tourville may also have been involved in the plan, as well as Joe Reader.

"Now, I want you to tell us everything you know about Walt Lamb and his associates. I'm sure I do not need to remind you of the seriousness of your position."

34

K ate and Chief Bridger watched the chastened Officer Larose walk out of the office when they had finished.

"Can we trust him, Les?" Kate asked, when he had left and closed the door.

"I am almost certain we can, Kate. His career means a lot to him, and he knows full well that I could have suspended him—maybe even fired him. I also think that, while he may have a somewhat casual attitude towards some types of petty crime, he would never condone murder or shelter anyone, including Walt, involved in a murder."

"Well, everything he's told us about Walt Lamb and his cronies fits right in with what I found out. Walt plays the pipe, and the others dance to his tune. Les, what do you think about the way he described Alan Brooks and Billy Tourville?"

"That was interesting, wasn't it? He said that Brooks is a 'loose cannon', that he's fearless and reckless and ruthless and will do anything Walt wants him to do, sometimes just for the thrill of it, while Billy is cautious and reluctant and has to be persuaded."

"Les, this is pure speculation, but do you think maybe Lamb has something he's holding over Billy? I keep getting the feeling, based on what people tell me, that Billy doesn't really want to be involved in any of Lamb's criminal activities, but he seems to be under some kind of compulsion. Maybe it's just because he needs the money—that's what I got from his girlfriend—but maybe there's something else."

The intercom buzzed.

"Yes, Ginny?"

"I've got the handwriting analyst on the phone for you, Chief, and the Medical Examiner called while you were busy and wants you to call her back."

"Okay, thanks, Ginny."

He picked up the phone.

"Chief Bridger here."

As he listened, a broad smile lit up his face.

"That's great; send me your official analysis for the file. Thanks!"

"Good news, Les?"

"Carol Tetrault not only delivered that note; she wrote it."

"Alright! That makes her guilty, even if she wasn't the one who struck the blow, doesn't it?"

"Guilty of conspiracy to commit murder and accessory to murder. Kate, let me call the M.E. right now."

"Sure."

It was a brief conversation, and just what the chief had suspected; the piece of pipe could absolutely have been the murder weapon, but there was no way to prove it. The rushing water had scoured it clean of any forensic evidence.

The chief sat back in his chair and twiddled his thumbs while he glanced up at the clock on the wall.

"I want to get Carol Tetrault behind bars today, Kate," the chief said, "but I have to do a couple of things first. I need to talk to Ray Everett first; if we can confirm when Walt Lamb and Peter Plouffe were at his store, that will go a long way toward showing us how this went down. Then I want to go back to the crime scene again."

"So do I," she replied. "I'm going out to Sunrise Farm to visit my mare, then I'll take one of Linda's horses out and ride out to the scene. Do you want to meet me there? About twelve-thirty?"

"That sounds good. I'm calling in both my sergeants for a meeting this afternoon at three-thirty. Jim Maroney will be back from Barton by then. We're going to go over everything we've got and decide what to do."

"Do you want me at the meeting, too, Les?"

"Yes, I do. Don't worry about what the sergeants think; they'll get used to it."

Dolly was looking healthy and happy and was pleased to see her mistress again. Kate spent some time with her horse while Linda Norman saddled Brutus.

Linda did not know that Kate was working with the police, but she had heard people talk.

"You're spending a lot of time with Chief Bridger, aren't you, Kate?"

Kate laughed.

"I guess I am. Are people gossiping about us?"

"Of course they are, that's what people do. I don't think many people actually believe you're having an affair with the Chief, though. If they believe you're a rich, scheming seductress, they'll have more appropriate targets in mind for you."

"'Targets'? Does that mean any man I show an interest in is a target?"

"Of course! You're the rich bitch from Connecticut, whose sole mission in life is to wreck marriages and leave broken hearts all across the valley!"

"Wow! If only I were that powerful!"

As Kate was about to mount the black gelding, Linda asked, "Do they think Billy Tourville did it?"

"Well, Linda, he has to be a suspect, don't you think?"

"Yeah, sure, I guess. But I hope those high-and-mighty Fremantles don't get their way and ruin him. I mean, if he didn't do it, and I don't believe he could have, they're still trying to blackball him."

"What do you mean, Linda?"

"That old bitch, Doris, has called me and every other horse owner, trainer, breeder, etc., and told everyone that Billy is a pervert and probably a criminal and no one should hire him. I'm hearing this from all over Vermont and New Hampshire."

"That's awful. Will people pay attention? Will they do what she says?"

"A lot of them will."

"What about you?"

"Not me! I don't care what those people think!"

"Do you have any work, Linda? Would you hire Billy?"

"Sure I would; the guy is great with horses. I could use him twenty hours a week right now—maybe more."

"Well, listen. I can't tell you everything I know, Linda, but I believe it will all become clear in a few days. Meanwhile, I think Billy is in a low place right now and he could really use a lifeline. Why don't you call him and offer him a job?"

Kate was sitting atop Brutus and slowly moving along the trail while staring across Wandering Brook when the chief's cruiser pulled up and parked. He got out of the driver's seat and walked around toward her, a brown paper bag in one hand and two bottles of water in the other.

"I brought us a couple of sandwiches, Kate."

"Oh, thanks, Les. I forgot all about lunch. Let's sit down at one of the picnic tables by the bend. Then I want to walk back down from there to where the body was found."

They were not far from the bend of the brook, where the huge concrete slab still stood at an awkward angle, water flowing around it on both sides. The two picnic tables were far enough from the bank that they were not endangered by the erosion that had resulted from the flood, so Kate and the chief sat down at one of the tables to eat their sandwiches. Kate was looking all around while she ate, trying to get a better understanding of what had transpired on that tragic Saturday.

Chief Bridger was doing the same thing. When he had finished half of his sandwich, he said, "Listen, Kate, let's talk this through. If we accept that Rory was lured here to the brook by that note—and we really have nothing else—then the killer or killers had to be waiting for him."

"Right. There's plenty of cover, in spots. There are clumps of trees and bushes all along the east side of the trail."

"But the kids came along. They wouldn't have expected that, so they would have taken cover and waited to see if they would have an opportunity."

Kate glanced along the trail, first one way and then the other.

"There's no cover to the south, just open fields for quite a distance. So they must have been hiding somewhere along there." She pointed towards the line of trees along the east side of the trail. "They would have been waiting there for Rory to come along, and they would have stayed hidden while the kids were here.

"Rory came along the trail from the Fremantle property and stopped here when he saw the kids. Whoever was waiting saw what happened—saw Rory jump in and saw the two boys run along the trail downstream."

"Right. Let's walk down toward where he pushed the girl to safety."

They walked north, finishing their sandwiches as they went. The mild-mannered Brutus walked along happily beside Kate.

"You know, Les," Kate said as they rounded a bend in the trail and approached the ledge where the two brothers had pulled their sister out of the brook. "It's looking less likely that Rory was hit on the western side of the trail. It makes sense only if the killer walked straight from the junkyard to the brook with that piece of pipe. But nobody could have crossed the brook anywhere along here that day, and besides, they were expecting to meet Rory somewhere along the trail, on this side."

"Right. If this was planned and executed the way we think it was, they were waiting for him on this side. I talked to Ray Everett, and he confirmed that Walt and Peter were at the store at three-thirty. So, if they brought the weapon with them, they parked somewhere along the road—plenty of places they could have parked—then walked across the meadow and waited for Rory."

They stopped, and Kate pointed toward the bushes along the trail.

"These bushes here, Les..."

"Raspberries, still green. Lots of raspberries along here."

"The killer—or killers—could have easily hidden behind the bushes and seen everything that happened. Then they could have gone downstream, staying behind this line of bushes. One of the boys rode off on his bike, and the other was taking care of his sister, so it isn't surprising that they wouldn't have noticed anyone. Once the killers got around the next bend, they could have run along the trail without worrying about being seen. Let's walk farther down."

It was a longer walk to where the body was found—about a quarter mile. The distance between the horse trail and the brook varied from only about ten feet to nearly a hundred. For most of this stretch, the bank on this side—the eastern side—was high enough to hold the flood, but there were a few places where the water had reached almost to the trail itself.

"What would they have thought, Les?" Kate asked as they approached the murder scene. "Did they expect to find him already dead?"

"It seems likely, don't you think? The brook was still at its highest flood stage, or nearly. I've heard that Rory was a strong swimmer, but still, you would think it would be surprising for him to survive in those waters."

They reached the spot where the body had been found. Standing at that spot and looking across the brook to the west, it was easy to see how high the water had been that day. The bank on the west side clearly showed where the high mark had been.

The two of them stood silently for a minute or so, both trying to envision what the same view would have shown them when the flood was at its highest. Then Kate pointed to the spot directly across from where they were standing.

"That spot right there, Les; that's where somebody has stood with a fishing rod."

"Right. There's a trail—not very wide or very much used, but plain to see—and it leads straight over that ridge. On the other side of the ridge is the 'machinery graveyard' and the farm road that leads back to the Plouffe house and barnyard."

"So, if the killer had walked straight to the brook with that piece of pipe, and if Rory had been trying to scramble up the bank on that side..."

"Then the attack could have taken place right there. But then the body would have to have been washed back across to this side."

"The M.E. said that he would have died instantly from that blow, didn't she?"

"Yes, she did."

Kate slowly shook her head back and forth.

"I just don't see it, Les. We can't know for certain what the current was like that day, but it just doesn't seem possible that the body would have been pushed across without going much farther downstream. Besides, it doesn't fit everything else we know. I'm sorry that I mentioned it as a possibility."

"Don't be sorry, Kate; we have to look at every possibility and then eliminate the ones that don't fit. Look, Kate..."

He pointed at a stretch of the western bank south of the fishing spot.

"You see how the bank curves there, pushing out a bit?"

"Yes, I noticed that."

"Well, like you said, it's impossible to know for certain—until the next flood, anyway—but it looks like the bank might have pushed the flow out this way at that point. So, if Rory was still alive..."

"The current could have pushed him right towards this side."

"And whoever was waiting for him would have seen him struggling to get out here, where the brook was much shallower, and hit him over the head while he was trying to get to his feet."

"That's a theory that works, Les, and it fits in with our theory of why Rory was here and how he got here."

Chief Bridger turned around and gazed across the meadow. A little used dirt track led across towards the line of trees a couple hundred yards away that lined Tower Road. It was that track that the emergency vehicles had used to reach the brook before the trail from Sunrise Farm had been opened for motorized vehicles.

"They could have parked right over there, along Tower Road, and come across the meadow. After it was over, they threw the pipe in the brook and walked, or ran, right back to where they parked."

"That looks logical, and likely. Les, we've been saying 'they,' rather than 'he.' We know that Walter Lamb and Peter Plouffe were at the hardware store at three-thirty. It seems like—up to now—no one has wanted to consider Peter as a likely suspect. But we have to, don't we?"

The chief looked very sad as he said, "Yes, we do."

35

Ben Fremantle walked into the Tiff-Toff Shoppe just as a customer was leaving. He held the door for the portly middle-aged woman who was exiting with a well-wrapped package.

"Can you manage that alright, Mrs. Prentice?" Tiffany called out, then to Ben she said, "Honey, can you give Mrs. Prentice a hand?"

"Sure. Is this your car right here, ma'am?"

"Oh, thank you; such a gentleman. Yes, it's the Lexus."

Ben took the package from her and waited for her to open the trunk of her car then made sure the package was securely placed where it was safe from harm. She thanked him again and waved goodbye to Tiffany, who was standing in the doorway.

When the happy customer had driven off, Ben and Tiffany went back into the store together.

"I'm sure she didn't really need help, Tiff; it wasn't very heavy."

"I know, but when somebody spends eighteen hundred on an antique tea service, I give them all the help they want, whether they need it or not."

"Sure, I get it. Sorry I couldn't get away for lunch, hon—important meeting."

"No problem, I had some soup from the cafe. So, what was your mom upset about?"

"Well, it's about Robert. He's in a real funk, apparently. He feels that he's let the family down somehow, but he won't say how or why or when. Says he can't talk about it until 'it's over.'"

"Until what's over?"

"I don't know, and Mom doesn't know. It's probably something to do with the murder; Chief Bridger had Robert in to question him again. But I'm sure nobody thinks Robert had anything to do with it."

"Of course not. Honey, do you think they're getting close to an arrest?"

"I hope so. Do you remember Joe Reader? I think I told you about him."

"I don't remember."

"He was the hired hand who worked at the Plouffe farm. He's been gone from town for six years or so, but apparently he's still in touch with some of the low life in the valley, including Billy Tourville. I'm not sure what the connection with Rory is, but Joe Reader is considered a suspect in the murder and he's now fled to Canada; stole his boss's pickup truck and drove across the border."

"So they're after this guy for the murder? And he's a friend of Billy's? I knew that creep had something to do with it!"

"Well, I can't say for sure."

"Chief Bridger should tell you what's going on, Ben. There's no reason our family should be kept in the dark; we need to know what's going on!"

Kate walked into the police station at three-thirty. Ginny gave her a big smile and said, "They're all in the conference room, Ms. Stone; go right in!"

"Thanks, Ginny!"

Chief Bridger and the two sergeants were sitting at the big, oval table, all with coffees in front of them. Sergeant Meadows gave Kate a smile when she walked in; Maroney wore a frown.

"Have a seat, Kate," the chief said, "and pour yourself a coffee. I'll fill you in on what I've got arranged."

After Kate had seated herself, the chief began.

"First, I'll go over what we believe was the course of events that led to the victim's death. We believe that this was a conspiracy to commit murder; a conspiracy to lure Rory Fremantle to the horse trail by the brook, where one or more people were waiting to attack him. The plan was almost certainly hatched by Walter Lamb, who has openly stated that he had a grudge against the victim. Lamb is the de facto leader of a group of small-time criminals who operate all over the valley. His cronies include Alan Brooks, who has a criminal record, Billy Tourville, and Carol Tetrault, who is a former girlfriend of the victim.

"There is no obvious motive for Tourville, and it is possible that he was not directly involved, but the others had motive, opportunity, and the means to commit the murder."

"What about Joe Reader?" Sergeant Maroney asked. "Shouldn't he be included in this group of suspects?"

"Well, yes, he was certainly involved with the others in drug dealing and may very well have been involved in planning the murder, but we know that he was in Barton on Saturday and could not have committed the act. There is one other person, though, that we have to include as a suspect. Peter Plouffe was with Walter Lamb that afternoon. Until we have evidence to prove otherwise, we have to consider the possibility that Peter was with him when the murder was committed."

"Chief," Sergeant Meadows asked, "we know about all of these people—they have been on our radar as petty criminals for years—but what exactly did Walt Lamb have against Rory Fremantle? What was the grudge?"

The chief looked at Kate, and she responded.

"They were competitors," she said. "Rory was involved in drug trafficking since his college days, sometimes in direct competition with Walt Lamb. At some point, Rory apparently hijacked a deal that Lamb had set up, and Lamb claims that it cost him ten thousand dollars."

Both sergeants looked a little stunned.

"Do you know this for sure?" Maroney asked. "I mean everyone knows Rory was a rake, but you're saying he was a drug dealer at a pretty high level. You're talking about a man from the oldest and richest family in the valley."

"I know, Sergeant. Look, I'm very new here, but one thing I have learned already is that there are two levels of community here in Merryfield, or maybe I should say in the valley. The people at the top—the respectable people—believe that the Fremantles are above suspicion, that they are perfect law-abiding citizens. But on the lower level, everybody seems to know what Rory was doing. As for how I know this—Walt Lamb told me himself. I can't vouch for the truth of what he told me, but it doesn't really matter. What matters is what Walt Lamb believed, and his exact words were 'he got what was coming to him'."

"He told you?" Meadows asked.

"Yes. I went to Bucky's Tavern last night, in disguise. I talked quite a bit with Carol Tetrault and with Walt. He was trying to pick me up, so he did a lot of bragging. I did not talk to Billy or to Alan Brooks. There was another woman there—Daisy Millette—who is seeing Billy Tourville, and she told me and my friend, when we gave her a ride home, that Billy would not have done anything to hurt Rory, but that he feels compelled to keep hanging out with Lamb and his cronies because he just lost his job and he needs the money."

Both sergeants looked at the chief, who grinned and nodded.

"Ms. Stone has uncovered a lot of information for us, at no small risk. Now, I'm going to go through this in as much detail as I can, or as much as we have."

Chief Bridger proceeded to outline what happened leading up to the murder and how he and Kate believed it took place.

"Sometime earlier—maybe that day or maybe in the days just passed—Lamb, and possibly Peter Plouffe as well, had gone to the junkyard on the Plouffe property and picked up a heavy piece of rusted pipe. Lamb must have realized that a weapon like that could be simply thrown into the brook afterwards and any forensic evidence would be erased by the water. On that Saturday afternoon, Lamb and Peter drove to the hardware store; they were there at three-thirty. We believe that, after leaving the store, they drove to a spot along Tower Road, parked the truck, and walked across the meadow to the brook, where they waited for Rory.

"We know what happened after that. The killers must have seen the rescue of the Cote girl then headed north along the trail to see what would happen. When they saw Rory struggling to get out of the water, one of them struck him over the head with the pipe then threw it into the brook. They made their escape across the meadow and back to Lamb's truck."

"So you think it was Lamb and Peter Plouffe?" Maroney asked.

Chief Bridger shook his head sadly.

"I hate to think Peter had anything to do with it, but..."

"I think," Kate said, "just from what I know about these people, that Walt Lamb would have wanted Alan Brooks with him. We don't have any evidence to that effect, but it seems likely that Lamb would have wanted someone with him he could rely on. Brooks has been described to us as 'ruthless' and as someone who would do whatever Lamb wanted him to do. He wouldn't have been expecting it to be that easy to kill Rory, so wouldn't he have had an accomplice with him? Someone capable and ruthless?"

"That wouldn't have been Peter," Meadows said. "He's a big, strong boy, but no one would describe him as either capable—not when it came to killing someone—or ruthless. I just can't believe Peter was in on it."

"Maybe they picked up Brooks somewhere," Maroney offered, "and maybe they left Peter in the truck."

"That's a possibility," the chief said. "Clearly, we've got to get Peter alone and try to get the truth out of him."

"What about Billy Tourville, boss?" Meadows asked. "He may not have been the killer, but he must know a lot about the others, and he's done nothing but lie to us from day one. We've got to get the truth out of him, too."

The intercom buzzed, and Ginny's voice said, "Officer Larose is on the phone for you, Chief; says it's important."

"Thanks, Ginny."

The chief picked up the phone and said, "Go ahead, Stan."

The chief listened quietly and a little smile grew broader as he listened. He picked up a pen and scribbled something, then, after a couple of minutes, he said "Thanks, Stan," and hung up.

The two sergeants looked puzzled, and Chief Bridger quickly explained.

"That was Stan Larose, as you heard..."

"He's off-duty today, isn't he?" Meadows asked.

"He is, officially, and he wouldn't have been able to arrange this otherwise. He is meeting Walter Lamb and Alan Brooks at seven-thirty at a spot in the woods behind the high school athletic fields. Jim, do you know where that is?"

"Uh, sure I do," Sergeant Maroney answered. "When I was in school, that's where we'd go to have a smoke."

The chief laughed.

"Things haven't changed much; I was in that school ten years before you were and that's where we would go back then. Well, Jim, you are going to go out there with two officers and find yourselves a place to hide. You don't necessarily have to be close enough to hear what they're saying, because Stan will be wearing a wire. He will be able to signal you when to close in, and you will then arrest both of them on suspicion of murder. You will take them straight to the lockup in Petersford; I don't want them here.

"Meanwhile, Carl, you will pick up Billy Tourville again and bring him back here. Make sure he gets a chance to call his lawyer; he's going to need him. Before you start interrogating him, tell him that Lamb and Brooks have already been arrested for murder. If that doesn't loosen his tongue, I don't know what will."

"What about Carol Tetrault?" Maroney asked.

"She's working a banquet out at the Tranmere tonight. She should be done at ten-thirty, and I have alerted the manager there to let us know if she gets out early for any reason. By that time, one of us will be available to pick her up.

"I will be out at the Plouffe farm. I've spoken to Reggie, and he will call me as soon as Lamb has left to meet Stan Larose. I'm going to sit down with Peter Plouffe and try to get him to talk. We think we know how this all went down, but we need Peter to prove it."

Kate was smiling as she listened to all of this.

"Les," she said, "I'm so glad Officer Larose came through. I wasn't entirely convinced that he would."

"I wouldn't have been convinced either," Sergeant Maroney said. "How did you get him to do that, Chief?"

"Well, I really didn't give him any choice."

Kate and the chief chatted as they walked to her car.

"I'm glad your sergeants appreciated what I did, Les," she said. "I wasn't sure how they would respond."

"Well, I wasn't entirely sure myself, but they're both good men. They both understood that getting any information out of that crowd was virtually impossible without somebody 'under cover,' and it had to be someone nobody knew. Like Jim said, 'That was good work and we're proud to have you helping us out.' At this point, it's down to straight police work, which you can't be a part of, but we might never have gotten to this point without your help. Thanks, Kate."

"You're very welcome, Les. You know, I've really enjoyed this; it makes me wish I were a real detective. Well, I've got to get home and get some supper. Let me know how things turn out."

"I certainly will, Kate."

She got into her Volvo, backed out onto the street, and headed off towards Merryfield and home.

Seconds later, a car parked across the street pulled out and followed right behind her.

"Yeah, it could be her, alright," the driver said. "The figure looks familiar; it's just the hair."

"Like I told you, Al, if they think I can't tell when someone's wearing a wig... Yeah, that's 'Kitty;' I'm sure of it."

36

Kate hadn't decided what to do about supper, but, as she drove through Merryfield, she saw an open parking spot near the café and decided to stop there.

The car following her continued along the street before turning a corner and stopping.

"If she's eating at the café, she'll be there for an hour, probably," the woman said, "and I've got to be out at the 'Tran' in twenty minutes."

The man cursed and said, "Yeah, and I've got to meet Walt as soon as he's done milking. No time to deal with her right now."

"Walt will know what to do with her—and Bitsy, too. 'Friend from college,' my ass!"

Bitsy Dufresne was in a splendid mood and delighted to see her friend again. She had several other customers at the counter, so they couldn't really talk about last night, but the shared experience was like a backdrop that no one else could see.

A stuffed pork loin with mustard cream sauce was the special Kate ordered, and it was perfect. The roasted vegetables and a side salad made it a splendid meal.

Kate was in the happiest mood she had been in since the tragic event of the previous weekend, and she talked merrily with several other customers, some of whom she had met and some she hadn't, until now.

"Hey, Kate," Bitsy asked her at one point, "I saw you talking with Ray Everett this morning. Was he trying to get you to go on the trip to Fenway?"

"Yes, he was. Are you going, Bitsy?"

"I don't usually go, but I might think about it if you're going."

"It's a lot of fun, Ms. Stone," said Walt Drake, who was sitting on her right. "A bunch of Red Sox fans from Vermont getting together for a game at Fenway Park; it doesn't get much better than that. You should come along!"

"Well, what if I'm not a Sox fan? Will I be tolerated?"

He laughed.

"Well, since you're from Connecticut, I'm guessing you like the Yankees, which makes it kind of problematic, but you won't be the only one. You should sit with Linda Norman; she loves the Yankees, and she don't take no guff from anyone!"

"Oh, that sounds fun; I like Linda a lot!"

"Walt," said Bitsy, "you'd better tell her about the bus ride before she decides—especially the ride back!"

The banker started chuckling while he had a mouthful of food, which was a mistake, but he recovered quickly.

"I'm sure you know, Ms. Stone, that they sell beer at the game..."

"Yes, of course. So, I'm guessing the ride back is a little livelier than the ride down."

"You might say that!"

When Mr. Drake had left, Bitsy explained in more detail.

"Remember I told you that Ray Everett goes to Bucky's every couple weeks and gets plastered?"

"Yes, I remember."

"Well, apparently Ray only drinks on payday, which is every other Thursday, and when he goes to a ball game. The bus rides back from Fenway are notorious, mostly because of Ray and a couple other guys. Not that there's ever any actual fighting, just a lot of loud arguing. Once Ray gets a couple beers in him, he won't stop talking sports and challenging everybody's opinion about anything. But Linda Norman keeps him in line. I heard that one time she actually pinned him in his seat and held him down until he agreed to stop."

"Oh, that's funny; I can see her doing that!"

Attorney Clare Sharp arrived at the police station in Wayford at seven o'clock and was granted a few minutes alone with his client before the interrogation began. When they were ready, Sergeant Meadows, along with Officer Bascomb, entered the conference room and sat down opposite Billy Tourville and his attorney.

"Billy," the sergeant said, "Officer Bascomb is going to start the tape recorder in a minute. I just wanted to tell you first that we have just arrested Walter Lamb and Alan Brooks on suspicion of first-degree murder in the death of Rory Fremantle."

Billy and his lawyer looked at each other; the lawyer nodded and Billy turned to look at the Sergeant.

"I had nothing to do with it," he said.

Meadows gestured to Bascomb, who pressed the button to begin recording. When each person in the room had identified themselves for the recording, the sergeant began.

"Mr. Tourville, on Thursday last, June sixth, you met Joe Reader at your apartment. He was accompanied by a man and a woman. You previously told us that you did not know who the man and the woman were. In light of the seriousness of the charges against Lamb and Brooks, I ask you again who those two people were; perhaps your memory has improved."

"Yeah, well, I was probably stoned, you know. Now that I think about it, I guess it was Al and Carol. I mean, those guys hang out together, so it probably was them."

"By 'Al and Carol,' are you referring to Alan Brooks and Carol Tetrault?"

"Yes."

"What was the purpose of this get-together? What did you talk about?"

"There wasn't no purpose. Joe has been a friend of mine for years, and those guys, too. He came to town to visit."

"You didn't talk about Rory Fremantle?"

"Rory? No, why would we?"

"What did you talk about?"

"I don't remember. We were just bullshitting, you know, like old friends do."

"You didn't plan anything that night? You didn't make a plan to lure Rory Fremantle to a place where you could ambush him and kill him?"

"No, of course not! Rory was a friend of mine; he was good to me. I would never have done that."

"But what about the others? Did they regard Rory the same way you did?"

Billy looked sad and hesitated before he answered.

"I don't... I mean, I can't say. I can't speak for them."

"Alright. Did any of them—that is, Joe Reader, Carol Tetrault, and Alan Brooks—did any of them take anything with them when they left your place?"

"No, why would they? I mean, like what?"

"We believe that one of them grabbed an envelope and some note paper from the top of your bureau. Is that possible?"

"Oh, well sure. But that's no big deal, is it? I think Carol asked if she could grab some paper. Why not?"

"Okay. Now, we know that the three of them met Walter Lamb at Bucky's Tavern shortly after leaving your place. But you didn't go with them. Was there a reason?"

"A reason for what?"

"A reason you didn't go to Bucky's with them. You don't miss many nights at Bucky's, but you didn't go with them that night. Why?"

"What do you mean, 'Why?'; I don't go out drinking every night. I shouldn't have to explain not going out. I work in the morning, you know—at least, I used to."

"Okay. You told us, previously, that Joe Reader did not stay the night, that he had to drive back to Barton early in the morning. But we know that Reader was in town the next night, Friday night. In fact, you were seen sitting with him at Bucky's on Friday night."

"Oh, well, I must have just got the two nights confused. Yeah, I guess it was Friday night he said he had to get back."

"Okay. Billy, do you remember when Chief Bridger found that note in Rory's shirt pocket? At the barn?"

"Yeah, sure."

"Did Rory show you that note when he came to the barn that day?"

"No."

"Did you ever see that note before Chief Bridger pulled it out of Rory's shirt?"

"No. I didn't see it after, either. He wouldn't let me see it. I ain't never seen it."

"Well, that note was what lured Rory to ride to the brook, where someone was waiting to ambush him. Do you think your friends wrote that note and hatched a plan to kill Rory Fremantle?"

Before he could even think of answering, Billy's attorney leaned over and said, "You don't have to answer that."

Chief Bridger pulled into the yard at the Plouffe farm a little after seven. He already knew that Walt Lamb had left in his truck right after milking; Reggie Plouffe had called to tell him, as they had planned.

The Plouffe family were still sitting at the table. The supper dishes had been cleared, but Reggie, Peter, Christy, and Matty each had a dessert plate in front of them, covered in the remnants of cherry pie. When the chief walked in the open door, Christy got right up to fetch another plate while the others greeted him.

"Just in time for dessert, Les; just like Ma used to say whenever you stopped in!"

"Well, I always knew where to get the best dessert, and my timing was pretty good, I guess."

"Here you go, Chief," Christy said as she served him a thick slice of warm pie. "We're having tea, but I can make you a cup of coffee if you'd like..."

"Oh, thanks, Christy, but I think tea would be fine."

There was whipped cream for the pie, of course, and the chief dug right in while the others finished theirs.

"Nice weather since the storm, Les," Reggie said. "Looks like most folks survived it pretty well."

"I guess. Seems like folks were prepared this time, and it could have been a lot worse. I haven't heard any damage estimates yet, though. It's going to cost the town of Merryfield a pretty penny to repair that slab at the bend, of course. Have you seen how it looks?"

"Oh, yes, we've been there and seen it. Never underestimate the power of water, my old man used to say."

"Can I ask you a question, Chief?" Peter Plouffe asked.

"Well, Peter," the chief answered, "I've actually come here to ask you some questions, but sure you can."

"Wait a minute, please, Chief," Christy said, then, to her boy she said, "Matty, I think that show you like is coming on in a couple minutes; you want to watch it while we talk?"

The boy silently nodded, and Christy led him into the living room, turned on the TV, and found the right channel for him then came back to the kitchen.

"What would you like to ask me, Peter?" the Chief asked when Christy was seated again.

"Who killed Rory?"

No one had expected that, and both Christy and her dad looked a little shocked.

"Well, Peter," the chief answered, slowly, "I guess it might as well come out now." He looked up at the clock on the wall and said, "Sometime in the next few minutes, my officers are going to arrest Walter Lamb and Alan Brooks on suspicion of murder. We think they killed him."

Peter dropped his head and said nothing, just looked down at the table. Christy put her arm around her brother's shoulders, and Reggie wiped his brow with a handkerchief, looking very sad.

"Now, I have to tell you, Peter," the chief continued, "that because you were with Walt practically the whole day, we have to consider you as a possible suspect until we can prove otherwise, and, before I go any further, I have to tell you that you are entitled to have a lawyer with you while I question you. Do you understand?"

Peter slowly shook his head back and forth and said, "I don't need no lawyer. Just ask me what you want to."

Reggie Plouffe said, "Peter's nineteen, Les, and he can make up his own mind. I already told him I could call a lawyer, but he said 'No,' so go ahead."

"Alright. Peter, you were with Walt Lamb when he drove to the hardware store on Saturday afternoon, weren't you?"

"Yeah, I was. We was mending fences, and he said he needed something at the store, so we drove there. I don't remember what it was we needed."

"It doesn't matter. You were there about three-thirty, weren't you?"

"Yes. We was only there a few minutes, then we went to pick up Al."

"Al? Do you mean Alan Brooks?"

"Yeah, that's him."

"Where did you go after you picked him up?"

"We parked the truck on Tower Road, over by the horse farm. Walt called somebody on his cell phone..."

"He called someone? Do you know who?"

"No, but I heard her voice. It was a woman. I didn't hear what she said, but it was only a few words, then Walt hung up. Then he told me to hand him a piece of pipe that was in the back."

"He told you to hand him the pipe?"

"Yeah. I was in the back. When we picked up Al, I got in the back of the truck, 'cause there's not much room and I hate sitting beside Al anyway. Then Walt told me to wait for them, and they walked across the field."

"That's the field between Tower Road and the brook, right?"

"Yeah, that's it. They was gone ten or maybe fifteen minutes, then they came back."

"Did they have the pipe with them when they came back?"

"No."

The chief paused for a moment to think. He pulled a handkerchief out of a pocket and wiped his forehead before continuing.

"Okay. What we think happened, Peter, is that somebody else—somebody working with Walt and Al—had a note delivered to Rory asking him to meet them by the brook, and those two waited for him and then they killed him when he was trying to get out of the brook. We think that one of the two—we don't know which—used a piece of pipe that they picked up out where all that old machinery is..."

"Walt said he needed it for something. He picked it up one day last week."

"Was that the same piece of pipe that you handed to him?"

"Yeah, it was."

"Well, I think one of them used it to kill Rory. Does that surprise you, Peter?"

"No. I know Walt didn't like Rory. Walt's smart and he's good to me, but he didn't like Rory. I hope it was Al, though. I hate that guy; he's mean and stupid. He treats me like I'm an idiot."

"We don't know yet which one of them did it, but it doesn't matter to the law. The people who helped plan it are just as guilty as the one who killed him."

Peter looked really sad and a little scared.

"Does that mean I'm guilty, too, 'cause I handed him the pipe?"

Christy reached over and took her brother's hand. She looked scared, too.

"No, Peter," the chief replied. "You didn't know what they were going to do, and you didn't have any reason not to hand it to him. But you did do something wrong by not telling us—meaning the police—about this before. Why didn't you tell us?"

"Walt told me not to. He said I should only say what he told me to say and that I would be a snitch and a rat if I said anything more to the cops, and I didn't want to be a rat. Are you going to arrest me now?"

Reggie looked at the chief and said, "Les, please…"

"Don't worry, Reg, I'm not going to arrest Peter. Peter, will you be willing to testify in court? Will you tell a judge and jury what you just told us?"

Peter nodded his head and said, "Yeah, I will."

The chief stood up and said, "I've got to get going. Thanks for helping us out, Peter; it's really important." Then something occurred to him. "One more thing, Peter. You usually wear gloves when you're doing farm work, right?"

"Yeah."

"Were you wearing gloves when you handed Walt that pipe?"

"No. But he was."

Chief Bridger's phone buzzed with an incoming text message from Sergeant Maroney.

37

Sergeant Jim Maroney knew the patch of woods behind the athletic fields like the back of his hand, and it was easy for him to find a place for himself and Officers Watts and Dubrul to hide. He knew exactly where Stan Larose was and had a perfect view of the track Lamb and Brooks had to follow.

He was surprised, though, to see Walter Lamb walking along the path by himself; he had been told to expect that Alan Brooks would be with him. The plan was to arrest the two of them together once they got the signal from Larose. Maybe Brooks was coming along later. But if he wasn't, they had to make another plan to pick him up. He'd better let the chief know.

Stan Larose was nervous. For good or ill, this was the defining moment in his career. He had always enjoyed this sort of double life he had been living—being a working police officer while maintaining a connection with some of the valley's petty criminals. But he had been growing increasingly uncomfortable with Walt Lamb's criminal activities. This was no longer fun, and it was standing in the way of his career. His erstwhile friend had gone far beyond "victimless" crimes, and it was time to turn the table on him.

There he was now, but he was alone. The plan was that both Walt and Al Brooks would meet him; that's what they always did.

Walter Lamb didn't mince words.

"What's going on, Stan? You never told me that Stone woman was helping out the chief? What gives?"

"Well, I'm telling you now! None of us knew until yesterday, and I didn't find out until last night. You know I can't just call you anytime I want; it has to be safe."

"Yeah, I get that, but it could have been big trouble for us. Why is she even involved?"

"Well, the chief seems to think she's really smart. She's some kind of expert on murder mysteries, I guess, and he decided her brains could be a big help to us. Hey, where's Al?"

"She ain't as smart as all that. She's gonna get what's coming to her, and Al's taking care of that right now!"

This wasn't working out at all the way they had planned. They had hoped to get Lamb and Brooks talking and get some incriminating evidence on tape, but if Al Brooks was after Kate Stone, there was no time for that. Officer Larose pressed the little button under his belt and, seconds later, Sergeant Maroney was pinning Walt Lamb's arms behind his back while Watts and Dubrul pointed their weapons at him.

Lamb was quickly overpowered. He didn't cry out or curse; he simply looked his former friend in the eye and quietly said, "You're dead, Larose."

Sergeant Meadows was still in the conference room with Billy Tourville when the urgent call came in from Chief Bridger.

"Carl, Alan Brooks is not with Walt Lamb. We've got to find him ASAP."

"Okay, Chief; I'm finished with Mr. Tourville, so I can head out right now. We know what Brooks drives; we'll find him."

Over the next two minutes, Sergeant Meadows told Billy Tourville he was free to go, with a stern warning not to leave town, and he instructed Ginny, the dispatcher, to put out an APB to all departments, with a description of Alan Brooks and his car. Then he ran to his car, with Officer Bascomb right behind him.

Kate arrived home, feeling well-fed and pleased with herself. What to do now?

There was work to do, of course; a few things she had put off because she had spent so much time playing "detective" over the last few days. But it was Friday night, and there was nothing that couldn't be put off until tomorrow. She decided she'd relax on the front porch for a while, just enjoying the view.

She poured herself a glass of brandy, then she heard the distinctive sound of a car on her gravel driveway.

Chief Bridger was getting ready to leave the Plouffe farm, having reluctantly turned down a second piece of pie.

"Sorry, Christy," he said. "It's a great pie, but I've got to go."

They had a suspected killer on the loose; one who may or may not realize he was being pursued. Then his phone rang.

"Yes, Jim?"

"Al Brooks is after Ms. Stone! We've got Lamb in cuffs, and I'm headed out to her house right now with Officer Larose. Watts and Dubrul are taking Lamb over to the lockup."

"Jesus! Get out there as quick as you can; I'll call in to the station!"

Without time for niceties, he waved a goodbye to the Plouffes and ran out to his car. While backing out, he called in on the car radio.

"Ginny, I want everyone available to head out to the old Andrews house; Al Brooks is after Ms. Stone, and he should be considered armed and dangerous!"

Kate was just about to walk out onto the porch to see who it was when her phone buzzed.

"Les, what's up?"

"Kate, you're in danger. Al Brooks is after you. Lock all your doors and windows, and don't let anyone in. We're on our way!"

She wasted no time in answering, just put the phone down and rushed to the front door—just in time to see the thin redhead open his door and start to get out of the car. She locked the door and threw the deadbolt, then hurried to the kitchen door to lock that one. *What about the windows,* she thought. She knew that not all of them locked properly; it was one of the things she had put off for later.

What to do? Where to hide? How to defend herself, if it came to that?

Somewhere, in the bottom of an unpacked box, was the thirty-eight caliber pistol her husband had given her—much against her wishes—but she had never bothered to practice with it, and it wasn't loaded anyway.

She heard his footsteps on the stairs up to the porch; she had to do something. Well, if she could hear his footsteps, he could probably hear hers. She walked quickly to the cellar door then took off her shoes and opened the cellar door. She slammed the door shut then quickly grabbed her phone from the counter and, shoes in hand, ran around to the main staircase and hurried upstairs.

If he checked the cellar first that would give her some time, but time for what? She could hide in any of the rooms on this floor or go on up to the attic. But she wanted to be near a window that faced the front of the house and the driveway, so she could show the police where she was when they showed up. If they showed up in time.

The front door was right below her, and she heard the rattle as Alan Brooks tried the door. Seconds later, she heard the crash of a window breaking; he wasn't wasting any time. Then she heard his footsteps as he hurried into the kitchen.

Would he try the cellar door? If he went down the cellar stairs, that would buy her a few minutes.

She heard the creak of a door opening then hesitant footsteps on the cellar stairs. At least, she hoped that's what she was hearing. She was in her bedroom, and she moved as quietly as she could to the window. She had a perfect view of the front yard and the driveway, but, as she looked down, she realized she was in the wrong room. The window was beyond the end of the sub roof that covered the porch; if he found her in there, it was too far to safely jump out. The spare bedroom next door was the place to be; she could drop onto the roof of the porch.

Her shoes still in her hand, she walked quietly to the door. Should she risk moving to the other bedroom? What was he doing, and did she have enough time?

Footsteps. He was walking back up the cellar stairs to the kitchen. She opened her bedroom door and walked quickly and quietly to the spare bedroom. The door was open, but when she closed it behind her, it made a noticeable noise.

She locked the door behind her, but she knew it wouldn't resist a powerful push. The four-poster bed was too heavy to push against the door and so was the bureau.

She heard footsteps again; he was coming up the stairs. At the same time, she heard a vehicle on the gravel driveway but no sirens.

No sirens?

She rushed to the window and saw Chris Doran driving in, his pickup filled with firewood.

She tried to lift the window, but it was stuck. It was too late to change her mind and try pushing the bed against the door; Al Brooks was at the top of the stairs. She had to get out.

Then she heard her dial tone; her phone was ringing in the other bedroom. Al Brooks rushed to her bedroom and, finding the door locked, he started crashing his body against the door.

Kate knew that door wouldn't hold for long; she had to get the window open. There was a lamp on the bedside table that looked heavy enough. She grabbed the lamp, backed up a couple of steps and threw the lamp as hard as she could towards the window.

Chris had just stopped when he heard the window smash, followed by Kate's scream.

"Chris! Help me!"

There were shards of glass sticking out of the window frame, so Kate grabbed a pillow off the bed and held it awkwardly against the bottom of the window frame as she climbed over and dropped to the roof just as she heard her attacker crashing through the door behind her.

Chris looked up to see Kate climbing out of the window and dropping to the roof. As he rushed toward the house, he saw that Kate had hurried to the edge of the roof and was standing there, hesitant to jump.

"Kate!" he yelled, as he ran toward the house. "Don't jump! Try to hang from the edge and drop!"

Then somebody else was climbing out the window; a somebody with a hunting knife in his hand.

Kate got down on her hands and knees. She was at the end of the porch roof, and there was a corner post right beneath her. She took one look up at Al Brooks's leering face then swung her legs over the edge, hoping she could get a hold on that post.

"I'm right here, Kate! Just drop!"

She let go and fell right into Chris Doran's waiting arms. She heard her attacker's angry curse, and then she heard the sirens.

Finally, the sirens.

Al Brooks heard them, too. He looked up to see the first police car entering the driveway, shoved the knife back into the scabbard on his belt, then ran along the wrap-around porch roof and disappeared.

"Oh, my God, boss! You have got to be kidding me!"

"I wish I were, Millie. It was terrifying!"

"But are you alright, Kate? Are you hurt?"

"I've got a few cuts from the window glass, but nothing serious. God, Millie, I can't believe how foolish I was, to think I could just walk into that redneck bar and talk to a bunch of murderers and think I could get away with it. What was I thinking?"

"Oh, my God! So, what happened to the guy who was after you?"

"He jumped off the porch roof over the kitchen door and ran up into the woods, but the cops were waiting for him on the road on the other side of the ridge."

"Oh, that's good. What about the others?"

"They already had Walt Lamb in custody and the chief told me they were going to go get Carol Tetrault. She's working a banquet out at the Tranmere—the restaurant we went to—and they were going to wait until she was finished, but just in case Brooks managed to get word to her, he said they were going to go pick her up right away.

"I don't know the whole story yet, Chief Bridger will fill me in tomorrow. I do know that going to Bucky's Tavern was the worst mistake I've made since... Well, since I married Jim Stone! Anyway, Patty Doran is coming over to spend the night. Not that I really need protection anymore, but..."

"Yeah, yeah, I get it. Will you be able to sleep after all that?"

"I don't know; I hope so."

38 |

Kate didn't get to sleep very quickly, but she eventually got in a few hours, helped along by a stiff drink and a joint she shared with Patty. It wasn't something she usually indulged in, but if ever there was a time, this was it.

When she awoke, she could smell coffee and bacon. Patty was in her kitchen, preparing breakfast for them. She threw on a robe and went downstairs to join her friend.

"Good morning, Kate," Patty said, cheerily. "I hope you got some zees!"

"Yeah, I did, eventually. You didn't have to make breakfast for me, Patty."

"Ah, no problem; it's what I do every morning. How do you want your eggs?"

The two women had a leisurely breakfast while they talked over what had happened. Kate filled Patty in on her night at Bucky's and her conversations with Chief Bridger.

"It sounds like the two of you figured things out pretty well," she said, "but it was kind of dangerous playing the 'undercover cop.' I'm surprised the chief let you do it."

"Well, I didn't ask permission, and I didn't tell him exactly what I was doing. It was my decision entirely."

"Well, you certainly met some of the valley's characters, alright."

"Do you know all of these people, Patty?"

"Yeah, I know them. It's been a few years since Chris and I stopped drinking and hanging out in bars, but, yeah, I know just about everyone you mentioned. So, tell me, was Billy Tourville in on it? In on the murder, I mean?"

"Well, I don't know everything yet. I'm going to meet with Les this morning, and he'll fill me in. The last I knew, we were certain that Lamb, Brooks, and Carol Tetrault were in on it, although Carol couldn't have actually committed the murder. But I'm still not sure how Tourville fit in, or Peter Plouffe, either. One of the parts of the chief's plan was to get Peter away from Walter Lamb, so he could get him to talk."

"Poor Peter. That boy's been through so much in his life already."

"I haven't met him, or any of the Plouffes, actually. The only people I actually talked to were Carol, Walt Lamb, and Billy's girlfriend, Daisy."

"Daisy?"

"I think Bitsy said her last name was Millette."

"Oh, okay. She's a little younger than the others, and I don't know much about her."

"Well, she seemed like a sweetheart; she was very worried about Billy being involved with the others."

"Hmm... so you didn't actually meet Alan Brooks that night?"

"No. I was told who he was, but I never spoke to him."

"Just as well. He's an animal. You're lucky he got scared off in time."

Ginny was all smiles when Kate walked into the police station.

"Ms. Stone, I'm so glad you're alright," she said. "Everybody knows what you did, and I, for one, am so proud of you." She looked around the lobby, where two officers were chatting while the chief looked on from his office door. "I wish you were actually on the force; we could use a little feminine diversity around here."

The two officers just grinned and continued their conversation.

The chief smiled and said, "You're right, Ginny. But we'll have to do with what we've got for now. Come on in, Kate."

Kate sat down opposite the chief and poured herself a coffee. There was a plate of doughnuts on the desk—no surprise—and she happily took one of them to go with her coffee.

"Well, Kate," the chief began, "everything is looking a lot clearer this morning. It looks like we were right about almost everything."

"Almost everything?"

"Some of the details are still a little fuzzy, but our suspects are starting to talk, so it's all coming together. Walter Lamb, who's neither as dumb nor as brave as Al Brooks, is already trying to bargain his way out of this. He claims that he just wanted to talk to Rory and scare him a little, but Al Brooks got carried away and killed Rory before he could stop him. Carol Tetrault broke down when she realized that she could face the same penalties for being an accessory, and she's ready to testify against both of them."

"What about the Plouffe boy: Peter?"

"Well, technically, he withheld information, but he was certainly under duress. We're not going to charge him. It looks like Lamb and Brooks were trying to set Peter up to take the fall by having him handle the pipe. If they had thrown the pipe into still water, the fingerprints might have survived..."

"Or not thrown it into the water at all..."

"Right. We don't know yet what they were thinking, but it will all come out."

"What about Billy?"

"I really think he's telling the truth, finally. It looks like he was duped; the others planned this knowing Billy wouldn't have anything to do with it. Hopefully, that will all become clearer soon. The Montreal police picked up Joe Reader last night, and, as soon as he's extradited, we'll get his side of the story."

"Oh, that's good. It seems like he was involved in the planning, at least."

"Absolutely. Anyway, our three suspects have all been arraigned this morning on first degree murder charges. There will be additional charges against Al Brooks, of course, for his assault against you. He's not going to see the light of day for a long time."

When Kate walked into the Maple Leaf Café, a squealing Bitsy DuFresne came racing around from behind the counter to give her a big hug.

"Oh, Kate, I'm so glad to see you!"

That was all she said, but she wouldn't let go, and the customers in the café started laughing and calling out to Kate.

"Well done, Ms. Stone!" someone said, and others repeated it, then someone started clapping. Ray Everett, who was sitting with Walt Drake, got up and walked over to shake her hand.

Kate managed to free her right arm, if nothing else, from Bitsy's grasp and shake Ray's hand.

"You helped find Rory's killer, and we're all so proud of you!" he said.

"Thank you, Mr. Everett. I guess everybody in town must know everything by now."

"Of course we do!" someone called out, and there was general laughter.

"Come and sit down, Kate," Bitsy said, finally releasing her.

Kate stayed at the cafe for half an hour or so, just having a salad and chatting with various townspeople, who kept stopping on their way in or out to say something. Everybody did, in fact, know that she had helped the police to solve the murder of the town's favorite son, and any lingering animosity toward the "rich bitch from Connecticut" seemed to have disappeared.

Tom and Lila Bennett stopped to say hello. Mrs. Bennett warned Kate to be careful; she had heard of "strange goings-on" at the old Andrews place.

"That's right, Miss Stone," her husband echoed, "strange goings-on."

"Well, thanks for the warning; I'll be careful."

When she walked out of the cafe, Kate nearly bumped into Ben Fremantle, who was on his way in.

Ben's face lit up in a bright smile and he said, "Ms. Stone, Chief Bridger told me this morning how much help you have been. I am so grateful, and Mother will be, too, when I've explained it all to her."

"Oh, well I appreciate that, Mr. Fremantle..."

"Ben—please call me Ben."

"Of course, and I'm Kate."

Just then, having parked her car around the corner, Tiffany Thompson appeared. She took one look at Kate and her fiancé chatting happily together and turned on her heel and stormed back to her car.

Ben threw his arms in the air in a gesture of helplessness.

"Sorry, Ben," Kate said ruefully.

It didn't look like she and Tiffany were going to be friends.

The end.

Acknowledgements

I would like to thank my friends Leesa Guay Timpson, Rocky Nelson, and Bonnie Epstein, as well as my wife Jude, each of whom read my drafts and encouraged me. Also big thanks to Rachel Fisher and Rachel Carter at Onion River Press.

Dan Marshall is a life-long resident of Vermont. He was raised in Essex Junction and currently lives in Burlington. Mostly retired from a work life of cooking and bookkeeping, he reads, writes and feeds his beloved wife and three cats.